WALKER

ALSO BY SHANI STRUTHERS

EVE: A CHRISTMAS
GHOST STORY
(PSYCHIC SURVEYS
PREQUEL)

PSYCHIC SURVEYS
BOOK ONE:
THE HAUNTING OF
HIGHDOWN HALL

PSYCHIC SURVEYS
BOOK TWO:
RISE TO ME

PSYCHIC SURVEYS
BOOK THREE:
44 GILMORE STREET

PSYCHIC SURVEYS
BOOK FOUR:
OLD CROSS COTTAGE

PSYCHIC SURVEYS
BOOK FIVE:
DESCENSION

PSYCHIC SURVEYS
BOOK SIX:
LEGION

PSYCHIC SURVEYS
BOOK SEVEN:
PROMISES TO KEEP

PSYCHIC SURVEYS
BOOK EIGHT:
THE WEIGHT OF THE SOUL

BLAKEMORT
(A PSYCHIC SURVEYS
COMPANION NOVEL
BOOK ONE)

THIRTEEN
(A PSYCHIC SURVEYS
COMPANION NOVEL
BOOK TWO)

ROSAMUND
(A PSYCHIC SURVEYS
COMPANION NOVEL
BOOK THREE)

THIS HAUNTED WORLD
BOOK ONE:
THE VENETIAN

THIS HAUNTED WORLD
BOOK TWO:
THE ELEVENTH FLOOR

THIS HAUNTED WORLD
BOOK THREE:
HIGHGATE

THIS HAUNTED WORLD
BOOK FOUR:
ROHAISE

THE JESSAMINE SERIES
BOOK ONE: JESSAMINE

THE JESSAMINE SERIES
BOOK TWO: COMRAICH

REACH FOR THE DEAD
BOOK ONE:
MANDY

REACH FOR THE DEAD
BOOK TWO:
CADES HOME FARM

CARFAX HOUSE:
A CHRISTMAS GHOST STORY

THE DAMNED SEASON:
A CHRISTMAS GHOST STORY

SUMMER OF GRACE

REACH FOR THE DEAD
BOOK THREE

WALKER

SHANI STRUTHERS

Authors Reach
www.authorsreach.co.uk

ISBN: 978-1-7399581-4-5

ACKNOWLEDGEMENTS

Reach for the Dead Book Three: Walker, is my twenty-fourth supernatural thriller. I've been writing books full-time for nearly nine years now and what a journey it's been, but not one I've taken alone. I've had so much help along the way, from my family, friends, beta readers, editors, designers and formatters, all of whom I thank my lucky stars for. After writing a book (again not a lonely process, as you live with so many characters in your head), it goes to beta readers, in this case Rob Struthers (my most ardent critique!), Sarah England (my most favourite horror author), Sarah Savery, Kate Jane Jones, Lesley Hughes and Louisa Taylor – huge thanks for helping to shape the book with your feedback. After confirmation from beta readers that I do have a viable story on my hands, Walker heads off to the editor, Rumer Haven (also a brilliant author of Gothic fiction), for further shaping. Then it's formatting and cover design. Gina Dickerson has created so many incredible book covers for me and once again she came up trumps for Walker, she really is the best in the business. After a long old haul, finally the book is in your hands, the reader. A huge thank you to you too, for choosing one of my books to lose yourself in. I hope you enjoy the latest in the Reach for the Dead series, with Shady Groves, Ray Bartlett and Annie

Hawkins at the helm!

Please note because the book is set in America, it's written in American English.

All things truly wicked start with innocence.

Ernest Hemingway

PROLOGUE

1972

Freedom.

The sweet taste of it.

Unexpected. A gift.

There'd been a car wreck, the driver and his passenger killed instantly. It was on some news channel, the TV blaring night and day. Despite this, I only just caught what the newscaster said: *"...a man and a woman, thought to be in their late twenties or early thirties. The vehicle they were in is registered to the State of Oregon but belonged to a man long since deceased and is therefore possibly stolen. The couple had no ID on them, so if anyone knows of two people missing who fit the description, please come forward."* Jane and John Doe, the man christened them. *"We need your help to identify them."*

Ma and Pa had been on their way to Vegas, abandoning me again. Not that I cared. I wanted them to go; I longed for it. Trouble was, they always came back. And when they did, they'd burst through the door, the pair of them laughing like hyenas, their limbs entwined. For two people so hate-filled, they sure did love each other. They were kindred spirits. Crazy twins. Up one minute, higher than the clouds, the next lower than the worms beneath my feet.

Of all the things I despised about them, it was that, their lack of control, how randomly emotions ran riot, trampling all over them and me.

I didn't have friends back then. I wasn't schooled. All I had was them. The woman who called herself my momma smothering me one minute, declaring I was her baby, her sweet boy, then beating me the next, saying what a burden I was, a gross mistake. My pa also beat me sometimes. And when he did, I was almost grateful because at least he saw me then, acknowledged my existence. Otherwise, I wasn't even worth a glance.

For so long I used to wonder why they were like this, what was wrong with them, and why I existed too, why they'd brought into the world something they clearly never wanted. A kid has to find a reason for being, and so I'd wander far and wide into the scrublands, toward the foot of the mountains, and stare upward, feeling even more insignificant, and I'd yell out, "Why?" If there truly was a God living above the range in His kingdom of clouds, He didn't give a shit.

So much of my early life was spent at those mountains, just staring, just waiting. I never dared to go higher; I was too afraid for that, too young. Did animals do what Ma and Pa did? Mistreat their young so badly? Abandon them too? Were they as vicious as humans? I was busy contemplating this when I saw her in the scrub, a vixen, her red coat patchy in places and flecked with gray. She was swollen right around her middle. From the entrance of her burrow, she turned her head toward me, narrowed her eyes as I narrowed mine, and our gaze held. Ma's belly had swollen like that once, a couple of years back. She was pregnant, she'd told me, about to have another baby. I don't know what happened to it, though. There was never any other kid in that house but me. The fox's belly was swollen because she was about to be a mother, which got me thinking some more. Would she be like mine or better? One that cared.

Curious for an answer to something, *anything*, I visited that vixen every day. I didn't get too near because I didn't want to spook her, but that was okay; I was happy to keep my distance and observe her, as she would observe me, the pair of us with nothing much else to do anyway. Then, finally, as the sun began to sink behind the range, the day saturated in a golden glow before the darkness of night claimed it, she screeched—a sound that echoed off the mountain slopes and grew more intense each time she expelled those that had grown inside her. I stayed until her screeching ceased and they'd all been born, witnessed how she immediately nuzzled her brood, licked their coats clean as they gravitated toward her, mewling, blind, pitiful things, intent only on suckling, on survival. Eventually, she lifted her head and gazed in my direction again, those slit-like yellowy-orange eyes with a warning in them still, her teeth bared. She was a good mom, I decided. Protective. That realization brought tears to my eyes when a damned good beating at the hands of my folks couldn't, my lack of emotion sending their temper skyrocketing further. But here, in the wilderness, it was different. There was order and hope.

The only hope I'd ever known.

I continued with my visits to the vixen and her cubs, and slowly, slowly, she came to trust me, let me inch closer, watching as her babies grew bigger and stronger. There was something in me, something new that I couldn't define, not then, a feeling that was alien. I can now, though. It was awe, and it was admiration. Jealousy. There was also that. Of those born to the wild, living by a different set of rules.

I didn't think to bring them food. I had little enough of my own. I went so often without eating that the growl in my stomach often became a roar. Yet my folks would eat; they'd drink and smoke, the tang from their "special" cigarettes lining my own mouth and leaving such a bitter taste there. I didn't think they'd *become* food…the foxes. The joy of visiting them would brighten days that otherwise held nothing. But what I saw on that day, the last of that brief period, made my mouth roar as well as my stomach, squeezing more tears from my eyes, hot and salty, enough to flood a creek.

A slaughter had taken place. The mother and every one of her babes butchered, some half devoured, others left whole but bloodied, as if killed only for sport. There they were, the cubs I'd watched grow, begin to move and play, the mother that had looked on and kept them safe, tried her best—destroyed, every last one. But the wild is exactly that: wild. Bigger animals prey on smaller. As humans do. To survive, you must hold dominion.

How?

I was nine years old. How does a nine-year-old triumph? Reign over chaos? That was the question that replaced "Why," but again there was no answer.

I buried the vixen and her cubs as deep in the ground as I could dig. And there was movement, someone watching me, I swear it. I felt eyes on me, eyes that were…different somehow. Neither human nor animal. Halfway through the dig, I glanced up, over toward where the scrub thickens into bushes, and thought I caught a flash of something red. The eyes that grazed me. I was nervous and peered harder. Was this creature the killer? So hard I stared, now spying something hanging from its jaws—something limp and bloodied too. The true perpetrator, perhaps? Our gazes held. What kind of animal was this that reared up, that walked on two legs?

That rectified?

It disappeared, leaving behind a mystery.

I returned home, any joy I'd had gone. Would the foxes' fate be my own? Would I also be torn apart one day? Pa had come close on occasion; Ma had often. Would they bury me as deep? Do what I'd done and leave the grave unmarked? At least I'd mourned the foxes, stood by that mound of raised earth and wept. Would anyone ever weep for me?

It was not long after those small deaths that Ma and Pa hauled themselves out to Vegas for Ma's birthday. It was a special one, apparently; she'd be thirty. I heard them say they might get married, have themselves an Elvis wedding in a cute little chapel, Ma squealing at the thought, clutching her belly and laughing. They threw an old suitcase in that rusting hulk of a car Pa ran around in, and didn't once look back. They just left me there, waiting for their return, dread mounting as the days passed. I was such a hopeless, helpless thing, like the cubs had been, blindly awaiting my fate. After a trip, the most severe downers happened, when Ma in particular would go mad, a railcar speeding right off the tracks.

Fate, though, had other plans in store. The car on the TV screen, I recognized it, its dusty blue front mangled.

I was alone. At last. In the wilderness. *Truly* alone.

Nobody knew their identity, and nobody knew about me either.

The wilderness was all I had, a place of such wonder, such

terror.

It had been Ma's birthday but also mine. The day I heard was the day I turned ten.

They were dead. John and Jane Doe.

And I was reborn.

CHAPTER ONE

Current Day

"Can't this thing go any faster?"

"Hey, come on, don't diss my old lady!"

"She's making weird kinda noises, though."

"That's just her huffing and puffing like she does. She's done plenty of miles in her lifetime, this dame. Just chill out, be patient. She'll get us where we want to go."

"Okay, fine, whatever. Reckon I could walk quicker, though."

"Be my guest."

Brett, who was defending the campervan they were all packed into, and Teddy, the one providing the critique—*good-natured* critique—were up front. Brett was clearly proud of his "old lady," as he called her, a recent acquisition he handled with tender love and care. Shady Groves, Ray Bartlett and Sam Hope sat in the back. Five friends in their early twenties, they were off to see an old friend, grabbing the chance of an adventure together. Their destination was northeastern Oregon's Baker City. It should have been a six- to seven-hour drive from Idaho Falls, where they all lived, but the van had its own pace. Josie Lea, the old friend in question, had moved there a year or so back with her parents, and it was long past time for a reunion. Combining this with two days in a historic hotel in Baker City and two days in the wilderness, camping at Smoke Ridge RV Resort and Campground in the rugged Elkhorn and Wallowa mountains, and you had yourself a ball.

All had booked some much-needed time off work, Brett from the record store, Sam from her role as manager in a clothes store, and Teddy...well, Teddy was actually in between jobs and had been for a while now. Shady and Ray worked together at the Mason Town Museum in Bingham County, thirty miles south of Idaho Falls, alongside Annie Hawkins. It was the first time the two of them had had a break since Christmas, and now it was spring, the skies tantalizingly blue and the memory of ten-feet deep snow all but forgotten. As Brett and Teddy continued to jibe, Shady admired the scenery and smiled. She was looking forward to this time. Strange, though, how much she missed the museum, finding being away from it such a wrench. She glanced over at Ray, took in his crazy red hair, forever sticking out at odd angles, and his expression, one of pure contentment, loving life. Sam was snuggled up close to him, catching a few z's, as she'd been out late the previous night.

Did Ray feel the same as Shady did? she wondered. Did he find it hard to be away too?

As though catching her thoughts, he turned to her, matched her gaze, a grin developing and becoming wider. Maybe he did. Maybe he didn't. She could hardly ask him, not right now in the company of others. What they did at the museum wasn't just a job, it was a vocation. In the last few months, she'd come to understand the true meaning of that word.

The stuff they took care of—a huge assortment of items,

anything from vintage clothing to baby carriages to mirrors and dolls—was the kind that *needed* it, for the protection of the public. Stuff that somehow, some way, had become charged with energy, sometimes benign, sometimes not, and if not, its influence could be destructive. Annie was more than capable of holding the fort in their absence; it was her museum, after all. She owned it. She'd been custodian a long time now, Shady and Ray relatively recent inductees. It was a calling for Annie too, a lifelong one, a "responsibility," as she described it, inherited from her father, who'd owned an antique store in a place called Lavenham in England, one that had a mysterious back room, away from the prying eyes of the public...

Devoted. She, Annie *and* Ray. It was just...with Shady's gift and what she'd experienced so far, particularly with Mandy as well as a mirror that had once belonged to a member of a notorious cult, she wondered if there was ever such a thing as time off. The world was full of objects, and though some of them held the sweetest of human emotions, some held the worst.

As Brett and Teddy continued to banter—some obscure playlist on the stereo courtesy of Brett, but his van, his rules, she supposed—Shady shut her eyes, tried to do the same as Sam and chill. Before the museum, she'd worked as a server in a highway diner, a job she wouldn't give a second thought to right now if she were still in it. Maybe there was something to be said for employment you could forget about as soon as you left the premises. Her eyes indeed closing, she leaned her head against the window, relishing the coolness of the glass against her cheek. Tonight in Baker City was bound to be a late one. There were several bars there, including an artisan one Josie favored that made the best beer, apparently, a few likely to slip down their throats all the way to closing time.

Finally, she drifted, images of Josie Lea's face popping into her mind. The friends had all gone to school together in Idaho Falls at Fairmont High, she and Josie bonding from day one when they'd been seated next to each other in class and asked to draw something. Shady might be gifted in some ways, but she was no artist. Her picture had consisted of some terrible scribble she'd now forgotten about, but Josie's picture had been something else. She'd drawn a dragon, its wings flapping, its face compelling, scales and feet highly detailed.

"Wow," Shady remembered saying. "That's…amazing."

Josie Lea, her pale face framed by jet-black hair, had beamed. "It's my pet dragon."

Shady frowned. "Your pet?"

The girl nodded. "Uh-huh. What's your name?"

"Shady. I'm Shady Groves."

"That's pretty. I like it."

"Your name is…Josie, right?"

"Josie Lea Wong."

"I like your name too."

Josie smiled again. "Thank you. And your picture's every bit as good as mine."

It wasn't. They both knew it. But that was Josie all over. She was kind, sweet and funny, and she had stayed that way all through growing up, the pair of them remaining friends through thick and thin, falling out with some along the way, maybe, but never with each other. She was the best friend a girl could have. God, Shady missed her! Wished she was still close enough that they could get together as regularly as they used to. Just call each other up and say, "Whassup? Wanna head out somewhere?"

As Shady drifted further into sleep, Josie's face was replaced by that of the dragon. She'd colored it red, such a vibrant shade, black eyes with flashes of red too. They were eyes that bored into the very heart of you, a wild thing, not of this world. A creature of myth and legend...and yet still it existed. Had found a way to. Beautiful *and* dangerous.

Those eyes really were piercing, holding Shady's dream gaze as it drew closer, the maw that was its mouth opening to reveal teeth sharper than needles. A pet dragon? She had no idea why Josie had called it that. No way could it be tamed! It couldn't even be understood. And why was it opening its jaws wider? Did it intend to swallow her whole, devour her? Or would it bellow fire, as dragons were supposed to do, and burn her alive?

"Josie!" she wanted to yell. "What did you create here?" But Josie, in the dream, had vanished. It was just Shady and the dragon. She was in mortal danger, and it was all her friend's fault because she was the one who'd breathed life into this creature, and it had lived ever since in Shady's memory, waiting to strike.

"Josie! It's going to kill me. It is! Tear me apart. It's real because you imagined it! We have to be more careful, don't you see? There's so much we don't understand. JOSIE!"

"Hey, hey, hey, what's going on? Brett? Shady? What's happening?"

Sleep abruptly released its clutches, the dragon's face fading. She could see only Ray now, concern and confusion on his face.

She was confused too as she blinked her eyes and sat up straighter. His hand had been on her, shaking her—she must have shouted out or something, alerting him to the fact that any dream she was having had turned sour. He'd since retracted his hand, though, and she was still shaking. Scratch that, she was *shuddering*.

"What the fuck?" she murmured.

"Crap." Brett was also complaining. "I don't think my old lady's too happy."

Awake too, Sam called out. "Can we call her something besides your old lady?"

"Huh?" Brett said, clutching on to the steering wheel. "Why?"

"It's just…" Sam screwed up that pretty upturned nose of hers. "It's not cute enough."

"Cute?" This time Brett twisted briefly in his seat to glare at her, as did Teddy. "She's about to give up on us, and the only thing you're concerned with here is cute?"

Unfazed, Sam shrugged. "Dorothea. We'll call her that from now on. And no way will she give up on us, Brett! Don't lose faith so easily. She needs to cool down awhile, that's all. Look, there's a motel on the right-hand side. Pull in there."

Brett did as he was told, hopping out to check the engine when the van had stopped.

Meanwhile, Teddy was nodding. "Dorothea," he mused. "Cool name, Sam. Nice."

Ray opened the side door and jumped out, Shady close behind him.

"Hey, man," he said, approaching Brett to the rear of the van, "what is it?"

"She's done for," Brett replied, his head now beneath the hood. "At least for today."

Shady checked her watch. "We're only halfway to Baker City!"

Brett closed the hood and focused on Shady, his eyes much clearer than she was used to. Brett, as great a guy as he was, was something of a stoner, stubbing out one reefer, then lighting another, his glazed look his trademark. He pulled a face as he shrugged.

"Think you'd better call her, tell her we'll be a day late."

"Oh man, really?"

"Really," Brett said. "To be fair, the previous owner never warned me about this, said she was as good as gold. Wouldn't let you down. Not on short journeys, anyway."

"Brett," Shady said, her nostrils flaring, "just how much did you pay for...for..."

"Dorothea," Ray said, trying to help a girl out.

"Okay, whatever. Dorothea," Shady duly replied. *Crock of shit* was more the description she had in mind. A Westfalia, circa the last century. She bet if she looked underneath, it'd be nothing but rust. No point in her looking at the engine either; she was no mechanic and doubted any of them were, especially Brett, who was simply scratching his head and sighing. Sam and Teddy were out of the van now too and looking equally mystified.

As uncharitable as her thoughts were, one thing Shady couldn't deny was that the Westfalia had a happy air about her, indicating she'd helped forge many good memories in the past. Maybe she should be more like Sam, who had reached out, one hand stroking the beleaguered side panels of the campervan and murmuring, "Poor Dorothea. Can't help it if you're tired, can you?"

"So, what do we do?" Teddy asked as he pulled a reefer from his pocket, immediately firing a hunger in Brett's eyes.

"Teddy..." Shady said, her tone beseeching, she knew. "Brett...what if we wait an hour and then try again?"

If they started smoking the stuff Teddy had on him—the "good stuff," he always called it, powerful—they really would have to wait till morning.

Brett took the reefer. "Sorry," he said. "I reckon my old lady...sorry, *Dorothea*, tells you when she's had enough, and when she does, best thing you can do is listen."

"Or what?" challenged Shady.

Sam reached across and took the reefer from Brett. She then proceeded to light it and take a drag before placing it in Brett's mouth, blowing him a kiss of gratitude afterward.

Brett inhaled, his eyes closing in bliss. "Or she can be a real badass," he drawled.

"Jeez, fuck and shit," cursed Shady. Despite that odd dream, she'd been so looking forward to seeing Josie today, and she knew how excited Josie was too.

Ray reached across and squeezed her shoulder. "Shady, if we give Dorothea time to rest, have ourselves a good night's sleep too, then we can set off real early in the morning, be in Baker City in time for ham and eggs with a side of home fries. The last thing we want is for her to give up entirely and be towed home."

"Sure, Ray, but—"

"Just call Josie and explain. Sure, she'll be disappointed, we all are, but you gotta look on the bright side."

As Shady watched the reefer pass back to Teddy, she sighed. This was a disaster! What bright side could Ray possibly mean?

He thumbed behind him.

"We may be in nowheresville, but at least we got ourselves a place to stay."

14

CHAPTER TWO

"Whoa," said Brett, his eyes widening. "What a place!"

"Not quite the luxury we were expecting on our first night," Sam pointed out.

"Silver lining, huh, Ray?" Shady's every word dripped with sarcasm.

"D'ya think Norman Bates had a brother or something?" asked Teddy.

"An older, meaner brother?" Sam elaborated.

Ray nodded. "With just as much of a mother fixation."

"Hey, come on!" Brett shook off any misgivings. "It's not that bad. And it's…available."

Sam glanced at Shady. "For 'available,' read 'deserted.' Totally."

Shady nodded, trying not to think badly of Dorothea again.

It was Ray who took the lead and began walking the long row of single-story rooms for hire, the yellow paint on them peeling, toward a building that had an unlit "Office" sign hanging in the window. After some hesitation, the others followed.

"Shit, look!" Teddy practically yelled.

"What?" Sam said as several heads turned in the direction he was pointing.

"It's only the frigging house on the hill! *Psycho*-style."

Shady gulped. He was right. Beyond reception was a pathway with steps leading up to what must be the proprietor's house, a Victorian-esque Gothic building complete with gables and a turret. It looked every bit as deserted as the motel, the windows achingly black. This was a lonely highway they were on, the kind America was renowned for, with long ribbons of asphalt reaching toward a horizon that remained forever elusive. Again, she had to work hard not to sully Dorothea's name, but why the hell had she chosen this place to take a rest? Words not from *Psycho* but *Casablanca* flashed in Shady's mind: *Of all the gin joints in all the towns in all the world...*

Before they entered the office, the reefer was finished, dropped to the ground and snuffed out in the dirt. Ray told them the smell of it clung to them so to leave any negotiations to him.

Shady immediately protested. "Hey, I'm a smoke-free zone too. I can come with."

"Okay," he agreed, "but the rest of you stay put!"

A bell tinkled half-heartedly as Ray pushed at the door.

If Brett had exclaimed on first sight of this place, now Ray did too. "Man!" he said, looking around him as Shady, who was behind him, nodded avidly.

"This place...it's like a...a..."

"Museum?" Ray offered.

"Kinda."

It was stuffed with ornaments, all displayed on shelves—knickknacks, really, including little china ladies and animals, and old editions of classic books: *Gone with the Wind*, *Of Mice and Men*, and that ilk. There were several photographs too, all framed, one in particular that caught

Shady's eye and which she headed toward.

Ray stopped her. "Don't."

She turned to face him, genuinely confused. what?"

"Touch anything."

"Huh? Why?"

He rolled his eyes. "You know why!"

"But—"

"Shady, we're on vacation, okay? We're taking a bre. deserve it, and God knows so do you. Remember w Annie said, everybody needs time out to recharge the batt pack. Well, that's what we're doing here. *All* of us. So, s where you are, keep your hands by your side, and for Goc sake, don't touch a thing."

Shady looked again at the photograph she'd been heading to—a family group, comprising a mom and dad and grandparents too, two kids in front of them, a girl and a boy. The girl was gap-toothed as she smiled, and the boy, who was older than his sister, had his chest puffed out, either imitating a pigeon or feeling just so damned proud to be there. A happy family photograph, set against a backdrop of scrub and sky—this land before it was built on, perhaps? The family staking their claim? Everyone was smiling in it, so how come Shady felt a frisson of something when studying it? Unease?

She was prevented from further musings as another bell rang—this one loud and clear, on the countertop, where Ray had pressed it.

"Do you really think someone'll come?" Shady asked. "It just seems so—"

Someone *was* approaching them. At the back of reception was another door that had, until now, remained

closed. It opened, creaking as it did, Shady and Ray briefly tearing their eyes from it to look at each other. Ray mouthed one word at her: *Norman?*

It wasn't one of Alfred Hitchcock's creations that entered, though Shady guessed the woman might have been offered a bit part had he known she existed. Brown hair threaded with gray was cut into a severe crop, and her fragile frame was slightly stooped, although not with age, Shady realized. As the woman lifted her head, it became obvious she wasn't as elderly as first impressions suggested; rather, she was somewhere in her forties, the skin on her face still relatively plump, with a smattering of freckles across her nose. She placed her hands on the countertop, and Shady surreptitiously studied them. Yellow tipped, the nails were slightly ragged. A few age spots had also developed, but otherwise her hands too were smooth enough.

"Guests," the woman said, eyeing them, her tone matter-of-fact.

"We sure are!" replied Ray, summoning enough enthusiasm for both of them. "We're looking for...two rooms. You think that'd do it, Shady? Boys in one, girls in another?"

"Should be fine," Shady agreed, her eyes now darting between the woman and the family photograph, wondering all the while if this was the girl.

About to open her mouth to start a conversation about this place and whether it was family run, perhaps, Ray continued.

"Okay, that's sorted. Two rooms, please. They don't have to be your finest. This is just a pit stop. Unexpected, actually. We've got another four hours' drive ahead of us, but the van we're in, one of those Westfalias, the vintage

type, you know, the kind everyone loves—Dorothea's her name, just christened that—she's decided enough's enough for one day, and she needs a rest. So here we are! On your doorstep."

Babbling. That's what Ray was doing. But why? Even the woman looked bemused.

"Dorothea, huh?" she said. "Okay."

"Oh, and I'm Ray, by the way, and this is Shady. Sorry, we didn't get your name."

"I didn't give it to you, that's why," the woman said, but not unkindly. Her tone was blander than that. "It's Missy. Missy Davenport. And two rooms are fine. We're not busy."

Shady raised an eyebrow—with no vehicles parked outside except theirs, that was perhaps the understatement of the week. As Missy Davenport turned, presumably to fetch some keys and paperwork, Shady couldn't resist drawing a little closer to the photograph. Ray noticed immediately and stepped forward a little as if to block her. She raised her hands in a gesture of defeat. *Okay, Ray! Have it your way.* But when Missy turned back to face them, Shady had to comment.

"Great office you have here. So much to…admire."

Once again, Missy eyed her. Eyes that weren't the gateway to the soul but guarded.

"Spend a lot of time in here," she said at last. "No harm in making it homey."

"Oh. No harm at all. I didn't mean that—"

"So, where is it you're heading?"

"To see a friend—" Ray began, but Shady cut across him. "Baker City."

There was silence. Just a moment, but it felt loaded suddenly.

"Baker City?" Missy responded. "The base camp for Eastern Oregon, or so they say. Yeah, I know it. What are you doing there?"

"Spending a couple of days in the city, then we're off to the mountains."

"The mountains." Again, Missy repeated their words, her gaze shifting to the photograph on the shelf, something managing to cloud her eyes at last. Sadness?

Shady frowned. "You know them too?"

"Kinda. Not as well as some." She shook her head as though trying to focus. "You used to the mountains?"

"We're from Idaho," Shady told her. "Can't vouch for Ray here, but I used to go fishing with my dad, and hiking too, in the Blackfoot Mountains and along Palisades Creek Trail."

Missy nodded. "Even so, gotta take care. You know that, don't you? Be on the lookout."

"The lookout for what?" Ray said, grinning.

There was no amusement on Missy's face, though. She shot him a look that could have withered stone. "Be careful is all I'm saying! Here's your keys. Boys are in number thirty-eight, the girls next door in thirty-nine. Checkout is at ten a.m. prompt."

"Oh, we'll be gone long before then," Ray assured her. "Anywhere to eat around here?"

"Does it look like it?" Missy said, still clearly perturbed he hadn't taken her prior warning seriously. "You have to go about fifteen miles up the road for that kind of thing, and if you say that van of yours needs to rest…"

"No problem," he assured her. "We brought some snacks along with us."

"Right. Okay." After typing their names into an ancient

yellowed computer, Missy took a card payment. "You're all set. Have a peaceful evening."

She then turned her back on them, but not before glancing again at the photograph, sadness stuck to her like molasses now.

* * *

Shady, Ray and the others gorged on potato chips, Twinkies and beef jerky, although—aside from Ray—not strictly in that order. What punctuated each course, however, was weed, smoked while hanging out the bathroom window, Sam and Ray making the most of the unexpected situation they'd found themselves in, with nowhere to go and no one to see, no responsibilities of any kind, imbibing as much as the other two.

"If I had an ice-cold Coors to go with this," Teddy professed, exiting the bathroom, his eyes at half-mast, his feet dragging slightly, "life would be damn near perfect."

"Tomorrow night, bro," Brett told him. "We'll drink our body weight in beer then."

Shady smiled. Brett, although a stoner, was big-hearted enough. He hadn't had the best home life either, his mom walking out on him and his dad when Brett was barely knee high, getting in touch but only once in a blue moon. Teddy, on the other hand, had a similar background to Shady—he came from a loving home and was cruising along in life, not exactly overachieving but on track, or he would be once he started working again. Watching them as they turned chilling into an art form, the four of them hanging out in the boys' room as the girls didn't want theirs messed up, she wished she could really join in, be like them, but smoking weed and drinking more than one bottle of beer at a time didn't tend to agree with her. It enhanced her gift but not in a good way, seeming to open the floodgates for more darkness to come pouring through. Annie agreed with her that abstinence, or as near as possible, was the best way forward for someone like Shady.

"You have an extraordinary gift," she'd said early on in their friendship, "that seems to be developing rapidly. It's essential, therefore, you remain in control of it rather than *it* controls *you*. I know kids love to party. I did too when I was your age, but that's where the similarity between us ends. I might be sensitive to the paranormal, but I can't sense what you can. I can't see as far. Alcohol is a great relaxant, and I'm sure drugs are too, some of them—" here she'd paused, pursing her lips slightly "—but they can open doors, gateways to other worlds. Oh, Shady, there's much to this existence we don't understand, but you, me and Ray, we're making a stab at it. Recklessness, though, is not an option, not for you."

And so, while her wayward amigos slumped either on the bed or in chairs around it, Shady sat upright, laughing along but also continually losing the thread of the conversation as thoughts spoken out loud meandered down various random pathways that only the inebriated had full access to.

"Hey, Shady," Teddy said, gesturing toward the bathroom as he offered his latest smoke to her, "sure you don't want a toke? I mean, a tiny little one."

Shady declined. "As generous as your offer is, Teddy, no thanks. You know what I really need? Some fresh air. I'm gonna head outside, okay?"

Ray raised an eyebrow. "You want me to come along?"

"I'll be fine, Ray, thanks. If I'm not back in ten…"

"We'll send in the cavalry."

"You got it." She shot him a smile as she rose from her chair and left the room, that smile growing wider as she stood for a while outside the door in the coolness of the night and listened as their chatter dissolved into giggles. She didn't mind their behavior, not in the least, and one saving grace was that Josie didn't drink or smoke much either. She'd have solidarity with her, at least. Josie had been so upset when Shady had called earlier to explain they'd be late, but, typical of Josie and so like Ray, she'd erred on the positive.

"When you do get here," she'd said, "we're just going to make even more of the time we have together. Not waste a minute."

Evening had fallen, the sky not black, though; rather, it was streaked with gray patches of low cloud, a few stars valiantly trying to peek through the gaps. It had been warm during the day, but now Shady pulled the hoodie she was wearing tight around her as she left the porch that ran the length of the low-rise building and stepped onto the gravel.

A lonely, lonely highway, and theirs was the only room lit up. They'd taken the back roads into Oregon because Brett thought the main highways would be too much for the Westfalia, wanting to cruise at a relaxed speed without some asshole on their tail, continually blasting the horn at them. This road, though, had sadly proved as arduous.

Heading over to the van, nestled under a post that bore the motel's name—The Lazy Stay Motel, written in an orange squiggle—Shady reached out and touched her paintwork.

"How you doing, Dorothea? Enjoying your rest?"

Another burst of laughter erupted, this time nothing to

do with the occupants of room thirty-eight but an echo from the past, from an entirely different set of people. Ah, it was hard to continue being pissed at a van saturated in such happiness.

"See you in the morning, huh?" Shady continued. "Bright and early, mind you."

As she turned on her heel, she noticed another light, a yellowish glow, the merest hint of it, coming from the office. Was Missy still in there? The house beyond was shrouded in darkness, an abandoned feel to it as though it was somehow being avoided. Deciding to check who it was, Shady headed over, quickly reaching the door and pushing at it, the bell hardly tinkling at all this time, as subdued as everything else around here.

"Oh, hi," she said on seeing that Missy was indeed there, sitting at the counter, something in her hands that she seemed to be examining.

Missy set it down, below the lip of the counter. "Can I help you? Something wrong?"

"No, no, nothing like that. I was just out and about…wandering."

"Wandering?"

"Yep, getting some fresh air."

"Everyone else okay?"

"They are. They're chilled, right to the bone."

Missy frowned, as if guessing in what way Shady's friends might be "chilled," and then she reached down, picked up what she'd been holding and held it up for Shady to see.

"I was reminiscing," she said, by way of explanation.

As soon as she'd come in, Shady had noticed the photograph missing from the shelf, and so she ventured forward. "I saw it earlier. Is the little girl you?"

"Uh-huh, it's me, my brother, ma and pa, and one set of grandparents on my mother's side. Who my pa's parents were, we have no clue. He grew up in foster care." A sigh escaped her. "It was a good day this was taken, one of those warm, hazy summer days you thought might last forever. I guess they do in a way, at least in a photograph."

Shady nodded. "True."

"This was a professional photo," Missy continued, an unexpected smile revealing the telltale gap between her teeth. "Grandpa wanted one of the entire family to keep by his bedside. Said it was the last thing he wanted to see as he went to sleep and the first thing on waking."

"That's really sweet."

"He was a sweet old guy, lasted about a year or so after this photograph. Grandma soon followed him home. As for my parents..." She swallowed deeply, lowering her head briefly. "You know what? It's been a long day. I have to lock up."

"Oh yeah, sure. I'll get out of your way."

"I don't want to appear rude or nothing..."

"No, not at all. Do you want me to put the photograph back on the shelf for you?"

"What? Oh...okay. I guess."

It was with seeming reluctance that Missy handed it over, Shady feeling bad about that, wishing she hadn't ventured in and disturbed the woman's reverie. Reaching out, her hand enclosed the silver frame, which, despite being so recently handled, felt cold to the touch. Bringing it closer, her eyes connected with the Missy of old. Happiness shone from her, a little girl who was loved and knew a secure home. Laughter. There'd been plenty of that, family banter around the dinner table, the teasing good-natured, people that thrived when together, appreciating every precious second, Missy's father in particular, knowing at last what it was like to have a family, how sacred it could be.

And yet…laughter had, at some point, faded, replaced instead by silence. A void into which they had all fallen. Not only a lingering sadness, Shady sensed utter bewilderment too. She didn't want to drag her eyes from Missy, but the pull was magnetic, landing on Missy's brother. As she stared at him, she couldn't help but gasp. Something had befallen him, some kind of…*horror*?

"Shit!" Shady's hands released the photograph.

"What the hell?"

Missy darted out from behind the counter with the agility of an athlete, lunging for the memento and catching it before it could hit the floor.

"What do you think you're doing?" she yelled.

Shady was the one feeling horror now. "Sorry. I'm so sorry. I didn't mean—"

"You coulda smashed the glass!"

"I know, I…um. It's just…" How the hell could she even begin to explain?

"It's okay," Missy said, although her voice retained its rasping harshness. "No harm done."

She placed it back on the shelf herself, her breath slightly ragged as she dusted off some imaginary speck of dust on it, the hint of a cough bothering her too.

"I know it's precious to you," Shady said. "That everything here is…"

"Memories are all I have," Missy said, positioning it just right.

"You miss your family, huh?"

"Every damned day."

"Your brother especially."

Missy glared at her. "You need to leave."

"Missy—"

"You need to go back to your room and lock the door."

Shady frowned. What was she talking about? "Lock the door? Out here?"

"Yes!" hissed Missy.

"Why?"

"Because there's danger, that's why. It doesn't matter where you are and what it is you think you know. Keep your wits about you. There's danger everywhere."

CHAPTER THREE

"Halle-frickin'-lujah! You made it!"

"Josie!"

Shady rushed to greet her, forcing stiff limbs from the journey to quickly ease as she hugged her much-missed best friend, the pair of them laughing. When they were done, it was the others' turn to hug, a group of five becoming six.

Afterward, Josie immediately began apologizing. "I'm so sorry we can't put you up at our house. Like I told you, it's lovely but...a little on the snug side. The hotel, though— look, there it is, just along the road. You're gonna love staying there! Honestly, when it's fully done up, it's going to be amazing. The grand old lady of Baker City come back to life."

They'd spotted the hotel on the way in; it was hard not to. Taking up an entire block on Main Street, it did indeed have the kind of façade its name—the Grand Willmott— suggested. Even amid renovation, with scaffold covering half the front, it was impressive, complete with a clock tower with a flagpole on top, Old Glory flying. A little before noon, it was heaving, not with guests but construction workers.

Josie, her black hair trimmed into the same neat bob she'd had ever since a child, winced at their confusion. "The construction work finishes around four, then we'll be able to go to our rooms, no hard hats needed. Wanda McIntyre, the owner, is a friend of Mom's. She's the one who said we can stay as a favor to her. There're a few rooms at the back ready and completely safe to reach, away from construction. And, hey, it's in the heart of town!" When still there was silence, she added, "My bedroom at home really is tiny, guys, and at least this is only for one night now, not two. That motel you were in sounded creepy. The Willmott's gotta top that, surely?"

"It's perfect!"

"Love it."

"Wow, a grand old lady, huh?"

"Just like Dorothea!"

These were all the responses and more to the pleading in Josie's voice.

Shady hugged her again. "Honestly? This is great, really great. It'll be a real privilege to stay at the hotel. Thanks so much for organizing. We're grateful."

Josie squealed and clapped her hands. "Great! I guess first up is a tour of the town, starting with what drew us here in the first place, Halcyon Days."

Halcyon Days, also on Main Street, was a general store, the kind found in practically every town in America, selling a mind-boggling array of items that you never knew you needed. Josie's Mom—Lulin—was behind the counter when they entered the store, stepping out from behind it to greet them as warmly as Josie had.

"It's so lovely to see you all," she declared, her smile more than a match for Josie's. In fact, the two were more like twins than mother and daughter—same height, mannerisms and even choice of hairstyle. "You're going to have so much fun together."

"Oh, we will, Mrs. Wong," the group agreed, Shady adding, "It's lovely to see you too."

"Is the hotel all right for you?" Lulin checked.

"The hotel?" Ray said. "Yeah! Sure! It's amazing. Can't wait to get in there."

"Ah, you'll enjoy it," Lulin told them. "Wanda's doing a great job. It's had plenty of owners these past twenty years, but none that took particular care of it. The story goes it was pretty run-down even before that. Wanda's passionate about the restoration, so, so meticulous. People are going to come from miles around, itching to explore this great town and the amazing landscape. Best you experience it now. It'll be hard to get into soon!"

As Lulin delivered her spiel, Josie was backing toward the door, tugging on Shady's sleeve. "Come on," she said, also leaning in and whispering, "or we'll be here for hours."

The other four duly got the hint and backed away too while continuing to listen dutifully to Lulin, who was now talking about Baker City in general and what a lovely place it was to live, everyone so friendly and the atmosphere relaxed. Despite Josie's efforts, Shady stood firm, at least for a few minutes, nodding attentively and responding occasionally, something Mama Wong clearly appreciated.

"Oh, Shady, Shady, Shady! We really have missed you so much. You've got a new job, I hear. In a museum, of all places. How interesting! You must tell me about—"

"Shady!" Josie hissed at her from the doorway. "Come on!"

"Sure, I'll tell you all about it...um...pretty soon. Sorry, I think the others are waiting...sorry." She turned to go, five pairs of eyebrows raised that it had taken her so long. Feeling bad, though, Shady turned back to wave at Lulin, only to find she was already busy chatting to a customer.

"Ensnaring her next victim," Josie said, but she was laughing. Shady knew just how close she was to her parents and how protective too. Second-generation immigrants, they'd overcome some real hardships in their lives. "Come on, let's get on with the tour."

As Lulin had said, the vibe was truly relaxed, the sun shining in a blue sky and a smile on just about everyone's lips. In the time she'd been here, Josie had clearly gotten to know practically everyone local, introducing her friends to a variety of people, from store owners to barkeepers to those who ran cafés and restaurants—some establishments a little yesteryear, others more up-and-coming, their owners, like Wanda, determined to bring Baker City into the twenty-first century without any loss of charm.

When the tour was done, and it really only covered the length and breadth of Main Street, they hopped back in Dorothea, who transported them happily enough to the outskirts of town to Josie's house so she could pick up her backpack.

The 'burbs that surrounded the main town were even more relaxed, sleepy, Shady would call them, green and leafy too. Not a huge city—the population was fewer than ten thousand—it was named after Edward D. Baker, the only US senator ever to be killed in military combat. A place with a proud heritage, it was also ideally placed, the base camp for Eastern Oregon, as Missy Davenport had mentioned, for those who wanted to immerse themselves in the great outdoors, the Powder River running right through it, leading on to Snake River. Like just about everywhere else, though, there were some cool areas and not-so-cool ones, the west regarded as the safest part and where the Wongs lived.

As Dorothea chugged to a stop outside her house, Josie was the only one to clamber out, rushing up a path flanked by two narrow strips of lawn before entering the house to grab her backpack. The home was indeed modest but, as there were only three of them in the Wong family, plenty big enough, Shady able to see in her mind's eye the bright décor Lulin favored, cheerful shades of yellow and orange punctuating everything.

"Color makes you feel alive," Lulin had said once, Shady nodding, then glancing down at the clothes she'd been wearing: black jeans, black T-shirt and black boots, similar attire to what she and the rest of Dorothea's passengers wore now—Josie too, for that matter, who soon returned, climbing back inside and snagging the seat next to Shady.

"Okay," she said, that trademark beam of hers in place, "to the Grand Willmott we go!"

* * *

By the time they reached the hotel, the construction workers had left, but Wanda McIntyre was there to greet them. A blonde in her middle years with a ruddy, outdoorsy complexion, she was, unlike the owner of The Lazy Stay Motel, all unbridled joy and enthusiasm.

"Hello, hello," she greeted, "and welcome to the newly revamped Grand Willmott Hotel!" Ushering them in through a side door by the kitchen area rather than the main entrance, she led them through a corridor and down a shallow ramp to reception. "It's coming along, don't you think?"

Although reception was clear, ladders and paint pots could all be spied in the distance.

"Of course we haven't officially opened our doors to the public yet," she breezily continued, "but when we do, the celebration is going to be monster! It was one of the first hotels in the Northwest, did you know that? Dates back to 1899 to the gold rush itself, people stopping here on their way to them thar hills and it gaining quite a reputation for itself. What we're doing, renovating it but keeping as many original features as possible, is certain to attract the crowds again, vacationers this time rather than prospectors, putting Baker City right back on the map where it belongs, the gateway to the mountains! Come on, let me show you what will be the restaurant. Such a shame you're only here for the one night instead of two, but hopefully you'll be back when we're hosting real guests."

As they followed her, Ray nudged Shady. "Last time I looked, we were real enough."

Shady smiled. "Real guests pay the going rate, I guess."

"Here it is," Wanda said, leading them through a set of double doors to what was a very impressive space with marbled floors and crystal chandeliers plus columns, crown molding and paneling in matching mahogany. High above was the most magnificent stained-glass ceiling that flooded the area with light, a pattern etched upon it in turquoise and gold.

"Wow." Sam's eyes were on stalks. "Will you look at this?"

"Palm Court," Wanda said, delighted by her reaction. "And isn't the ceiling magnificent? Original, of course, and thankfully largely intact."

"Gourmet dining?" Ray asked.

Wanda shook her head. "At the Grand Willmott, we're all about keeping it real. Baker City folk are like that. Oh, I'm not saying the food won't be top quality, it will, but it'll also be accessible, with plenty of favorites, including mesquite smoked prime rib, salmon and spaghetti. For dessert, there'll be a good old peach cobbler pie and chocolate torte."

"Jeez, man," Brett sighed, "I'm starving already!"

Teddy agreed. "Too bad we can't order room service."

"There are plenty of places in town doing great food that'll welcome your business," Wanda assured them. "Now"—she went from being ecstatic to brisk and businesslike—"although we're coming to the end of works, on the bedrooms, at least, the place is still something of a construction site. As I've told you, your rooms are complete, and I'm sure you'll find them just about perfect, but, please, can you promise me you won't go wandering around the building? I don't want any accidents. And absolutely no smoking."

Six voices solemnly promised.

Returning to the staircase off reception, so grand, so sweeping it'd make Scarlett O'Hara weep, they ventured to the second floor, the boys intending to share one room and the girls another like before. When the doors to the first room were thrown open with nothing less than a theatrical flourish, all of them gasped. A vision in cream and gold greeted them, with floor-to-ceiling windows and two queen beds adorned with cushions.

"Will it do?" asked Wanda, fit to burst.

Sam was the first to reply. "Absolutely! And thank you so much for letting us stay."

"You are so welcome," Wanda said, moving to the next

room and repeating the procedure before handing each group a set of key cards. "And afterwards be sure to leave a glowing review on TripAdvisor, won't you, and tell all your friends and family about us too. I always say the best form of advertising is word of mouth!"

Wanda left them to it, the girls entering their room, closing the door behind them and then running to the beds and throwing themselves onto the quilts and cushions.

"See?" Josie said in between laughter. "It's not what you know, it's who you know!"

"Sure is!" agreed Sam. "It'd be great to do a ghost hunt later, don't you think?"

Shady sobered slightly. "Wanda said not to go exploring."

"Yeah, but…how would she know? She doesn't live on-site, does she, Josie?"

Josie shook her head. "She has a house on the edge of town."

"She'll know if one of us trips over something and has that accident she's afraid of!" Shady reminded them. "She's sticking her neck out here. We have to respect that."

Josie reined herself in too. "Shady's right, Sam. We're heading out soon to the bars. By the time we come back, it'll be late and we'll be pretty lit."

"Sure, but a ghost hunt, in this place… Come on! It reeks of history."

"It's against the rules," Shady reiterated.

"Okay, okay." Sam kneeled on the bed now, hugging one of the cushions to her chest. "What if we compromise? What if we don't look around later but *before* we go out drinking, while we're stone-cold sober? Just to get a feel for the place."

A feel for the place. Shady had to admit, it was tempting.

As Sam had said, the place reeked of history; you didn't need to be sensitive to realize that. An exciting history too—so many people filled with so much hope had stayed here, en route to the West, not just to scour the hills for gold but intent on making new lives for themselves. She could almost hear the excited chatter that would have filled the air, people drinking and dining, all sorts of meetings taking place. *Meetings.* That word, that *concept*, stood out the most. There would indeed have been many meetings held here, a place that was designed for it.

Realizing Shady might now be on side, Sam jumped up, smoothing down the tight-fitting shorts and top she was wearing. "Please," she cajoled, "just a little peek."

"Should we ask the boys?" Josie said, also rising.

Sam shook her head. "Brett mentioned grabbing some sleep for a while, and Teddy agreed with him. Pretty sure Ray'd be going with the flow."

"Okay," said Shady, "the less people the better anyway. Just a quick scoot around, nothing more."

"You got it!" Sam was already heading for the door, Josie and Shady following her. Before they went anywhere, though, they stopped outside the boys' room and listened intently.

"Pretty sure I can hear snoring in there," Sam whispered.

Tiptoeing away, trying to suppress laughter and their own excitement, they headed along the upstairs corridors, peeking into rooms wherever doors had been left ajar, finding various spaces in various states of cosmetic overhaul.

"You know what?" breathed Sam. "I've been thinking about moving away from fashion and into interiors. D'ya think Wanda might give me a job?"

"You can ask, but it looks like she already has someone

pretty good," Josie said, leading them downstairs and back to the public rooms. "Be great to have you here, though. There's a bar and café as well as the Palm Court restaurant. Think they'll be pretty jumping places. Here, come and see."

The bar and café areas were to the left of the building, close to where they'd come in, and still in their infancy regarding updating. All they could do was gaze through glass doors into rooms that would indeed be thriving one day. For now, though, more work tools littered the floors.

"There are more public rooms up here," Josie told them, leading them across reception toward a corridor on the right before reconsidering. "They're just function rooms, though. Wanda told Mom there'll be a lot of events going on here. It'll form the backbone of the business, keep 'em going all year round. Can't really get into those rooms either at the moment. I came here with Mom about three weeks back—Wanda likes to chart her progress with her friends—and they've been totally stripped back. So, really, we've seen the best parts. Time to renovate ourselves instead, I think, and get ready to hit the town!"

"Sure," Sam said, taken with that idea now. "Before we do, though, Shady, tell me, you think there are any ghosts here?"

Josie cocked her head to one side, intrigued too. "Yeah, is it actually haunted?"

Both girls knew well enough Shady was sensitive. "Fey," they used to call her, marveling at her knack at finding objects when they were lost—rings, necklaces, earpods, keys, those kinds of things. Both also knew she worked in a museum, one that was a little different to the norm. They'd been surprised by her sudden change in career—Shady had once harbored ambitions to be an English teacher—but hadn't, as of yet, questioned it too much. If they had, if they realized just how much that childhood skill of hers had developed, they'd be either stunned or horrified. Likely both.

"Shady?" Sam prompted.

"I…um…it's hard to tell."

"Why?" Josie asked, still so curious.

"I think…because of the building work. The energy's kind of—"

"Tainted?" suggested Sam.

"Altered," Shady amended. "But you know what, it feels nice enough to me. A great place to stay. Really friendly and upbeat and—"

"Shady?"

There was something up ahead, on the wall of the corridor that Josie had said led to the function rooms. Something that, as with the photograph at the motel, drew her to it.

"Can you excuse me for a second?"

Not waiting for an answer, Shady entered the corridor and saw exactly what it was—another framed photograph. Like the one in the motel, it was of a group of people and taken some time ago, judging by its washed-out, grainy quality. But that was where the similarity ended. This group—all fully grown males—were wearing masks, *animal* masks: lynx, wolf and bear, pretty authentic-looking too. One masked figure in particular stood out at the center of the group, hands spread wide as if in welcoming and knees slightly bent. His was the mask of a mountain lion, perhaps one of the wild's most formidable creatures, the kind you prayed you wouldn't bump into while on a Sunday hike.

As Shady stared, Josie and Sam arrived by her side.

"Shit," muttered Sam, also peering hard at it. "Who are these guys?"

"Mom wanted to know the answer to that question too when we were here last," Josie told them, "but Wanda had no clue. Said it was hanging on the wall when she took over, and so she'd keep it, a bona fide part of the building. But, yeah, I agree, it's weird. Not bona fide at all when I come to think of it. It doesn't seem to…fit."

Shady also pondered this and agreed; it *was* at odds with its surroundings. And yet here it was, the words of Missy Davenport returning: *There's danger everywhere.*

CHAPTER FOUR

Even a heavy night on locally crafted beer at Barley Brown's couldn't dampen their spirits. All six woke bright and early the next morning, despite not rolling in until the early hours, Shady glad they had the place to themselves because of the racket they'd made. *Enough to wake the dead*, she'd thought as she'd helped both Brett and Teddy up the stairs while Josie had assisted Sam and Ray. Peeling off from the boys, the girls had entered their own room, Sam snagging a bed to herself, falling headlong into it, and Shady and Josie sharing the other.

Too tired to speak, they'd fallen into a deep and dreamless sleep, a strip of daylight entering their room a few hours later courtesy of drapes that hadn't been shut properly.

Wilderness Day, that's what they'd dubbed it. Time to head toward the mountains for two more days of unadulterated fun. Feeling exhausted but admiring the stamina of her companions—particularly Sam, who'd been the first of the trio in the girls' room to pull back the covers and leap from bed—Shady showered and dressed, then repacked her backpack.

Settled in Dorothea, Brett at the helm, Sam offered a brief lament about leaving the Willmott behind. "I'd better start earning big bucks if I ever want to stay there again."

"Unless you change careers," Josie reminded her.

"Clothes or brick walls?" she mused. "Better work it out, see what's the most lucrative."

"My mom's friends with an interior designer," Ray told her. "Earns a fortune."

"Just for slapping on a little paint?" Teddy snorted from the front seat.

"Bit more to it than that," Ray insisted, also settling back to admire the vista.

Smoke Ridge RV Resort and Campground was rated pretty highly for its beautiful mountain views and endless hiking opportunities. How far they'd actually get as far as hiking was concerned, however, was anyone's guess. Brett had been talking about hoisting up the hammock he'd brought with him beneath some trees and just chilling, Teddy nodding enthusiastically at that idea. Sam too was looking forward to swimming in a lake there and playing tennis, Josie promising to give her a game. As for Shady, as much as she didn't want to wish this precious time away with friends, she couldn't wait for night to fall, to be sitting out under the stars. A yearning was growing inside her to be closer to nature, especially now that she knew more about her mysterious Native American grandmother, her mother's mother, from whom she'd inherited coloring darker than her mother's, Ellen, who was blond. Ellen's coloring was her father's, a man who'd raped Kanti and then gone on his way, never knowing such a terrible act had resulted in a child. A tragic history, and Kanti was long gone, having died when Shady was a babe in arms. But since finding out about her, Shady had forged a connection, able to vividly imagine her face, the sharp and soft planes of it, her hair dark and flowing.

In whichever jacket she was wearing, Shady kept a scrap of leather that once belonged to Kanti and had been gifted to her by Ellen, one of the few things Ellen had of hers. Kanti and Ellen had been estranged from each other, Kanti a broken woman, not just because of the rape but because she'd had psychic ability too—could see like Shady could see, but, according to Ellen, only the dark stuff, the demons that had plagued her, her mental health deteriorating further. In death, Shady liked to think of her as healed, no longer frightened but powerful, as guiding her granddaughter, the stars guiding her also, the ones etched by Kanti's own hand onto the leather, which Shady clutched at now, her hand in her pocket, savoring the softness of it.

Tonight, there'd be stars for real, and perhaps more comfort to be had from them, because right now she felt in need of it. She felt…unsettled. As excited as she was to be camping with her friends, to get closer to nature, to be at one with it, unease was doing its best to nudge all those feelings aside. The photographs she'd seen—at The Lazy Stay Motel and the Grand Willmott—it was like they'd engraved themselves upon her mind.

Photographs… They had several at the museum too, definite energy attached to each. But energy as disturbing as she'd felt from those two? She wasn't sure. One of the photographs at Mason Town Museum, taken around the early 1900s, was of a little boy standing by a lake, the same lake he'd later drowned in, Shady had quickly realized. The sadness the photo exuded was understandable, that of the mother who'd sat with the image, pressing it to her chest and crying and crying, her heart shattered. Whenever Shady picked the photograph up, she felt the full force of that grief, as had its previous owner, another woman who collected old photos but who'd grown quite depressed over that one, suicidal even, and who'd brought it one day into the museum, located just a few miles from her home. Right away, Annie had connected the photo to the present owner's decline in mental state and asked if she could keep it to be studied.

In spite of her sorrow, the woman had been reluctant. She'd grown attached to the photograph, to the little boy, had grown comfortable too with the misery. She said she would sit and stare into his eyes, wanting to reach him somehow, to calm and comfort him. Though Annie sensed the woman wouldn't appreciate being called psychic or sensitive, she obviously was, identifying not just with the drowning boy but his stricken mother too, a powerful combination. Eventually, Annie had persuaded her to relinquish her grip on the photograph, at least temporarily, hoping against hope that the sorrow of an accident long gone would also let go. It worked. Less than three weeks later, when Annie had met the woman again, she'd looked completely different, her skin and eyes much brighter.

"Would you like the photograph back?" Annie asked.

"The photograph?" the woman replied. "Good Lord, no! Throw it in the trash if you want. I don't care. Can't think why I had such a thing about it, about any old photographs, for that matter." She'd then squinted her eyes. "I can barely even remember the boy's face."

Throwing it in the trash was, of course, an option, but for one thing…Annie and, in turn, Shady and Ray were never quite sure if there was more than residual energy attached, in this case something of the mother's spirit. If so, to dispose of her in such a brutal fashion when she'd suffered so much was not acceptable. Part of their job description was to sit with the charged object, all three of them at different times, to drench it in love and understanding, their aim to lessen the emotions attached, break down the energy but gently, returning anything that lingered to Source, considered the true home of spirit.

The photograph of the boy was still a work in progress. Others, however, were not in a controlled environment but out in the world, one hanging in a hotel, for God's sake! And no matter that it was down a darkened corridor, because that corridor was a thoroughfare that led to function rooms, causing Shady's concerns to increase further. Was that where those masked figures had met? Where the photograph had indeed been taken? It'd been hard to tell the background, as the men had filled it entirely.

"Hey, hey, hey, we're climbing higher!" Brett informed them, Sam squealing about what a steep road it was, the drop at the side really quite alarming.

Josie squeezed Shady's arm. "You okay?"

"Huh? Yeah. Why?"

"You got that faraway look in your eyes. Something on your mind?"

Turning toward her, Shady caught such earnestness in Josie's gaze. Thought too of all the photos they'd taken together all through their youth, selfies on their cell phones, either grinning or pulling faces or pouting. Must be hundreds of them, thousands. Precious photographs, imbued with happiness. How could she tell her about those not as good? As Ray had said, they were on vacation; this was downtime. And yet she couldn't forget the photographs—two in two days—that held such negativity, the masked figures something more than that, something

44

darker. Evil? A strong word, harsh, but even so…

She clutched at Josie rather than the leather scrap in her pocket and forced a smile. The masks had distorted the people behind them, turned them into something alien, their expressions hidden but not their eyes. Their eyes…they had glowered right back at her.

"There it is. It's coming into view!" Teddy yelled. "Smoke Ridge, we're coming atcha."

A cheer went up, drowning out any further thoughts plaguing Shady. She cheered too, tuning in to the excitement of the moment. Although the two photographs were similar in some ways—both of a group of people and with energy attached, one drenched in despair, the other in something akin to predatory glee—they had nothing, absolutely *nothing* to do with each other or with her. Their history was not her problem.

The campground wasn't busy, holiday season still a way off yet, and so they picked a prime spot by a large lake with views right across to the mountains, the blue of them indeed lending something of a smoky quality. The camping gear they'd brought with them, neatly stowed at the rear of the van, was retrieved and tents duly erected, although Brett and Teddy—tentless—had opted to sleep in the campervan. The day passed, Brett in his hammock as he'd promised he would be, the rest heading to a store on-site to get a few last-minute provisions for their evening meal after having gathered an assortment of sticks to throw in the burner so they could sit around a campfire at sundown.

"We're having s'mores, right?" Sam asked.

"'Course," Ray replied. "No camping trip would be complete without them."

Teddy piped up. "D'ya think we'll be able to—"

"No!" the group said in unison, Shady adding, "Seriously, Teddy, stick to Coors, okay?"

Although Teddy looked disappointed, he shrugged amicably enough, and ice was also duly purchased from the store to be put in buckets for the dozens of bottles of beer that Dorothea had hauled all this way from Safeway in Baker City.

As they headed back, Sam shivered a little, despite the day's warmth.

"Whassup?" asked Ray, noticing.

"It's just…it feels like we're the only ones here, doesn't it? A bit, like…isolated."

As Shady glanced their way, Ray said, "There's a few people on-site. We just have no neighbors, that's all. That's better, though, right? Gives us more freedom."

Although Sam agreed, she didn't seem convinced.

"Sam, what is it, what's bugging you?" Shady asked this time, Josie having gone up to Sam and linked her arm through hers, trying to impart comfort that way.

"It's nothing," Sam said before faltering. "I shouldn't have done it, not really."

Shady was even more intrigued. "Done what?"

"Oh, it was dumb. If I could kick my own ass, I would."

"Okay, Sam," Ray interjected as he stopped walking, "what are you talking about?"

"The film I watched a few nights ago," she confessed.

"What film?" asked Josie, patting at her arm now.

"A slash horror?" guessed Teddy. "Set in a campground? A *deserted* campground?"

"Fuck you!" Sam said, immediately angry at him, but then she faltered again and nodded. "But yeah, a slash horror set in a campground. Freaked the living hell out of me!"

"Sam!" Shady couldn't help it; the word burst from her, full of accusation. Teddy, meanwhile, was laughing so hard he had to put his bags down.

Sam raised her hands. "I know! I know! Like I said, it was a dumb thing to do. But…it looked kind of neat. Thought it'd get me in the mood. And then everyone just started dying! I mean, really, really dying, gruesome deaths, the most horrible you can imagine."

"Who was the murderer?" Ray wanted to know.

"One of them, of course," Sam told him. "The group that went camping." She then narrowed her eyes at Ray. "The sweetest one, the one you'd never guess would be guilty. Like…the hero, you know? Who you thought was saving everybody, not slaughtering them and then hiding their bodies!" Tearing her gaze from Ray, she then turned to Shady. "Guess you can never tell who's evil and who isn't, huh? It's like people wear…masks."

Shady's breath hitched. Why had Sam said such a thing, singled her out when she'd said it too? Another coincidence?

"Eyes," murmured Shady in response. "You can't disguise the eyes."

Sam, though, denied it. "This guy, the murderer, had cute eyes, big and dark. The kind you'd *want* to look into. So…you know, I don't think that's true. Eyes *can* fool you."

There was silence as they continued walking, each mulling over that point, wondering just who was right, Shady or Sam, and then Teddy burst out laughing again and pointed.

"Jeez, y'all," he said, "will you listen to that?"

They were only a few feet from camp now, a sound like a pneumatic drill emerging out of nowhere to assault their ears. Still laughing, Teddy shook his head.

"If Brett snores like that tonight in the van, there'll be murder for sure!"

CHAPTER FIVE

The sky was everything Shady could have hoped for, the stars silvery pinholes in night's curtain, as someone famous had once said, forming celestial patterns older than time itself.

She and Ray were lying back on a patch of grass, a bottle of Coors beside each of them, Ray's empty, Shady's barely touched.

"See that one?" Ray said, pointing. "That's Perseus, and that there, that's—"

"Gemini, yeah, I see it. And Ursa Minor, right up above us."

"And Ursa Major too, the Big Dipper."

"You know what I love most about the stars, Ray?"

He turned his head toward her. "That they're big and shiny and…hopeful."

Shady smiled. "All of that. But also that there are people just like us all over, looking up and seeing the same thing. You ever think about patterns?"

"What do you mean?"

"Patterns," she repeated. "And how they form. Connections that are…surprising."

Ray looked upward again. "Well, yeah, I suppose so. Getting from A to B doesn't always go the way you think."

"Yeah, I'm learning that more and more. Ray?"

"Yeah?"

"This job we do, it teaches you, doesn't it, to trust your instinct? To listen to yourself?"

"Sure does. I guess that's the only thing we *can* rely on." He pushed himself up onto one arm and gazed down on her. "Has something happened?"

"You told me not to touch."

"Did I?"

Shady laughed. "You know what, Ray? When you screw your nose up like that, you look like a little kid!"

"A little kid?" He reached out and tickled her, immediately causing her to collapse into fits of giggles.

"Ray, come on, stop it!"

"Who looks like a little kid now, huh?"

"Hey, you two, quit what you're doing and come on over here!"

Teddy's voice brought them both to their senses. As she sat up, playfully thumping Ray on his arm while she did so, Shady hollered back. "What is it?"

"Story time, of course," he replied. "Around ye olde campfire."

Sam giggled, as did Josie. "*Ghost* stories," she elaborated.

"Really?" Shady said, Ray helping her to rise.

"Yeah, sure!" Brett asserted. "It's tradition, right? Ghost stories and s'mores. Come on, hurry. Let's get this party started!"

As they approached, Josie beckoned for Shady to come and sit with her, Shady happily obliging. "So, who's going first?" she asked as Teddy handed them both their s'mores, toasted marshmallow and Hershey's chocolate oozing out of the graham crackers.

Josie licked at her fingers, then straightened. "The story I've got isn't about ghosts, but it is a true story, and it is pretty gruesome. That okay?"

"Shoot!" Teddy encouraged.

"All right. Sam, you sure it's okay to go ahead? You're not gonna get spooked?"

Sam waved her bottle of beer in the air, her fourth or fifth by the looks of the empties by her side. "Like Teddy says, shoot. Don't know why I got so freaked earlier."

"Here goes, then," Josie said, shifting a little to get comfortable. "There was a family years ago, can't remember how long exactly, but they went camping right here in Oregon, just like we're doing. It was a mom, dad and two kids, both girls. One was aged around nine, the other twelve or so." She cocked her head to the side. "Hey, what if it was this campground they'd stayed at?"

"Do you think it was?" Despite her earlier bravado, Sam sounded edgy again.

Josie thought for a moment and then shook her head. "Nah! There are campgrounds like this all over Oregon. It could have been any one of 'em. So, they were having a great time, it was busy, kids were making friends, the parents just chilling out, planning some day trips to keep them all occupied. Shame they did, though, that they didn't just stay put."

"Why? What happened?" Teddy asked, gooey marshmallow stuck to his chin.

"They struck out from camp one day, and that was it. They…disappeared."

"An entire family?" Sam breathed. "Really?"

"Uh-huh," replied Josie, continuing to pick at her s'mores. "The police got a big search underway, as they do, but couldn't find 'em. Eventually, they had to call off the search. The family was gone, joined the ranks of the missing."

"Heavy, man!" said Brett.

"Real heavy." Having devoured the s'mores, Josie then clapped her hands together, indicating she was far from finished with the story. "Six months later, though, and whaddya know, the family was found! Miles and miles from the campground and completely by accident, by a hiker just out there doing his thing. As decomposed as their bodies were, it was obvious they'd met with gruesome deaths, that they'd been…torn apart. They thought it might be a bear. If it was, though, it was one hungry motherfucker. The twist is, the guy that found them, he went on record as saying it *wasn't* a bear that did it, that the injuries to all of them were too violent even for a big old pissed-as-hell grizzly. He insisted something else was responsible, something…mythical."

"Mythical?" Teddy was clearly confused. "Come on, have you seen *The Revenant*?"

"*The Revenant*?" Josie asked.

"Yeah, there's a bear attack in it. Leo DiCaprio barely survives. Grizzlies can be mean!"

Brett just shrugged. "Wouldn't know one bear attack from another, honestly."

Shady nudged Josie. "What do you mean, 'mythical'?"

"Skin walkers," Josie said, that sweet smile of hers completely at odds with all she was saying. "This man, this hunter, he believed their deaths to be the work of a skin walker."

Sam almost choked on her beer. "What the fuck is a skin walker?"

"Actually," Ray said, looking a little more somber, "I've heard of them. Shady, you know about them? It's a Navajo thing."

Shady shook her head. "Sorry, Ray, still got a lot to learn about my ancestry. It's like I've barely even lifted the lid. So, come on, Josie, what are they?"

Josie happily continued to educate them. "Skin walkers are, like, demonic creatures," she said, dramatically lowering her voice even though there were no immediate neighbors. "They're like humans, they walk on two feet, but they're not. They're *transformed* humans that've become half animal too, with powers above both, like, a breed apart."

Shady was further stunned that Josie, whom she still thought of as exuding childlike innocence, knew about such creatures. Dragons were one thing, but...skin walkers? Her own s'mores discarded and, like her beer, barely touched, she frowned as she probed further. "Okay, right. But if they're mythical, then why did the hiker think they're responsible? A myth is just that, something made up, a tall tale."

"Because there's more to the myth than we think, that's why!" Josie replied. "He said he'd seen one once, out in the wild, the *Oregon* wild. Said it was three times bigger than a wolf, walked on two legs and had eyes that glowed red. Said he was lucky to escape it too, that it was only by pure fluke he did. It had its eyes trained on him, and then something else seemed to attract its attention, and off it went, faster than the speed of light."

"Man," Brett said, drinking deeply from his Coors bottle.

"And maybe..." Josie continued, clearly on a roll. "It was a walker responsible for Alisa Jones's disappearance too.

Although, she was never found, poor thing. And it's been twenty years for her. Twenty long, long years. You ever heard of Alisa Jones?"

Five heads shook. "Should we have?" Sam asked.

"It's just…she's kind of like a superstar, in these parts, anyway. Her picture was pasted everywhere at the time and kinda went viral. She had this white blond hair, blue eyes and the biggest smile you've ever seen. Real pretty. Real accomplished too. A serious hiker and a very skilled hunter. She was from a place called Bend in Oregon. People still talk about her to this day. Well, in Baker City they do, anyways—I've heard them, about the mystery surrounding her. I looked her up online. There're loads of theories about her disappearance, YouTube videos, stuff on TikTok, Twitter, that kinda thing, and, yep, there's a lot of people out there who think that a walker got her. Devoured her whole."

"Jeez, Josie!" Shady gasped.

Josie winced. "Going a little too far?"

"Just a bit."

"It's…interesting, that's all. And sad, of course, real sad. Alisa's camp was found, you know, with all her gear still there, including her rifle. Why would she bring all that stuff, then strike out with none of it? Especially her rifle. No one does that. Especially not someone experienced. So, what happened? What lured her? She really was very pretty."

"You lie awake thinking about this stuff?" Shady was intrigued to know.

Josie laughed as she denied it. "No! But being out here, camping, it reminds me of shit like that, makes it more real somehow." She tilted her head and gazed outward. "Come on, guys, look out there at the darkness. What's in it? *Truly* in it? What kind of secrets does it hide? Sometimes it seems like anything's possible." A brief silence was followed by more laugher. "Will you listen to me? All this fresh air must have gone to my head!"

Everybody insisted it was fine, Brett adding, "It's what we're here for, to have a little fun, and fun for me includes scaring the shit out of myself."

"Just don't go wandering from camp, anyone," Teddy said, friendly sarcasm in every word. "If you need to pee, go in twos. Like Josie said, you don't know what's out there."

Ray, however, was contemplative. "There's a skin-walker ranch, did you know that?" When it was clear no one did, he went right ahead and enlightened them. "Yep, not here, though, in Utah. Yeah, yeah, it's coming back to me now, what I read about it. It's right out in the wilderness. And it's called that because…nope, hang on, I have to Google it…" Ray reached for his cell and tapped the screen. "Here we go," he continued, the screen lighting up his face ghoulishly as he read. "It's the site of paranormal and UFO-related activities. A load has gone on there, including sightings of skin walkers, who focus on cattle, mutilating and killing them. In contrast, the skin walkers are impossible to kill. Here we go: 'According to ranch owner Terry Sherman, he shot one three times at close range, and the bullets just seemed to bounce right off its hide.'"

"Guys, guys," Shady implored, "can we change the subject?"

"Getting spooked yourself now, Shady?" Brett asked.

"No…yeah…look, I want to sleep tonight, that's all."

"Actually," Sam said, "so do I. I know, let's play some music instead!"

On hearing this, Ray did the honors and opened a

playlist on his phone. "Taylor Swift anyone?"

There were various groans, but when "Shake It Off" belted out, no one could help but join in. An hour or two later, with everyone exhausted from continuingly shaking it out to that and other Taylor tunes, the music was lowered and something more ambient chosen instead.

Stifling a yawn, Shady rose.

"Where you going?" Josie asked, her head on Ray's shoulder as she too yawned.

"The bathroom."

"Want me to come with? We need to go in twos, remember."

"You're okay," Shady said, smiling. "The restrooms are just there. I'll be fine."

"In the middle of the night, though—"

"It's not the middle of the night."

"But when it is…"

"When it is, then you can come with, okay?"

As Shady ventured out, Teddy called after her. "Watch out for the walkers!"

"Will do!" Shady replied, rolling her eyes.

"And any passing axe murderers," Brett added.

"Yep, thanks for that, Brett."

Farther away from them now, Shady's smile faded. The shower facility *was* a short distance, but even a few feet from her friends, the darkness closed in, became more potent. It wasn't like she needed to pee either. What she'd wanted was some peace. All that talk of skin walkers had unsettled her further. A myth—a *Navajo* myth—it was one she didn't particularly want to know about. *Because of the photograph. Because of them…* Was that it? The masked men—*hybrids*—still playing on her mind? The other photograph too, such a source of grief and loss. Both of them stumbled upon in less than twenty-four hours. *Is that the only connection?*

Time alone was what she sought, she reminded herself, to try to quash this unease, replace it with something more positive. From her pocket she retrieved Kanti's scrap of leather, studied the stars on it, then looked up at the sky again and studied the stars there. Stars that blinked and twinkled, had done so for billions of years and would no doubt for billions more. With nothing to pollute the air, no neon city lights, the night truly was breathtaking, able to harbor such mystery and wonder, as Josie had said. Her ancestors, had they believed in skin walkers too? Had they feared them? Had some…idolized them? *Become* them? Like a shape-shifter, able to transform themselves?

She laughed, the sound of it really quite startling in the silence.

Looks like Josie got you good tonight! It's a myth, no matter what anyone says. Fabrication. Go back to the others before a passing bear decides you're his dinner.

About to turn, she stopped, saw something in the trees by the showers, movement of some kind. A night owl, perhaps? Taking a couple of steps closer, she craned her neck forward and squinted. Bigger than a night owl, something that squatted.

She frowned. What the heck would squat in a tree?

Cold fear gripped her.

And how come it had red eyes that glowed?

CHAPTER SIX

Higher up the valley, about thirty miles or so from Smoke Ridge, was a lake renowned as a popular beauty spot, the reflection of the mountains surrounding it shimmering in cerulean-blue waters.

It was Ray who was Googling the local area at breakfast the next morning. "It's considered sacred to the Native peoples," he said, reading the description. "There's a quote here from a tribe elder. He says, 'Nowhere else in the world is quite like Mazuma Lake. It is surely one of our most blessed places.' Sounds pretty cool, huh?"

"Sure," Shady replied, rubbing at her eyes. She was tired, hardly able to sleep at all in the tent between Sam and Josie, and when she had, her dreams had taken a strange turn, including those in the photograph at the Grand Willmott, all with glowing red eyes.

"Should we go?" Ray suggested, not just to Shady but the group, who were all lazing around the blackened aftermath of last night's fire. "It's a nice day for an excursion."

With everyone murmuring agreement, it took another hour for them to get ready, adopting their previous seats in Dorothea, who then burst readily into life.

"Atta girl," said Brett, almost caressing the wheel.

As Teddy set the GPS, they headed out of the resort,

more of Brett's woozy psychedelic music serenading them.

"I think I prefer Taylor Swift," Josie said, making Shady laugh.

"I definitely do!"

"So, you didn't sleep too good last night?"

Shady was surprised. "You noticed?"

"I woke up a few times, thinking I could hear someone snooping around outside."

"Oh shit, really?"

"It was just my imagination. Gave myself the creeps by talking all that bullshit. Did I give you nightmares too? Is that why you were tossing around so much?"

"No," Shady lied. "I was just hot. It got kinda stuffy in there."

"Yeah, I suppose. This place, the lake, you heard of it before now?"

"Mazuma? No."

"Me neither, and it's on my doorstep. Think we'll be tempted to go skinny-dipping?"

"You, maybe, not me! It's nowhere near warm enough."

"Actually, you're right, the weather's kind of turning. Look."

Shady peered out the window. Back at camp, the skies had been clear. Now, though, a fog was developing, gray-tinged and rolling in.

Even Ray appeared concerned. From his seat beside Sam, he also peered out. "Where'd that spring up from?" he wondered, scratching at his head.

"Keep within the white lines," Sam warned, still paranoid about the drop.

"Got it, don't worry," Brett assured her, but he turned the music down so he could focus, Shady grateful for small mercies.

Dorothea continued to rumble upward, although she was wheezing again, just like she had when they'd stopped at the motel.

"Shit, man." Teddy's voice was a half whisper. "Think she's gonna make it?"

"Sure," Brett said and then sighed. "How beautiful is this beauty spot anyways?"

"Very," Ray told him. "A must-see."

"A must-see, huh?" Brett muttered. "Okay, well, when in Rome and all that."

Silence reigned as Brett continued to focus on the road ahead. Chilled to a fault normally, the way he gripped the wheel and shifted in his seat showed he was taking his responsibility seriously. But just as Dorothea was struggling, so was Shady.

The previous night, in camp, they'd talked about the darkness and what lay within it. Now, Shady was wondering the exact same thing about the fog and what it concealed.

The higher they climbed, the thicker the fog became, Dorothea's lights struggling to cut through it. Another thing: it was deepening in hue, going from gray to greeny black.

"You know what," Teddy piped up, his voice also betraying his concern, "I think I've read about this phenomenon."

Brett looked over at him. "Is that what this is? A phenomenon?"

"Yeah. It's got something to do with cold air from the mountain running into warm air from the valley. It causes thick fog like this."

"Oh yeah," Brett said, just a second before slamming on

the brakes, bringing Dorothea to a juddering halt. "Shit! What the fuck was that?"

Sam also shouted. "Jeez, Brett, what the fuck was what?"

"I don't know!" His breathing had grown heavy. "Something ran past the van, something, like…really fast. An animal of some sort. Tall. Didn't you see it?"

Teddy shook his head. "Don't see nothing but fog."

Brett took a moment to compose himself before addressing Teddy again. "Maybe…maybe it was just my imagination. Or maybe some of your 'good stuff,' Teddy, is still pumping through my veins. Yeah, yeah, that must be it, some kind of buildup. Hey, do you think we can ride it out? That it'll clear the higher we go?"

"We can give it a shot."

"NO!" It was Shady who shouted now, nervousness making her chest heave. "We don't go another inch. We turn around." Her voice much smaller, she added, "Somehow."

"Turn around?" Brett twisted in his seat, as did Teddy. "This is a narrow road, Shady."

"With a sheer drop on one side," Teddy reminded her.

"Oh God," Sam exclaimed.

"It's like, I can't see the edge of the road, not well enough," Brett continued. "Might be easier to keep going. Hope that when we reach the summit, the fog'll be gone."

"You know what?" said Teddy. "I think when I read about this phenomenon—"

"Fuck's sake, Teddy." Ray sighed.

"No, hear me out. When I saw it on YouTube or whatever, it said you couldn't just ride your way out of it. It gets more and more intense. Man, if we ever wanted surreal, we got it right here, right now. Never seen a fog like this before."

"We cannot go any further," Shady insisted.

"But it's only a few more miles to the lake—"

"No, Brett, I mean it. We have to turn around! I can't…" Shit, she was struggling for breath now. Was this a panic attack? In front of an audience of five.

"Shady, come on." Josie was beginning to sound panicky too. "It'll be okay—"

"TURN AROUND! We can't carry on!" Once again, Missy's words flew back at her: *Keep your wits about you. There's danger everywhere.* What if she meant here, like this, in fog as dark as night? A fog that was…unnatural. "Please, please turn around."

In response to her pleading, Ray had already opened the side door and was jumping out of the campervan, telling Brett he'd help him navigate the turnaround.

Sam had scooted over to Shady's side too, and, like Josie, was trying to comfort her.

"We're turning, okay?" she said. "It'll be all right. We're getting out of here. Actually," she added, shivering as she rubbed her hands together, "maybe we should all jump out of the van. You know…just in case Brett gets it wrong."

Shady wouldn't do it, though. "Just…too much darkness," she said. "Sorry. So sorry."

"You have nothing to be sorry for," Josie assured her. "Brett, you got this?"

"Sure," he called back. "We're doing okay."

Everyone fell quiet, leaving just the sound of Shady struggling to get herself back under control and subdue too her mortification at her behavior. Sure, the fog was dense, a true phenomenon, but it didn't merit quite this reaction. Panic had sprung from nowhere.

Immediately, she realized that wasn't true. It had sprung from the unease that had been building and building ever since The Lazy Stay Motel and just kept being compounded. What was it that Brett had seen in the fog, running in front of them?

"Come on, baby," Brett muttered as he turned Dorothea, Ray shouting precise instructions.

"Back up, STOP! Now forward, another foot, that's it. STOP, Brett, STOP!"

The tension was palpable—Shady could feel both Josie and Sam trembling too. This was a narrow road by any standards, a narrow *mountain* road, which would of course plateau out, but not soon enough. They couldn't afford to make a mistake. Shit, the fog out there; Ray was barely visible in it, let alone the edge of the road, his voice muffled by it too.

Eventually, though, and miraculously, Dorothea was pointing her beautiful blue nose in the right direction, Ray jumping back in the van and high-fiving both Teddy and Brett, Brett putting her back into gear and driving them down.

"Sorry about that," Ray said. "Guess Mazuma Lake wasn't such a great idea." He leaned closer to Shady. "We'll be back at Smoke Ridge soon enough."

Twenty minutes later, they pulled into the campground. This far down, the fog had completely dispersed, although the day remained gray, clouds in the sky bursting open.

"Shit," Brett muttered, "rain. That's all we need."

As they parked, the atmosphere was so different to when they'd arrived the previous day, thanks to the elements and to Shady's disintegration. The girls continued to fuss around her as the boys erected a tarp over their seating area, Ray also trying to light some kindling that had become damp, several attempts needed.

For her part, Shady kept assuring Sam and Josie that she was fine, but the two girls stuck to her like limpets, pulling her over to the slowly developing fire and sitting with her there, seemingly in as much need of warmth as she was. The chill in her bones, however, refused to abate, her eyes traveling over the lake to the mountains beyond and the trees that covered the slopes between the scree. Mountain lions, lynx, cougar and bear were some of the animals that roamed this land, but what about others, those with glowing red eyes that crept around campgrounds?

It was no use. She couldn't settle, and neither could the others. As for the rain, it poured harder. A reefer might help settle her—she'd be sure to take a few puffs this time—but, strangely, no one was offering or cracking open the beers either. Everyone just sat and stared at the fire in silence.

Josie eventually broke the spell. Letting go of Shady's arm, she jumped up and clapped her hands.

"Okay, my house is kinda small, but what the heck? We can't stay here, we'll…catch our deaths," she said, wincing as her eyes flickered toward Shady, clearly wishing she'd chosen another form of expression. "Let's go back to my place for our last night together. It'll be snug in my bedroom, sure, but it'll be fun, and Mom can amaze you with her cooking. Some of you don't know this, but she does the best dim sum this side of Shanghai!"

"Oh man, I love dim sum!" said Teddy, needing no further prompt as he too jumped up and began to gather his stuff. The others quickly followed, Josie and Shady exchanging a glance, Shady grateful for such a suggestion, for not having to spend another night in the wilderness.

Maybe she'd feel differently if the sun were still shining, more able to put what she'd seen in the trees the previous night down to imagination. She guessed she'd never know, and she was cool with that. Four brick walls, some heat, and Lulin Wong's cooking were the things to look forward to now.

The journey back to Baker City was thankfully fog-free, the sun trying to make an appearance, no matter how weak. This break hadn't exactly gone as planned, what with the motel stay and only the one night at Smoke Ridge, but determination now replaced somberness in the group, false cheer becoming more genuine every mile they traveled on the highway and drew closer to civilization. When they eventually disembarked Dorothea, spirits were high again. Josie had called ahead to warn her mom they were coming, and she was duly closing the store early to come home and prepare a feast.

As all six goofed around up the pathway that led to the Wongs' porch and front door, another car drew up, parking right beside Dorothea on the street.

From it, a woman emerged and a young girl—likely her daughter, although the pair were as different as night and day, the mother blond, wearing a floral dress and flashing a toothy white smile, the daughter with stringy black hair, black clothes and decidedly sullen.

"Hello, hello," the woman said, waving to the group as she walked along her own path.

"Hello, Mrs. Hadley," Josie hollered back, stopping to introduce her friends to her neighbor. "Hi, Brandi," she added, the teenager issuing a grunt in response. Undeterred, Josie also told them her friends were visiting from Idaho Falls for a few days and that they'd just come back from camping at Smoke Ridge.

"Smoke Ridge?" Mrs. Hadley enthused. "We used to go there! Remember that, Brandi? You used to love to swim in the lake in summer. Oh, did you make it to Mazuma Lake too? Now *that's* the place for swimming. Out in the boonies for sure, but totally worth it."

"No, ma'am, we didn't quite get there," Josie replied. "The weather turned on us on the way, got real foggy. We were going to spend two nights at the campground, but, again, because of the weather, we've quit. It was sunny the first day but rainy today."

"Ah well, you had beautiful weather for part of it. That's something to be grateful for. So, let me guess, you sat around the campfire, telling each other ghost stories?" Here, Mrs. Hadley laughed, most likely recalling good times when she'd done exactly that too.

"We sure did," Josie told her, Shady noticing the girl beside her mother growing even more restless, bored with the chatter, contemptuous even.

Mrs. Hadley, however, was oblivious to her daughter's attitude or perhaps too used to it to care. "Did you tell the one about the knock, knock, knocking in the dead of night?"

"Um—" Josie said, but Mrs. Hadley didn't seem to need a reply.

"Well, sheesh, this banging, it's getting on everyone's nerves, okay? They can't work out where it's coming from. This family's staying in an RV, of course, on one of the campsites, but a little further out than normal. Who the hell could be doing that, they wonder? A ghost? A monster?" Lost in the storytelling, she seemed to gaze beyond them. "The wind's picking up, it's getting really stormy out there, and it happens again, one of the kids eventually saying they think it's coming from the back of the RV, the window there. Before his parents can do anything to stop him, the kid runs to the window and opens it, and, whaddya know, a severed head blows right in, all wrapped up in entrails, hanging from the boughs of the trees above. *That's* what the banging was!"

Shady's eyebrows shot up. "Jesus," she murmured.

Josie, however, was totally unfazed, something that astounded Shady. Back in Idaho Falls, she'd shudder at such tales. Not now, though; she'd gotten braver. "Oh, that's a good one, ma'am, but, no, we talked mainly about skin walkers."

Shady was the one who shuddered now at the mere mention of them. Even so, she noticed the kid lift her head, stop kicking the pavement in obvious boredom, her eyes narrowing as she did, her head tilted to one side, interested at last.

In contrast, a frown crossed Mrs. Hadley's face. "Skin walkers? Oh, well, I wouldn't know about that."

"Oh really?" Josie said. "We were wondering if they were responsible for some of the people that go missing, you know"—she nodded into the distance—"out there."

"Josie…" Shady tried to interrupt. Even Ray was looking surprised by this exchange.

"Well, if I knew what they were, then maybe. Sure, a lot of people go missing, and those that are found, well…perhaps it's best they stay missing, you know? Remember that poor family? Oh, and Alisa. What happened to her, d'ya think? Such a cute smile."

"Yeah, sure hope that what killed that family didn't get her," Josie replied.

"Josie!" This time Shady's voice was firmer.

Josie turned to her, her expression as sweet as ever. "Shady? You okay?"

"Let's just…get inside." All this talk of skin walkers, she didn't want it, wished she was like Mrs. Hadley and ignorant of them.

"Sure," Josie agreed. "Nice seeing you, Mrs. Hadley. You too, Brandi."

Mrs. Hadley waved again, as did the group, continuing onward to their respective homes, Shady once more noting the teenager, whose hands remained steadfastly by her side. Her eyes, however, met Shady's, the curiosity that had briefly enlivened them gone.

CHAPTER SEVEN

Josie cried as the group of friends left for home the next day, hugging Shady as tightly as she'd hugged her on arrival.

"We'll see each other soon," said Shady. "We won't let another year go by."

"Promise?"

"Pinky promise."

"And I'll come see you too in Idaho Falls. I love Baker City, but, man, I miss that place."

Everything had returned to harmony the moment they'd set foot in Josie's house. They'd set up another camp, this time in Josie's bedroom, Lulin having returned home not long after them to prepare dinner. That evening, all had squeezed around the family dining table—Josie's father, Huan, at one end, Lulin at the other—and enjoyed the most delectable cooking they'd had in a long while, Brett as theatrical as Wanda McIntyre and standing up and clapping afterward, declaring the meal "a triumph."

The laughter at the dinner table had continued in Josie's bedroom, the six of them reverting to being high school kids, no talk of skin walkers, severed heads, or mutilated families making it onto the agenda this time.

The journey home went smoothly too, although it took an extra couple of hours, Brett really taking it slow with

Dorothea, and Dorothea clearly appreciating the pampering. They didn't pass The Lazy Stay Motel on the way; Brett took a slightly different route, and Shady was disappointed *and* relieved, curious about what she'd encountered there but also wanting to rid herself of the last dregs of unease.

When she and Ray met at the museum the following day, Annie greeted them with fresh coffee and donuts, wanting to know how they'd gotten on.

With her hands wrapped around her mug, appreciating its warmth, Shady was happy for Ray to do the talking, Annie listening intently. It was only later when Ray had finished his shift and gone home, Shady staying behind to care for some particular items, that Annie cornered her. Shady might have thought she'd gotten away with remaining mute earlier, but she should have known better. Annie didn't claim to be psychic as such, but she knew well enough when something was up, that the trip had had some low points, for Shady, at least.

Annie…Rhapsody-in-Brown, as Shady still thought of her, a name she'd coined when meeting her that first time she'd come into the diner where Shady used to work and asked for help regarding a doll called Mandy. Annie had been christened such because of the clothes she always wore, all brown, sometimes from head to toe, her eyes and her hair brown too, although the latter was flecked with gray. Even the rims of her eyeglasses were brown. A woman who was her boss, her mentor and her friend, who'd changed Shady's life irrevocably, *helped* her. Could she help her now to make sense of these latest events?

It all came spilling out, not least about the confusion she still felt.

"That's the thing, Annie, with the photographs it's about feelings, nothing more tangible than that. And the thing I saw in the trees. I'd had a beer, just a few sips, but even so, maybe it affected me. Do you know much about skin walkers?"

"A little. I know they're a taboo subject, amongst the Natives, I mean. No one goes out of their way to talk about them. In fact, they *won't*."

"Really?" Shady said, wondering if that hesitation was somehow inherent in her. "And then when we were in the fog, Brett saw something run straight across the road in front of him. Something big…and hairy."

There was a brief silence, and then both burst out laughing.

"Big and hairy, you say?" repeated Annie, still grinning.

"Yeah, yeah. Sounds stupid, I know."

Annie shook her head. "Oh, it doesn't, not really, but again, it could be imagination at play. As for feelings, we've discussed this before, called it by another name: *instinct*. Maybe there's something to it, but, Shady, as you know, everybody, *everything*, carries history. If you're meant to get involved, another path will open up and lead you back there. Fate, if you like. Until then"—she gestured around her—"we've enough to contend with here. Now, do you mind if I push off? I'm meeting a friend for dinner, and I'd like to head home first to freshen up."

"Sure, I'll lock up."

"You're heading home soon, though?"

"Yeah, I will be. Just buffing up the gold on this ring here," Shady replied, holding up one of the items she'd been tending to.

"Ah, yes, jewelry, how it soaks up a person's energy."

Shady nodded. "Whoever wore this was troubled, that's for sure."

"Which is why it remains here, so it doesn't trouble anyone else by proxy." Annie leaned over and examined it. "It has interesting markings on it, doesn't it, the wavy lines."

Shady examined it further too. Annie was right, markings that had clearly meant something to someone a long time ago, a woman older than her, maybe in her thirties, who'd touched this ring a lot, spinning it around and around the ring finger on her right hand. A nervous habit, perhaps? But what had she been nervous of, exactly? The twirling of it became more and more frequent the more agitated she'd become. The ring had been precious to her, what she'd focused on when feeling such emotions, the gold imbibing them, becoming more than a ring, a mere object but something synonymous with her troubles. Found in a junk shop by Annie, who scoured such places regularly looking for charged items; the person behind the counter knew nothing of its history, as was so often the case. It had been part of a bulk buy from another dealer, so who the woman was, what the pattern meant and what she was afraid of were all a mystery, this ring—early twentieth century— her only legacy. A dangerous legacy in the wrong hands, or rather the wrong finger.

Annie at last bustled off, shouting another goodbye before closing the door behind her. Despite the dubious nature of the items at the museum, Shady liked to be alone there and would often make an excuse to stay behind; Annie and Ray, she suspected, were perfectly aware of this and indulged her.

The ring polished enough now and gleaming, something that made Shady happy, the brightness of it when it had been so tarnished, she placed it back in its velvet-lined box and made her way over to Mandy. This was another ritual she usually carried out, spending time with the doll, releasing it from the glass box it was kept in, just for a short while, tuning in to the good that inhabited it while sending light to the evil that was also deep inside, wondering as she did so about objects, about herself, and about photographs specifically and the world within worlds that they contained.

Shady might not know much about skin walkers, but she knew well enough the ancient Native belief regarding photographs. They held that the process could steal a person's soul, thus disrespecting the spiritual world. The technology alien to them, they regarded photography as magic—*bad* magic.

Smiling wryly at that, Shady gave Mandy a final hug, feeling both the longing in her and the doll's repulsion, then placed her back in the glass display. After that, she wandered over to another cabinet, where some old black-and-white photographs were kept. In particular, she sought out and focused on the one with the boy who had drowned in the lake behind him, the photo that had come to mind during the trip. Was a part of his soul trapped within it, as well as his mother's? Or was it just the residue of emotions? Emotions maketh the person, though, so could the two be separated? Such sorrow. It emanated from the photograph, the shock of a life cut short, a future unrealized. Tears sprang to Shady's eyes, the sadness of strangers becoming her own, so intense, able to fell an otherwise contented mind. As Annie was always at pains to point out, that was where the danger lay.

In amongst the other photographs was one of an Omaha Indian, just the back of him, dressed in a fringed jacket with a long, rather exotic feather poking from his hair. Shady was glad she couldn't see his face because if she could, there'd be anger in his expression, for that was the overriding energy that clung to this object. A justified anger, though. Some Natives had been forced to pose like this in full regalia, portrayed as savage, primitive beings, utterly different to the white man, lower, and this subject knew it, he *reviled* it, and his anger, justified or not, could still be contagious.

Her eyes traveling briefly to the clock on the wall to check the time—it was a little past six o'clock—she examined one more photo. This was, like the ring, from the Victorian era and, as far as she was concerned, the height of morbidity. It was of a trio of children, all sitting side by side, but one, the smallest, had her eyes closed. A dead child, propped up beside the living, her blond curls still resplendent, the white pinafore she wore pristine. Annie had told Shady and Ray all about the trend for postmortem photography back then. With diseases such as diphtheria, typhus and cholera commonplace, death had been very much a part of life. It seemed like a miracle that anyone made it into adulthood, nurseries also falling foul of measles, scarlet fever and rubella, all illnesses largely avoided now thanks to better diet, sanitary conditions and vaccines, but not then and which could prove fatal.

In having a photograph of a lost child, you had a relic, a permanent likeness of someone treasured. Not so morbid, when Shady thought about it, understandable even. If it comforted you, if it got you through, then how could it be criticized? The aura that clung to this photograph, however, had nothing to do with the family it once belonged to but, rather, the person who'd subsequently collected it and others like it. A person obsessed with death. A *black* obsession. And that's why it was held at the Mason Town Museum, beneath glass, Annie having placed crystals such as tourmaline and labradorite around it as well as the others to soak up any negative energy, cleansing those stones regularly so they could take on more, the aim to leave the afflicted objects something benign again—a token of history, merely that.

Shady sighed. It really was getting late, time to go home, grab some dinner and watch TV with her mom and dad. They were currently working their way through *Breaking Bad* for the second time, her mom having developed quite the crush on Bryan Cranston.

As she began turning off all the lights in the building, working from the coatroom at the rear toward the entrance, her coat shrugged on and her backpack slung over one shoulder, photographs were still on her mind. Even as she locked the museum door and got into her car, she thought about them, those that were still out there in the big wide world, two in particular. She thought too about feelings and instinct, just trusting your gut, and lastly about fate and the roads it could lead you down. The roads it *had* led her already. *The tip of the iceberg, Shady. It's just the tip of the iceberg.*

CHAPTER EIGHT

A few short weeks later and the trip Shady and her friends had shared passed into the realms of memory, life happening as life did, work filling most days from beginning to end, as well as shopping trips to the mall with her mom and evenings at The Golden Crown in the heart of Idaho Falls with Ray and whomever else was free. Also during those weeks, Ray had started talking about taking a course in ancient history.

"Whaddya think, Shady?" he'd asked one afternoon, both of them working the desk at the museum, a busload having stopped by, drawn there by articles on the Net about Mandy, including a TikTok video a visitor had posted that had gone viral. The doll really was quite the superstar, the concept of her being haunted tickling just about everyone's fancy. People equaled money, though, each one wanting to gawk at her having paid an entrance fee and thereby, voyeurs or not, supporting a worthy cause.

Ray had been looking at his cell when he'd posed the question, causing her to ask what he meant.

"Harvard or Yale?"

"Still not with you, Ray."

"For this history course I want to do. Where should I go? Harvard or Yale."

Shady laughed. "Yeah, right. Don't think your wages are gonna stretch that far."

"Only kidding," he said. "I wouldn't give this job up for the world. It's just ignited a thirst, you know, to learn more about the past, to try to see the bigger picture, become something of an expert. Annie is. She's got this whole English background in history and antiques, and you've got that superhuman ability of yours—"

"I'm not superhuman, Ray! Besides, everyone's good at something."

"Yeah, and I want to be good at this job, really good, an authority. I want to take it into the future, live and breathe it. I think a history course of some kind will help with that, you know. I'll be as relevant."

"Ray," she said, reaching across to squeeze his arm just as a burst of giggling erupted from a group standing next to Mandy, swearing she'd moved her eyes from side to side. "You *are* relevant. We're a team, the three of us. We work because we're different, because we complement each other. Together we can see what the other can't. But, yeah, I'm all for learning, for self-improvement. Just don't bankrupt yourself in the process."

Ray smiled and patted at Shady's hand. "I just believe in what we're doing, the power of it. I feel…fired up by it. You inspired me, you know, that night under the stars up at Smoke Ridge, when you talked about connections, joining the dots, that kind of thing, how we get from A to B. That's what we're doing here, traveling through life, an experience I want to enrich as much as possible." He shrugged. "The history course is an idea, that's all." Picking up an object in front of him, which was yet to be curated, an antique smoking pipe, a beautiful piece carved from mahogany, he added, "I want to know about the world stuff like this came from, the people who used them, who also wore those military jackets we have, who pushed the ancient plows in the field, the trappers, the days of the gold rush, beyond that, even, beyond this country, the history of the artifacts we have from all over the world—that ankh, for example, from Egypt. Now there's a history I could sink my teeth into. Learning about pharaohs, Cleopatra and the Nile."

"Ray," she said, "you took history at Fairmont, right?"

"Sure."

"And?"

"Never listened to a word of it."

"Gotta admire your honesty."

"It's different now, though."

"Yeah," she agreed. "It is. Completely."

The day soon passed, and this time Shady and Ray closed the museum together, then headed home.

A pleasant day turned into a pleasant evening, Shady having dinner with her parents, Ellen and Bill, telling them a little something about her day, them also telling her about theirs, that the stationery-supplies company they ran, after a bit of a struggle recently—competition from giants such as Amazon taking its toll—had picked right up, people remembering how much they appreciated the personal touch. As Josie's house in Baker City was modest, so was the Groveses' house in Idaho Falls. They lived in the numbered streets in Kate Curley Park, but as Ellen would always say, "We have everything we need as long as we have each other." Certainly, Shady's job at the Mason Town Museum might not be the key to riches; the wage meant she couldn't move out of her parents' house, not yet, anyway. But rich in experience? It ticked the box in that respect, Ray not the only one fired up about that.

After helping with the dishes, Shady watched another episode of *Breaking Bad* with her parents and then headed to her room. She'd left her cell in her room since before dinner and only now checked it, that easy contentment she'd been feeling rapidly fading. Josie had called. Several times. She'd texted too. *Where are you, Shady?*

"Shit," muttered Shady as she brought up her favorites screen and called back. "What is it?" she said, dispensing with any niceties on connection. "Josie, is something wrong?"

"Shady! Where've you been?"

"I was having dinner with my parents, and then we watched TV. Sorry, Josie, I left my cell in my bedroom. Mom doesn't like me looking at it at the dinner table. You know what she's like. Hey, your voice sounds funny. Have you been crying?"

"She's gone. Another one."

On the edge of her bed, Shady sat up straighter. "Huh? Who do you mean?"

"The girl from next door. You remember you met her?"

"Yeah…um…Brandi?"

"That's right, Brandi Hadley. Shit, I've babysat her a couple of times since I've been here. She's sixteen, but only just."

"What's happened? Tell me."

"She's gone, Shady, like I said. Missing!"

"When?" Shady breathed.

"We only found out a few hours ago, and I called you soon after, but…"

"Josie, I'm sorry. If I'd known—"

"Sure, sure. How could you? I understand that whole

thing about not bringing your phone to the table. My mom hates that too."

"How long has Brandi been missing?" Shady asked a second time.

"She was last seen this morning, on her way to school. She stopped off at Batemans, a corner store, like all the kids do, to buy a soda or gum or something. Joe Bateman runs it. He said she grabbed a drink from the fridge, paid her money and then left, nothing unusual about that. The only thing slightly off was that she crossed the street when she didn't need to and seemed to lift her hand slightly as if waving to someone."

"Who?" Shady asked, trying to picture the scene in her head.

"That's where the trail goes cold. She headed to wherever and then—boom! She disappeared. The school contacted her mom around midday to ask where she was, as it had finally been reported she'd skipped class, but Mrs. Hadley didn't know. It's late now, Shady, it's dark. And she's still missing. Where could she have gone?"

"The police are on it?"

"The whole damn neighborhood is."

"If she crossed the road, if she was meeting someone, that suggests she wasn't snatched, at least."

"That's what Mr. Bateman thought he saw, but apparently when questioned, he said maybe she lifted her hand for some other reason, I don't know, to scratch an itch or something. More customers had come in by that time. He had no reason to keep watching her."

"But the police know all about it?"

"Sure, yeah, of course. Oh, Shady, a girl's gone missing! Just like that. Another one."

Another one? She remembered Josie had said that before.

"Alisa Jones. Do you mean her?"

"Uh-huh. Another female."

"That wasn't in Baker City, though."

"It was the closest town! And she'd been here a couple days beforehand, staying at the Grand Willmott like everyone did, planning her hike, getting to grips with it. *Integrating.*"

"Josie, people go missing." She only just stopped herself from adding, *a lot of people.*

"I know. I know," Josie conceded. "It all just feels…so close to home, you know? I mean, like, literally. My parents moved here for a better life, a safer one. They wanted a small-town community, one that kind of wraps its arms around you in a warm fuzzy hug and holds you close. Sure, everyone knows everyone else's business, but there's a sweetness in that. Mostly. And then this happens. It doesn't feel safe here anymore. It's…ruined."

"It's been less than twenty-four hours. Brandi could still turn up."

"That's the most crucial period, isn't it? The first twenty-four hours. After that, the risk of finding them alive heads south. Who's got her, Shady? And who took Alisa?"

"They're twenty years apart!"

"They might be, but what if there were others in between?"

"What do you mean? I don't understand—"

"Just what I said. Alisa and Brandi are only the ones we know about linked to Baker City, but what if there were others? What if this is some kind of hotspot or something? I don't know, people are so vulnerable, women, kids. Shit, Brandi being on my doorstep, it feels kinda…personal, you know? I wish I was back in Idaho Falls!"

"I've told you, people go missing from here too, from every state in the US and far more frequently than that. Men as well as women, adults as well as kids."

"True, but you know what?"

"What?" asked Shady, Brandi's face foremost in her mind now and, indeed, how sullen she had looked until Josie had mentioned the skin walkers, then how interested.

"Better the devil you know, huh?"

* * *

It was late, and Shady was in bed. Her mom had just left her room, Shady having told her about what had happened and how agitated Josie was, as if all of Baker City's young women were now in danger, the specter of Alisa Jones gaining new substance. Ellen had sincerely hoped that Brandi would be found safe and well soon, had pointed out how kids could just take off on their own; after all, who knew what troubles existed behind closed doors. Even those closest to them could never really tell.

"It's easy to get paranoid when something like this happens," she'd said. "And Josie's right, women seem to be more at risk." She had sighed heavily. "Poor Josie. I expect she wants her old comforts at a time like this."

"I don't know what to do, Mom. I feel…helpless."

"Just be patient. Keep in touch with her, help to calm her fears. Missing doesn't mean dead." Ellen had then hugged Shady, hard. "Stay safe yourself, okay? You're right when you said people don't only go missing in Oregon. There's danger everywhere."

Yet again, Missy Davenport's words came back to haunt

her. It seemed it was true, though. Baker City had appeared safe, its shiny veneer full of bespoke stores and the people friendly. As for the wilderness that surrounded it, it might appear beautiful too, but what if it was plain hostile instead? No place for a person to be, experienced or not.

Although troubled, she was eventually claimed by sleep, both hands clutching at Kanti's star-etched leather, which was tucked in beneath her chin. Her dreams, as she suspected they would be, were filled with more strangeness. Eyes that glowed red, others—those belonging to the little drowned boy—fathomless pools instead. The Omaha Indian also made an appearance, no longer with his back to her; he'd turned toward Shady, her dreamlike self holding her breath, almost fit to burst, not wanting to see his eyes and whether they were deep black or glowed red. There were animals too. Those that stood tall, that towered over her, that couldn't be outrun, no matter how hard you tried.

Image after image shoved its way into her mind, all becoming more and more abstract. The creature in the tree? It seemed to stalk her as she ran through the wilderness. If it captured her, she'd be torn apart, limb from limb, as so many people had been before her. Alisa…a poster girl for the lost, that's what she was, capable of burrowing her way into your soul and staying there, no matter the passage of time since she'd vanished. Then there was Brandi—dark-haired, dark-eyed, sullen Brandi. Would she pass into legend too, or didn't she fit the bill? Not quite pretty enough, not as endearing. Would she just be forgotten, lying alone in the darkness, somewhere remote, off the beaten path? And if that wasn't her fate, if she was indeed found, then in what condition? Eviscerated too, like the family of four had been—mutilated beyond all imagining?

There was crying, sobs that were heart-wrenching. Mrs. Hadley? Missy? The mother of the Victorian boy, even? Lost in the wilderness of her dreams still, her head whipping from side to side, trying to see what lay just out of sight, who it was that sobbed, Shady watched as a thick wall of mist rose, obscuring everything further. Even so, there was movement within it, a figure—not another monster but a female. Petite. Like…Josie.

Josie, is that you crying? Oh, Josie! You'll be all right. Just be careful, that's all.

It *was* Josie; she was certain of it. Still, she tried to appease her, repeating Ellen's words: *Missing doesn't mean dead.* But it could, soon.

What should I do, Kanti?

Even though she was asleep, she was aware she was clutching the leather scrap tighter, remembering the stars on it, the stars in the sky too and how brightly they had shone. On one night, at least. So full of wonder, something beyond time and understanding. Fate. That was supposed to be written in the stars, wasn't it? But where would the stars guide you? Toward destiny or into hell?

Kanti, the photographs are connected, aren't they? Missy's family and the men with the masks. How, though? How? And Brandi's disappearance, Alisa's, is that connected too?

Shady tossed and turned, yelled out on one or two occasions, but with Ellen and Bill sound asleep in their own bedroom across the hall, there was no one to hear.

She was on a journey, each step she took significant. *Don't touch.* That's what Ray had said, but she had, she'd touched, she'd looked and tuned in. Because she'd been meant to?

The room was still dark when Shady woke, morning

having not yet broken. Lifting the leather, she rubbed it against her cheek, as ever basking in the softness of it.

The stillness of night was broken with a whisper.

"Thank you, Kanti. I know what to do now."

CHAPTER NINE

"And you're sure you don't mind?"

Annie pushed at the rim of her glasses. "Shady, if you feel you can help, if Josie needs comforting, then do it. We can manage until you return."

Although Ray nodded along with Annie, he was clearly a little more reticent. "If you're going back, if you've got a hunch about something, then maybe I should come with you." He turned to Annie. "Sorry, I know we're kinda busy—"

"It's not a problem," Annie assured him, but Shady was having none of it.

"Ray, you're exactly right. That's all it is, a hunch. I'm fine to go on my own, and I promise, I'll be back as soon as possible. I just want to help Josie. Brandi's disappearance has really rocked her, rocked all of Baker City, I imagine. Anyway, I'd actually kind of like to spend some time alone with her too. We never really got a chance to do that recently, and…I just think it's important, y'know?"

"You're being called there?" Annie surmised, putting Shady in mind of what she'd said to her only recently, after she'd first returned from Baker City: *If you're meant to get involved, another path will open up and lead you back there.*

"Yes," she answered. "In a way, but maybe just to be

there for her."

"If anything happens," Ray said, "if you need help, an extra pair of hands or, I don't know, just a different take on it all, call me, okay? I'll be right there."

"That goes for me too," Annie insisted. "Go comfort your friend by all means, but don't put yourself in jeopardy, Shady Groves. Remember—"

"There's danger everywhere. Yeah, I know."

"Okay," Annie said. "And you're leaving right away, or do you want coffee first?"

Shady shook her head. "I'll grab a coffee on the way. A few, most likely."

"Take care, then."

Annie stepped forward and embraced her. When she was done, Ray did the same.

"Keep in touch," he said. "I mean it. Just…keep in touch."

A few minutes later and Shady was in her Dodge Stratus, firing up its old but faithful engine and pulling out onto the highway. Such a long drive ahead, but the Dodge could go faster than Dorothea, so she just needed to put her foot on the gas and endure, some great playlists courtesy of Spotify to ease the process.

She'd have to make a stop along the way, retrace their tracks all the way down that lonely highway to The Lazy Stay Motel. It was midweek, early; she should reach the motel in around three hours if luck was on her side, so no need to stay the night. She just wanted…to talk. Something had happened to Missy's brother, and somehow it was connected to everything else, including this latest development, but she had no idea how. Maybe the fog that now existed in her brain, rather than courtesy of some phenomenon on a mountainside, might clear enough to reveal a clue if she could just get to talk to Missy Davenport, or rather if she could get Missy to talk to her.

Smashing Pumpkins, Pearl Jam, Soundgarden and Hole were the bands that accompanied her on her trip, Shady deciding she was in the mood for some '90s grunge. Gradually, the backdrop began to change. In Idaho, rivers, mountains and farmland formed the view. Oregon wasn't so different, at least not immediately, although she knew there to be dense evergreen forests and deserts too. The Painted Hills were supposed to be a sight to behold, yellow, gold, black and red glinting in the sunlight, those hues ever changing depending on what time of day and year you visited. Other sights she'd heard about included the Columbia River Gorge and Smith Rock, plus the coastline, home to soaring sand dunes and bustling harbors. It was such a diverse and beautiful part of the US, and Shady would love to see everything it had to offer if only she had the time, but, for now, she was on a mission, The Lazy Stay Motel at last coming into sight.

She parked in exactly the same spot that Dorothea had once occupied, aching for the company of friends, feeling truly alone. The motel was as deserted as before, a slight breeze gathering some dust from the road and lifting it in a mini cyclone.

Climbing out of the car, she took a deep breath as her eyes scanned the now familiar row of empty rooms before settling on the office, the sign that was supposed to glow neon still stubbornly refusing. There was no trace of Missy. Of anyone. America was full of establishments like this, new roads having been built, leaving the old highways and all that depended on them to fade into oblivion. Instead of scenery, people wanted speed, needing to arrive at their destination that little bit quicker. How long the motel would remain open, Shady had no idea; most of these places fell into disrepair eventually, were abandoned.

At last, she made her way toward reception, kicking at the dust and gravel beneath her Converse, hands stuffed in her jeans pocket, feeling the scrap of leather there.

On reaching the office, she pushed at the door, but it was locked. Leaning slightly backward, she double-checked another sign. It said "Open," but she could have sworn it was even dustier than before. *Where are you, Missy?* she wondered, peering in through the glass, hands shielding her eyes from the outside glare.

The interior, if not dark, exactly, was gloomy. As empty as it had been when she and Ray had first entered, occupied only by ornaments and old-fashioned books, as much a comfort blanket to Missy, perhaps, as the star-etched leather was to Shady, each one holding a memory of a past life. And then there were the photographs, one especially of a group of people; the others, as far as Shady remembered, were of the land, the various stages of building that the motel and the house had undergone—a sense of pride unmistakable, of creating something out of nothing, forging a livelihood. Once.

The photograph she sought out was at an angle. She could only see one side of it, that occupied by the grandfather, mother and little girl. It was the other side she needed to see, edging along the window and squinting harder.

Was this a fool's errand? In order to tune in properly, she had to handle the photograph, close her eyes and drift... No way could she glean anything from this distance. So why was she trying so hard? It was just a random picture in a random motel on a random road. Why did the thought persist that it was so much more, that it was somehow key?

It was no use. She couldn't see the boy and couldn't tune in. A foolish errand indeed. Best to press on, get more miles under her wheels. Josie was so glad she was coming, couldn't quite believe it when Shady had told her early this morning, bursting into tears.

"I couldn't sleep at all last night," she'd said. "Every time I tried, I kept seeing Brandi's face, imagining her somewhere dark and terrifying. Maybe even the same place that Alisa was, or is, or whatever. You know what, I can't seem to think of one without the other. Why is that, Shady? I just don't get it. Oh shit, maybe I'm just being stupid, overreacting, getting all dramatic, but like I said, it's all so close to home. I mean, God, Brandi lives next door! A few feet away. It makes you wonder who he's coming for next."

He? Shady had baulked at that. Women were just as capable of evil as men, every bit as merciless; she knew that from handling Gina's mirror last year.

Ah, quit thinking, Shady, quit chasing ghosts. Just get back on the road. As Annie had said, as she knew well enough herself, everyone had baggage, a story to tell. Although this had been the photograph that had kick-started the unease in her, although Missy and her family knew Baker City, that was likely the only connection there was. Yes, Missy's brother had known horror too, but what kind of horror and at whose hands would remain a mystery, one of countless murders left unsolved.

Murder?

Not only did that thought—unprovoked—make Shady flinch, she could sense something else, or rather someone.

She swung around.

"Missy!"

The woman was right behind her, looking even more disheveled than before.

* * *

"Sit yourself down. Make yourself comfortable."

Shady selected the chair closest to her at the kitchen table.

Missy had found her peering into reception, strange thoughts running riot in Shady's mind—*forceful* thoughts, those of murder. When the two women had faced each other, Shady had been unable to speak. She didn't trust herself, which was why she'd remained silent, sure that she was going to blurt out the words *Missy, was your brother murdered?* Luckily, Missy had broken the spell, asking a much simpler question.

"Back again, huh? You want a room?"

Shady had gone red, she'd stuttered, and then had finally shaken her head.

"No, no. I'm heading back to Baker City because…because someone's missing."

"Missing?" Immediately Missy's expression had darkened. "You a cop or something?"

Again, Shady shook her head. "No! Not a cop. An…investigator."

Why she'd said that, she didn't know, had no idea how Missy would receive it. It was only marginally better than if she'd said she was a psychic.

There'd been more moments of silence, Shady envisioning huge bundles of tumbleweed blowing down the highway behind them as they stood there.

"I'm sorry, I—" she began.

"The motel's been closed these past couple of days."

"Okay," Shady replied.

"But you're here now."

"Yes, ma'am."

"Investigating."

Shady gulped.

"Better come up to the house, then, hadn't you?"

Shoulder to shoulder, they'd walked up the hillside path to the Davenport residence, Shady trembling a little, unable to get thoughts of mummified mothers, of *murder*, out of her head. Entering the hallway, further tingles ran up and down her spine. The décor was dark, the walls on either side papered in a floral pattern that had long since browned with nicotine. In fact, the air reeked of cigarettes, from past residents, perhaps, as well as present; it was ingrained, hazy, as if everything that existed here did so in a blur.

Before being led to the kitchen, Shady caught a glimpse of the living room, spied two armchairs on either side of a sofa facing a large open fireplace, a traditional enough setup. *That's where Grandpa and Grandma used to sit*, she thought, the cushions on them placed just so, and on the arm of one chair a crocheted blanket, pink, green and white. Missy never sat in those chairs, Shady would bet; she preferred the sofa if she ever ventured in there at all. Because that was the thing, the room was stuffed with ornaments again, with everything the family had collected over the years, representing another museum, an homage to shadows, nothing more, an ottoman by the sofa that Missy or her brother would occupy as children. If she could go in there, if she could touch, she'd be able to see that young boy from the picture come to life, his grin a lot like Ray's.

The kitchen was to be her destination, however, and once in there, Missy had busied herself making a pot of coffee, which she then set down between them on a table covered in cloth, more flowers imprinted on it, as faded and as yellowed as those in the hallway.

An homage. The whole house was. Paying tribute to a time when happiness, innocence and, above all, security had lived there. A world that no longer existed, that had decayed into extinction, as lives so often did.

"You take sugar and milk?" Missy asked.

"Black is fine, thank you."

"Same as me. Mind if I smoke?"

"Of course not."

"Good, good," Missy muttered.

She took from her shirt pocket a pack of cigarettes and lit one, taking several pulls of it before pouring the coffee from the pot into their cups.

Shady reached out, took a sip and then gestured around her. "This is a beautiful home you have."

"Stop it."

"What? Um…" Shady placed the coffee cup back down. "I'm sorry—"

"Don't patronize me," Missy continued, pained eyes becoming steelier. "Don't you do that, come into my home, then start to patronize me."

"I didn't mean—"

"What is it you're investigating?"

"I—"

"You may be on your way to Baker City, but you could have gone a dozen different routes. Why choose this one again? What is it about this place, *me*, that intrigues you?"

However Shady explained it, she'd sound nuts, a hazard of the profession, she guessed. But she couldn't just sit there, mute again. The way Missy was staring at her, this house, the atmosphere—a mausoleum, that's what it was—all weighed so heavy. Whatever had happened, not to Missy but to her family, her *brother*, had stopped time moving, for Missy, at least, enshrined her in it. Lonely. Missy was that, all right. Whatever comfort these walls, photographs and ornaments lent, insufficient.

"Your brother," Shady said at last. "In the photograph in the reception office."

"What about him?" If Missy was surprised, she hid it well.

"What happened to him?"

Missy lifted the cigarette to her mouth, took a few puffs in quick succession, then drew an ashtray closer and stubbed it out. "How do you know anything about my brother?"

Shady took a deep breath. Here it was, the bombshell. Missy would either believe her or throw her out of the house, or worse.

"I...I have this ability. I can hold an object in my hand and detect certain things from it. Not all objects," Shady hastened to add, "but objects that have become...charged, with energy. It's like...being able to read a story. That's the best way I can describe it. The practice is called psychometry, and it's not unique to me. Others can do it too. Holding that family photograph in your office, I felt such happiness and contentment, bliss, if you like. I saw a family who loved each other very much, who were...each other's world."

As she said this, Misty's eyes glistened. It had clearly been too long since she'd remembered this.

"But then...something changed," Shady continued. "People die. Grandparents, parents. It's the natural order of things. But something happened to your brother too, didn't it? When he was still young. Something that tore you up inside. That still does to this day."

Missy went to light another cigarette, her fingertips as stained as the surrounding walls, but then she paused and pushed the packet away. "Psych...what?"

"Psychometry. I know it sounds out there, the stuff of science fiction, but—"

"You're psychic?"

Shady could feel her cheeks coloring. "Yes," she said, angry with herself that she was still so embarrassed about it, at least with strangers.

"And you know that something happened to my brother. You picked that up from a photograph? *Just* a photograph."

Oh God, this was excruciating. But how could she get out of it? She'd made the decision to come here, to find out more, and all because of a link, a connection, that right now seemed more tenuous than ever.

"There were all these happy feelings attached to the photograph, but there were others too—stuff that came later, after the photograph was taken, although I'm not sure by how long. Grief, anger, disbelief. An enormous sense of...loss. And your brother's the focus."

How bewildered Missy looked, how utterly defeated suddenly, her head lowering.

Shady wanted to reach out but kept her hands to herself. All she could do was apologize further. "I'm so sorry, coming here, saying these things. I don't mean any harm."

Now it was her own eyes swimming with tears, as if all the feelings she'd sensed were rising up to become her own.

"Missy…"

"What happened to him?" When Missy spoke, her voice was a whisper. "Who took him? Who…killed him?" Her head came up. "Because that's what I think happened. He was murdered. He's lying somewhere out there in the mountains of Oregon. And no one is ever gonna find him. Not now, after all this time. Unlike my parents, my grandparents, there's no grave to visit." She lifted her hand and tapped at her skull. "Here's the only place he still exists. And in photographs." Abruptly, Missy stood up. "Come with me."

Together they left the kitchen and headed to the living room, once again Shady keeping her hands to herself. One step at a time was how she had to play this, not let the Davenport family history become a freight train that overwhelmed her.

"This is where we used to sit, where all families sit, I guess," Missy continued, "come sundown, once dinner was done. Oh, I loved this room in winter! The fire would blaze, Grandpa and Grandma sitting right there in the armchairs, Ma and Pa on the sofa, me and my brother fighting over the ottoman. Well, we'd *pretend* to fight, 'cause I always knew I'd win, that he'd let me and take the floor instead. Grandma would knit, and Grandpa would tell us stories. He loved the mountains, did Grandpa. He'd go trekking, to hunt and to shoot. He instilled that love in his own son and his grandson too. The three of them would head out, Baker City way, to the mountain ranges beyond, setting up camp beneath the stars, keeping the old ways, Grandpa would say, far simpler, far better ways."

"I can imagine it all," said Shady, knowing she'd *see* it all too if she just reached out.

"I wish, though, I wish…" Missy's eyes briefly closed.

"Wish what?" Shady said, daring to come closer.

"That he *hadn't* instilled that love of the wild into my brother."

"Why?"

"Because," she said, still stricken, "it was something wild that took him."

CHAPTER TEN

Shady was reeling.

She'd been right. There was a connection!

Right after Missy had said something wild had taken her brother, she had then about-faced, not issuing another word, not until they stood outside at the rear of the house, Shady swallowing hard as she gazed at what lay before her.

Graves. Four of them. Those belonging to grandparents and parents. Headstones gracing each one, gentle words of love carved into hard granite.

"There'll be a fifth, one day," Missy said. "Mine. I'll be lying beside them. We'll be together again. But not my brother. Like I said, his grave is cold and lonely, with no one to stand by it, lay flowers or just say…hello. All that's been taken from us." She turned to Shady. "He's dead, because he wouldn't have done this otherwise."

"Done what?"

"Disappeared!" Something stirred in Missy's eyes—hope? "You said you're psychic. Is that why you're here? Because it's *you* who can tell *me* what happened?"

Shady swallowed. "It doesn't work like that—"

Missy wasn't listening, though; she was heading back inside to the living room, Shady once more following, something of a lost lamb. Once there, Missy selected a framed photograph and thrust it into Shady's hands. "This is him. His name was…is…Robert. He's twenty-three in this photograph, about your age. This was…" Again, her voice caught in her throat. "This was taken a couple of weeks before he headed off, hunting, to the mountains east of Baker City. It's the most recent picture I have. The last picture."

Shady stared down at it, saw the young boy grown into a man. Robert was handsome, as dark haired as his sister, dark eyed too, full of youth, the promise of it, and a certain…if not arrogance, then *certainty*. He'd been brought up to love the great outdoors and had maybe thought he'd tamed it. That mistake proving costly.

"What can you sense?" From being so downcast, Missy was full of eagerness.

"I…um…" Shady touched the man's cheek. *What happened to you, Robert?* So very full of promise, a man who had grown up on love and lessons, been taught just about every trick in the book when it came to his inherited passion for hunting. Who adored wide-open spaces, endless skies and the freedom they gave. He respected nature when many didn't. No complacency after all, Shady realized. Grandpa Davenport had taught him well. There was nothing negative attached to the photograph, perhaps not having been handled as much as the family one, Missy and her family preferring the nostalgia of the earlier years, how it represented them as a unit rather than as individuals— connected.

"He went missing while hunting?" Shady confirmed.

"Yes," Missy breathed. "His camp was found, his belongings, rifle, all there. Everything was. Untouched. And that wasn't like Robert at all. He'd never do that. Knew you never ventured an inch from camp without your gun. It'd be damn near glued to your hand. Can you see anything? What happened? It was something…terrible, wasn't it? I feel that too."

Something terrible. Something…plain wrong.

"How long's he been gone?" Shady asked, finding it ironic that all she could sense was the excitement of the man, no horror at all.

"Thirty years," Missy told her, reading Shady's expression, the hope that had flared fading. "Last we heard from him was thirty years ago yesterday, right before he made camp. He'd gone to a wilderness station and called us. Then he headed out into the arms of evil. A man like him, so experienced, so damned capable. Told you, didn't I? Evil's everywhere. There's no escaping it."

Shady left the Davenport residence soon after, extricated herself somehow, because Missy wanted her to stay, to touch everything and anything connected with Robert, but there was nothing more to be had, nothing useful, anyway—just more family memories, a jumble of them, becoming more and more confused the harder she focused in on them, like a mixture in a bowl being beaten, all the ingredients merging. She got back in her Dodge and drove away, Missy in her rearview mirror, just standing there, a forlorn figure staring after her, Shady feeling like a fraud that she hadn't been able to help more, offer some kind of comfort, some kind of answer. Not yet, at least. But would she? If she persisted? Because, as she'd hoped, a link had emerged. Brandi Hadley and Robert Davenport had both gone missing. And although thirty years apart, what had shaken Shady was that they'd vanished on the same day, April twenty-fifth.

As she drove farther, she had to rein herself in. Was it really a connection or, rather, mere coincidence? Nothing more to it than that. One missing from the town of Baker City, the other from the wilderness that surrounded it. Is that where Brandi could be, though? Out there somewhere? Or in another town, another state entirely?

Robert's case was as cold as the site of his unknown grave, but she'd Google it, see if she could find out any more details other than those that Missy had provided her with.

A vision of the family plot behind the house returned, Shady imagining the aching chasm beneath the earth that remained empty. Was Robert really dead? Was it possible he'd just decided to disappear, this man who'd relished freedom so much? Instantly, Shady dismissed the notion. He'd loved his family, and his family loved him. As Missy had said, he would never willingly put them through such torture.

Something had happened to Robert, something bad; she knew it every bit as much as Missy did. Evil stalking Baker City and the mountains that surrounded it. Omnipresent.

* * *

Shady rolled into Baker City with one question on her mind—the poster girl, the one she could see in her mind's eye with her wide smile and blond hair, Alisa Jones, what date had she gone missing? Because if it was April twenty-fifth too, it'd make it a hat trick and more than coincidence, surely? *And yet there's a time difference, Shady—a huge time difference.* They'd gone missing decades apart. *Connections,* her inner voice continued regardless. *That's what this is all about. And connections can be strange. Remember that.*

101

As she slowly cruised along Main Street to the Wongs' residence, she noticed that the place was quieter than she'd seen it before. Past six o'clock, most businesses were closed, including Halcyon Days and, of course, the Grand Willmott, windows like black mirrors that returned her gaze as she remembered the photograph that lay within its dark interior, the men wearing animal masks, one man in particular, *something wild...* The same street as before, except for one thing—posters had been put up everywhere. Baker City had themselves a new poster girl for the lost, black letters beneath a picture of Brandi begging for information to help find her. Brandi...with her dark hair, dark eyes and sullen expression. Would she elicit the same reaction Alisa had? Shady still couldn't help but doubt it. People liked a dazzling smile. As much as she'd like to bring the Dodge to a stop and examine Brandi's image more thoroughly, she couldn't, not right now. Josie was waiting.

Finally, with the sun sitting low in the sky, Shady reached her destination. Parking the Dodge, she grabbed her backpack from the trunk and then...stood there. Her eyes not on Josie's house but the one next door, which had most of its drapes closed, those inside trapped in such darkness.

The only thing to break her focus was the door to Josie's house opening, her friend emerging and running down the path toward Shady.

Haunted. That's how Josie looked, reaching Shady and hugging her as tightly as before, but this time for very different reasons.

"I can't believe you came all this way. Thank you! Thank you so much."

As they continued to cling to each other, Shady's eyes returned to the Hadley house, a sight that couldn't—

wouldn't—be ignored.

"Come on, let's get you inside," said Josie on releasing her. Grabbing her arm now, she almost dragged Shady up the path and into the house. If downtown had a desolate air about it, then so did the Wong residence, despite the bright décor Lulin favored—the yellow accents, the orange, the red and the blue—grief from next door like an invisible gas, seeping out from windows and doorframes, affecting everything and everyone.

Lulin Wong also hugged Shady. "It's lovely to see you again. I only wish it wasn't under such awful circumstances this time."

Huan greeted her too. Like his wife and daughter, his expression was pinched and disbelieving. People went missing all the time, everyone knew that, but as Josie had said, when it happened on your doorstep, it took on new significance.

Lulin had prepared dinner, a far simpler affair than before, which was just as well, as no one had much of an appetite. Conversation included Brandi but didn't dwell on her, everyone clearly desperate for some respite.

Later in Josie's bedroom, Shady emptied her backpack. She'd brought enough for three to five days, grateful for the flexibility that Annie had given her, her colleagues back at the Mason Town Museum on standby even now at this late hour, having texted her several times already. It warmed her heart every time they did that, as if they were guardian angels every bit as much as Kanti, watching over her from afar.

"Shady, what's that in your hand?"

As she'd swapped day clothes for the T-shirt and shorts that she slept in, Shady had also retrieved the scrap of leather from her jeans pocket, transferring it to her shorts pocket instead. Turning to Josie, she held it out for her to take and watched as she gently stroked it, one finger then tracing the pattern on it.

"Stars," she mused. "It's…beautiful. So soft. Where'd you get it?"

Shady was silent for a moment. It was such a simple question that Josie had asked, but the answer was loaded—with history, with emotion, but also with wonder. Crossing over to the bed, she pulled back the covers and climbed in, Josie doing the same.

As the two girls snuggled closer, Shady sighed, deciding she didn't much feel like sleep anyway, even after such a long and bewildering day.

"There's a lot to tell," she said. "If you want to hear it."

"Shoot, Shady," Josie replied. "And don't you dare leave anything out."

CHAPTER ELEVEN

Research. That's what was next. Eventually, Josie had fallen asleep. Shady, though, was still wide awake, buzzing. It had felt cathartic telling Josie all that had happened during the last year or so, starting with Annie and the diner, then Mandy and the trip to Canada, then Gina's mirror that had led her into the terrifying psyche of an infamous cult leader. As her best friend, Josie had, of course, known the bare bones of it, but that was all.

"The thing is, Josie, I'm still trying to understand this gift of mine that just seems to be…accelerating. You know, get my head around it. Annie's been great. She's been my mentor, my rock. She knows so much about all this stuff because she's been brought up with it. She's not psychic but more of a sensitive. Her father was too. He ran an antique store in a small village in England, where history's right off the scale! I guess what I'm trying to say is, I didn't mean to keep anything from you. Even my parents don't know the full deal yet. I'm sorry if you think I've been holding out."

Josie had squeezed her arm. "I can't pretend I'm not stunned, but…I get it, I do. Christ, Shady, you're like the skin walkers, supernatural!"

Skin walkers. There it was again, those words, that concept. Being drummed into her brain. Another coincidence? Because before the first trip out to Oregon, she'd never heard of them, despite her Native heritage. Quickly, she denied such a comparison.

"Josie, I'm just me, Shady Groves. Don't think of me any other way."

"But do you?"

"What do you mean?"

"Think of yourself differently? Just a little bit. This talent of yours, it's…extraordinary!"

"You know what? We all have talent. Take your mom—she's the world's best cook, whereas I cremate everything I touch. Some people can sew. Not me, though. They can paint, write, sing, play the violin, whatever. *Everyone's* extraordinary in their own way."

"Do you think you can use your talent here?"

"Here?"

"To help find Brandi! I know you came back to support me, but, deep down, did you also come back for that reason?"

"I…I…shit, I don't know. If I can help, though, then hell yeah, I'll do my best."

"*We* will, Shady, the both of us."

A short while later and Josie was asleep, Shady, in contrast, pushing herself upward, resting against the wall and reaching for her cell, which was charging beside her.

Missing, Alisa Jones, Oregon, was what she Googled first, typing those very words into the search bar. There'd been so much to say on arrival at Josie's that the burning question in her mind had to get in line. No matter. She could find out now via the internet.

An image of the missing girl immediately burst onto screen, and she was every bit as pretty as legend asserted.

There were other images of Alisa too, portrayed as an action girl, brave but petite, most of them set against a backdrop of rugged mountain, Alisa in the foreground, dressed in shorts, a gilet and with a rifle by her side, always smiling. An all-American superstar; even the internet seemed to have fallen in love with her. A teacher aged twenty-six, she'd visit the terrain east of Baker City regularly, always opting to stay at the Grand Willmott beforehand, as Josie had said.

The Grand Willmott…a lot of visitors to Baker City would stay there. It was a natural choice, even more so after its renovation. Her hackles were on the rise about it, though. Because of the framed photograph that hung in one of its gloomy corridors? *A photograph you know nothing about*, she reminded herself. Maybe there'd been a festival of some sort in Baker City or thereabouts, one where wearing animal masks and carrying pitchforks was tradition. Because now she came to think of it, one or two *did* have pitchforks in their hands. She'd been so focused on the masks, the sheer *bestiality* of them, it hadn't registered until now, but it added to the sense of savagery.

When did you go missing, Alisa? What date?

She clicked on the first article, and there it was in black and white.

The last known sighting of Alisa Jones was by fellow hikers near local scenic area Mazuma Lake on April twenty-fifth, 2002. It was a beautiful day, the sun was hot, and Alisa appeared happy and confident, greeting Ben and Jean Marsh, even stopping to chat to them for a while. She said she'd come from Baker City and had stayed at the Grand Willmott Hotel and now had a couple of nights in the mountains to look forward to. The Marsh couple told her to take care, and she promised she would, patting the rifle by her side. "Go nowhere without it," she assured them. As we know, however, Alisa did leave her rifle and, indeed, all her belongings at the camp she'd made a few miles from Mazuma. For reasons that remain unclear, she struck out with no protection at all, an experienced hiker who went against the golden rule and seemingly paid for that mistake with her life.

Sensationalist. That's what the article was. Taking advantage of a tragedy. It was the same date, though, exactly as she'd suspected, Alisa's camp being near Mazuma Lake, the very place Shady and her friends had tried to reach but failed, beaten back by the fog. What's more, she'd done the same as another experienced hiker ten years previously, Robert Davenport—set up camp and then…abandoned it, along with everything that would protect her. That date…Shady proceeded to Google the heck out of it, linking it with Oregon, but page after page revealed nothing more than a list of upcoming events and weather forecasts. When she typed in *Robert Davenport, Oregon*, there was an article concerning him, but it was all too brief, providing her with nothing more than what Missy had already told her. Whereabouts in that great expanse of trees had he gone missing?

She was disappointed by the lack of information concerning him. Contrary to what people might think, the world wide web wasn't some magical library that gave equal weight to all. She'd bet there were many who'd gone missing whose details never even made it on there or were buried so deep in pages as to be unreachable.

Missing People USA were the next words she typed into the search bar, Brandi, Alisa and Robert having ignited a morbid interest. She read that in 2020 more than half a million people had been reported missing. Of that number, more than 340,000 were juveniles like Brandi. Another interesting fact that jumped out was something called "missing white woman syndrome" in which white women—particularly young, attractive and blond—got most of the media's attention. That was Alisa to a T. Wealth and class also played a role, which was one point in Brandi's favor, at least, as she came from what was perceived as a respectable middle-class background. But what about all those that didn't? How quickly could someone fade into oblivion?

Sleep still eluding her, Shady then started searching various facts, stuffing information into her head, hoping some detail might later prove useful. Alaska had the highest rates of missing people in the US, with a staggering 1 out of 617 people disappearing, Shady knowing a high percentage of those were Indigenous peoples, the kind the police forces didn't tend to look overly hard for. Oregon, though, was in third place, just behind Arizona. Marvin Clark held the record for the oldest active missing-person case in the US. He'd disappeared in Oregon in 1926, aged seventy-three, on the way to visiting his daughter in Portland for Halloween. Nearly a century later, his disappearance was still a mystery. Most people, it seemed, *were* found, dead or alive, but there were always some like Marvin Clark who never turned up either way.

"Shit," said Shady, a low sigh escaping her. It was terrible enough for the victim, but what about the victim's family and loved ones? It'd destroy them. Shady thought again of Missy and the physical toll that losing her brother had taken, never mind the mental scars, the kind you couldn't see. She recalled too the look in her eyes when she'd thought Shady might be able to help her, and also how quickly hope had vanished.

Regarding Oregon national parks, she read that 189 men and 51 women officially remained listed as missing since 1997 alone. All of them had just walked into the big wide open and never walked back out. Sure, there were some pretty wild places out there, remote, but the likes of Robert and Alisa knew that, were *prepared* for it. Was there something sinister about such high numbers, or was it logical instead? Somewhere so untamed, people could easily meet with accidents, fall down ravines or into rivers, that kind of thing. Shady knew there was a code of behavior between fellow hikers and adventurers, that they kept an eye out for each other, which helped, but what about those that didn't? People that stalked the grounds for other purposes entirely?

People?

Skin Walkers. The subject made her skin prickle. She didn't want to know about them, but now that she *did*, she couldn't remain blissfully ignorant.

Her fingers reacted before her mind had time to convince her otherwise, typing out the words, then clicking on the first site, entitled *Legends of America*. Before she even began to read, her eyes fixated on the illustration there of a man, tall and powerful and dressed in skins, his eyes glowing red. *Sleep, Shady! Leave this till morning.* Her mind, having caught up now, tried to insist, but she was in too deep.

In Navajo culture, the skin walker was a type of harmful witch, she learned, called *yee naaldlooshi*, translating to "With it, he goes on all fours." One of several types of Navajo witches, it was considered the most volatile and dangerous, able to turn into, possess or disguise themselves as an animal. Her eyes widened. She'd never guessed it was a type of witch, one that sought to harness spiritual forces to cause harm or misfortune.

In order to become one, the person had to be initiated by a secret society that required of them the evilest of deeds: murder. With that task completed, the individual then acquired supernatural powers, giving them the ability to shape-shift into animals—coyotes, wolves, foxes, cougars, dogs and bears—capable of extreme speed, strength, endurance and stealth. A skin walker was also able to take possession of the bodies of human victims if a person locked eyes with them, thus making them do and say whatever they wanted. Shady shivered at this. *She* had locked eyes with something in the tree back at Smoke Ridge. Something that had shown mercy after all?

For what was a taboo subject, there was a ton of information on skin walkers. How the Navajo prohibited its members to wear the pelt of any predatory animal because of such a phenomenon. They were actively *afraid* of them and the havoc they could wreak, rarely venturing out alone after dark in case they were near, and yet the white people paid no attention to such things, probably dismissing such a fear as nonsense, a dark fairytale, *primitive*. But, if the Navajos and other Native tribes took the threat of them seriously—*her* people, those who knew the wilderness better than anyone, who considered themselves a part of it—then who was she to disagree? And what if there were those that didn't fear them? That welcomed the idea of such a creature, *worshipped* it?

She looked over at the sleeping Josie. When Shady had told her the truth about her ability, Josie had, just like Ray, called her superhuman. And when she'd said it, there'd been a hint of envy in her voice, Shady was certain. Ray too would complain sometimes about the limit of his capabilities, longing to increase what he saw as his relevance in other ways, most recently via the prospect of study. The fact was, people read about stuff like this, had easy access to it, a taboo subject or not, plus saw a whole host of characters in movies doing extraordinary things—Spider-Man, Iron Man, the Hulk and the Black Panther, to name but a few—and wanted some of that for themselves, craved it. What if some people, those in the photograph at the Grand Willmott, tried to find a way to emulate the skin walkers? Sought to live the dream, turn fantasy into reality?

Taking it one step further, what if the likes of Robert and Alisa had run into them while out hiking and camping? *It was something wild that took him*…that's what Missy had said about her brother. Okay, all right, that theory didn't take into account the modern-day disappearance of Brandi—who knew where she'd gone?—but, as Shady eventually put away her cell to sink down beside Josie, what she'd learned, what she'd *experienced* since heading west, various fragments of information, floated together that little bit more.

CHAPTER TWELVE

"Sorry about this, Shady. It's just for a few hours. Dad has to go pick up a delivery, and, well, Mom's the driver. You know how much he hates getting behind the wheel."

"No problem," Shady assured her. "You go man the store. I can occupy myself."

"You could always come with, meet more of the locals?"

"Do you mind if I don't?"

Josie frowned. "What are you gonna do, then? Don't go wandering!"

"I won't," Shady assured her, refraining from adding, *not far, at any rate.* "Josie, go. You'll be late opening up if you don't. I didn't sleep well last night. I'll probably just end up grabbing some more sleep, that's all, then I'll come down to meet you. Say around noon?"

"Perfect. Mom and Dad'll be back by then. Oh, Shady, it's amazing to have you here! And you know, what you said last night about your...talent? That's amazing too. I've always said it."

"Said what?"

"That you're something out of the ordinary, huh?"

The girls hugged, then Josie left the house, Shady not returning to bed but quickly showering and dressing and heading out. Again, before she got into her car, she turned toward the Hadley house. The drapes were still closed despite the bright sunshine, all except in one room on the second floor—Brandi's? With sorrow squeezing her heart, Shady drove toward Main Street, mindful she'd need to be careful not to be spotted by Josie from the window of Halcyon Days. What she had to do, she needed to be alone for so she could fully focus. All the information gathered since leaving Missy's yesterday was performing cartwheels in her head. Despite that, she planned only to add to the melee.

First stop was the Grand Willmott, which she parked around the back of rather than at the front. Finding the side door that she'd entered through once before, she pushed at it.

A man in a safety helmet immediately approached her. "Hey there, can I help?"

"Is Wanda here?" Shady said, having to think on her feet.

"Wanda? Yeah, she's around somewhere. Want me to go look for her?"

"No, it's fine. I think she said she'd be in her office, at the back of reception. I've got an interview for bar staff."

"Oh, okay. Sweet. Well, if she's expecting you…but go straight there, okay? Nowhere else." He pointed to the helmet. "Some areas you can't go without one of these beauties."

"Just heading to the office," Shady answered, neatly sidestepping him.

As soon as she'd gone a short distance, she looked over her shoulder. The man had disappeared, the vastness of the hotel swallowing him up. Reception was not where she was planning on going but the corridor beyond it that led to the function rooms, hopefully avoiding Wanda if she was in situ and any more workmen, gliding ghostlike.

Thankfully, the way was clear, although there was banging and laughter from up ahead, men chatting as they worked. Soon enough, the framed photograph was yet again before her, the gloom of the corridor in no way relieved by the fact it was daytime. After giving the area another quick scan, she reached out and touched him, the man in the middle who dominated it. *Dominated everything.* Those were the words that came to mind. *A thirsty man.* But thirsty for what? *Were you a hunter too?* The skins certainly suggested it.

After a few moments, she took a step back, lowered her hand and scrutinized the photograph instead, drinking in every detail, the pitchforks that some were holding, the plaid shirts and the britches. *Wild men. Men of the wilderness.* When was it taken? Thirty years ago, forty? Longer than that? *A regular goddamned Ku Klux Klan,* thought Shady. *Some kind of group that held meetings here? At the hotel. Something as weird as this in such a public space, though? Who are you? Are you connected with Robert Davenport, Alisa Jones, even Brandi? Are any of you still alive, even?*

Questions, questions, when all she wanted was answers. Unlike some objects, this wasn't giving them up so easily.

Exasperated, Shady turned and faced the function rooms, tentative steps bringing her closer. Busy rooms, both historically and now, some walls in the process of being plastered. A *huge* room, fancy, about a dozen workmen in there, all men, no women.

It was always the men.

Shady frowned. Where had that thought come from? Before she could question further, more words formed in her mind.

A select few. The chosen. The willing. Those who seek to

115

ascend. Whose destiny it is. To be reborn. Reborn. REBORN!

"What the hell?" Shady didn't realize she'd spoken out loud or that she'd raised her hands to her head. Not until someone—another workman—came forward.

"Miss, I don't know what you're doing here, but...are you okay? You hurt or something?"

"Hurt?"

"Something wrong with your head? You're clutching at it. Looking mighty pale too."

Immediately, she lowered her hands. "Oh no, no, I'm fine."

"Okaaay. Like I said, you're not supposed to be here, rules and—"

"Regulations. Yeah, yeah, I know, of course. I was just leaving."

"There's no exit this way. You need to turn around."

"Thanks, I...um...I was here for an interview. Bar staff."

"Really? Well, if you follow me, I'll show you out."

"Thanks," Shady replied, her cheeks red hot. "Sorry to disturb you."

A burst of laughter rang out, from someone to the left of the man. A flurry of conversation reached her too. "Don't think we're the ones who're disturbed here." Someone else telling him to hush but half-heartedly, also laughing along.

So much laughter. Great big sudden gusts of it that bounced around the room and off every wall, then flew back at her, *men* laughing, raucous, arrogant and self-congratulatory. Feeding off each other. Getting louder and louder, earsplitting.

"STOP!"

Shady pushed at the man intent on escorting her, just caught the bewildered look on his face before she turned, his

116

colleagues perplexed too, mouths not laughing at all but wide with surprise. She didn't care. She hurled herself forward, down that gloomy corridor with its wood paneling and horrid photograph, refusing to even glance at it this time, trying to expunge its inhabitants from her mind, because it had been *their* laugher she'd heard, not the present occupiers of the function rooms but the past coming to life.

As her feet continued to pound the floor, retracing her way to the side door, the mask-clad figures didn't fade, however—not the man in the middle, his cohorts, the pitchforks, nor that grainy black-and-white world they were suspended in.

Instead, they burned like fire.

* * *

Outside on the sidewalk, Shady leaned against the wall of the Grand Willmott, almost bent double, the breath leaving her mouth in huge gulps. She knew what she had to do next, encounter another photograph—one emblazoned on a poster on the opposite side of the street, stuck to a lamppost there—and tune in again, stoke those fires a little more.

When she could breathe more evenly, she did just that, pushed herself off the wall and crossed the road. Flyers of Brandi Hadley were everywhere, signaling a town desperate to reclaim one of its own. A kid this time, only sixteen.

"Oh, Brandi," she murmured, checking the vicinity, making sure there was no one nearby, then placing her hands on the pixilated face. She closed her eyes, thirsty too—for more information. If she got any impressions at all, however, they were vague. This was a photograph reproduced many times over, and in doing so, something had gotten lost in translation. A serious teen, introverted and solemn, those big brown eyes every bit as guarded as Missy's had been. A teenager, like most teenagers, who kept herself to herself and was careful about what she revealed. Maybe she was like that with friends, but did it extend to her family too? No way of knowing, not from a poster. Frustration rising again, Shady had one more pit stop before meeting Josie, skirting down a sidewalk that would lead her back onto Main Street to the place Brandi had last been seen: Batemans.

Ten minutes later, and she had it in her sights. Joe Bateman was the proprietor, and as she peered through the window, she spotted a man behind the counter that had to be him, sixtyish with a balding head and wearing a loose dark sweater over dark slacks.

The shop was empty as Shady entered, Joe Bateman immediately greeting her.

"Well, hello there! How are you this fine day?"

It *was* a fine day, but Shady realized she'd barely noticed it, too consumed with thoughts of missing people, Brandi at the helm.

"All good, thanks," she replied, wondering what to say or do next. Mr. Bateman, however, saved her the effort.

"New in town?"

"Visiting a friend," she explained. "Josie Wong, who I guess *is* new in town. She and her family have been here about a year."

"Ah, the Wongs, who own Halcyon Days. Lovely family. Baker City is glad to have them." A frown appeared. "They live next door to the Hadleys, right?"

Shady nodded, glad he'd mentioned them first, taking advantage of it. "It's so worrying about their daughter, isn't it? I gather she was last seen in here, on her way to school."

"That's right. She grabbed herself a soda from the fridge there like she did most days, like all the kids do in the morning, then she headed off."

"Alone?" Shady asked. "Or do you think she was meeting someone?"

Mr. Bateman shook his head. "I've told the police everything I know. I would think they've questioned just about everyone in town by now. But yeah, alone, although…she crossed the road, and she never normally does that, was raising her hand as if to wave to someone." How crestfallen he looked. "If only I'd stood at the window a little longer, seen whether there was someone waiting for her. It could have been just the information the police needed. But more kids came in, and…that was that."

"You shouldn't blame yourself," Shady said, offering a small smile too.

"Hard not to, especially if the worst happens. Sorry, miss, what is it I can help you with? Would you like something? A soda too, maybe."

Shady spun around to where the fridge was. "Sure. Thank you. I could use one."

"Help yourself," Mr. Bateman said as the little bell on the door rang, indicating more customers, another person to distract him.

As that person approached the desk, someone Mr. Hadley clearly knew, a regular, Shady made her way to the fridge and held on to the door rather than opening it, hoping that whatever the customer and Mr. Hadley were talking about would engross them.

The handle of the door was cold to the touch, sending shivers down her spine. Two days ago, that's all it'd been since Brandi's hand had touched this same handle. Was there some imprint of her left upon it? Of course, many others had touched it since, but a desperate situation called for desperate measures. *Brandi, were you meeting someone that morning? Going to high school…or somewhere else?*

She detected such a mix of energies, male, female, young and old. Some words breaking through the fuzz: *project, teacher, nice day, warm.* Nothing out of the ordinary and way too vague to attribute to anyone specific, let alone Brandi. A new puppy…someone was excited about that, about a football game too and…a meeting.

Shady flinched. What meeting?

She leaned forward so that her head was touching the fridge as well. *Come on, come on, what meeting?* Whatever it was, along with excitement, there was trepidation…Brandi's? If she'd crossed the street to meet someone, had she been nervous about it? Why? If planning on running away, was coercion involved?

"You okay there?"

If Shady had flinched before, she now yelped.

"What? Oh…um…"

It was Mr. Bateman, that conversation he'd been having not as all-consuming as she'd hoped. "Handle get stuck? It does that. Here, let me."

As Shady stepped back, the store owner quickly—and easily—opened the fridge door. "What soda you having?" he asked.

"Coke. Coke'll be great."

"One Coke coming right up."

Trailing after him to the counter, she paid for it, then took the bottle, said goodbye and headed outside. On the sidewalk, she opened the bottle and took a few good swigs.

One hand reaching up to wipe at her mouth afterward, she stared upward at the blue sky hanging over Baker City. A blue sky that was…dark at the edges.

She blinked. Not once but several times. Was that right what she was seeing? The sky, not a cloud in sight but still blemished? Like the fog, another kind of phenomenon.

She drank more Coke, realizing she was trembling despite the spring warmth.

Could everyone see this, or was it unique to her?

And if unique, was it an omen of some kind? A warning.

CHAPTER THIRTEEN

"Mrs. Hadley? I'm so sorry to disturb you, but we brought some food, lasagna. We didn't think you'd want to cook, and, well…you have to eat. We're all so worried about you."

Josie and Shady stood on the Hadleys' doorstep, Shady having to conceal how shocked she felt at the sight of the woman. Their encounter previously might have been brief, but Mrs. Hadley had been bright and bubbly, a woman obviously content with life. Sure, she might have a sullen teenager—her only child, Josie had told Shady—but she wasn't fazed by it, took it for what it was: a passing thing. Maybe she'd been sullen too, once upon a time, understood how the whole thing went. Now, though, she was wretched, her hair unkempt, blue eyes with no sparkle and dark circles underscoring them. Her clothes were also rumpled, as if she hadn't changed since discovering her daughter had gone missing, had kept them on day and night, slept in them, if she'd slept at all.

Rather than answer Josie, Mrs. Hadley just stood and stared, causing Josie to open her mouth again, to utter something, anything, when another voice broke through.

"Serena, Serena, who is it?"

In the hallway, Mr. Hadley appeared, only slightly less beleaguered.

"What's this?" he said, now addressing the girls.

"Lasagna," Josie said. "We made it. For you."

"Oh." Like his wife, the last thing on their mind was probably eating.

"We can…um…come back another time," Josie offered, Shady trying not to wince at that. They needed to get in there, and fast.

That dark-tinged blue sky—she was right about it being unique to her. Meeting Josie at the store at noon, she'd come clean about what she'd been doing that morning and what she'd found out, which was, in all honesty, very little, and therefore it needed to be built on. The next thing was to go straight to the source—to Brandi's house—and for Shady to find a way to get into her bedroom. Having established that, Shady had then asked Josie about the sky. "Can you see the edges of it, how dark they are?"

Josie had duly glanced upward. "Looks pretty glorious to me for this time of year."

Shady knew Native Americans used to read the clouds in order to determine what kind of weather was in store for them. With no clouds at all, Shady had to read the sky instead, understand it. As far as she could discern, a sky closing in on them meant only one thing: time really was of the essence, and it was running out. The police were on the case, they all knew that, but there was a bigger picture, and any clues she could unearth by visiting Brandi's bedroom, by *touching*, could aid their investigation, make a difference.

Josie had proffered the lasagna, but now she held it close again, made to turn. Shady, however, stood firm, locked eyes with Mr. Hadley, silently pleading with him. *Let us in.*

It worked.

"Darling," he said to his wife, "it's all right." Returning

his attention to the two visitors, he added, "That's very kind of you. Come in, please, please. You're welcome."

Mr. and Mrs. Hadley duly stepped aside, and Josie and Shady entered the house—as gloomy as that dark corridor in the Grand Willmott, owing to the closed drapes—and made their way to the kitchen at the back, where at least a chink of light shone through a set of shades.

With all four of them in there, Mr. Hadley went straight to the window and rolled up the shades, causing his wife to blink a little.

"Should I put this here?" Josie asked, indicating for the lasagna to be placed on the table.

Serena Hadley merely nodded.

"Coffee?" her husband asked.

"Please," Shady answered.

As they took their seats around the table, the only sound was of Mr. Hadley shuffling around, grabbing mugs from cupboards and brewing the coffee. A few seconds later, and all that changed. It was as if everyone raced to speak at once.

"I'm so sorry, Mrs. Hadley," Josie repeated.

"I am too," Shady said.

"Where could she be?" was Serena Hadley's lament.

"You take sugar and milk with your coffee?" from Mr. Hadley.

Another brief silence followed before Shady spoke again.

"We're young," she said, "me and Josie. We don't have kids, and so we can't even begin to imagine what you're both going through. But we are thinking of you." She gestured toward the lasagna. "And we want to help in whatever way we can."

Nice enough words, but coming from someone who was virtually a stranger, they might anger rather than placate.

Shady held her breath, waited to see.

Mrs. Hadley had directed her gaze back downward. Now, though, she lifted her head, her eyes flitting between Shady and Josie before several more words burst from her on a tide of grief that was primal. "Where is she?" she repeated. "Oh God, where is she?"

"Mrs. Hadley," Josie breathed, eventually reaching out, laying her hand on the table, closer to the woman.

Mr. Hadley also rushed to her side. "Serena, Serena, come on. The police will find her. They said they would. They promised."

"She'd never run off without telling us," Mrs. Hadley insisted through a torrent of tears. "She's a good girl. Never troubled us, not once. Our family is strong, solid. *Decent.* Why the hell have we fallen apart like this? This is the kind of thing that happens to other people, not us." She wiped at her eyes savagely and took a deep breath, shrugged off her husband also, too consumed with her own emotions to take his on board.

Clearly at a loss for what else to do, Mr. Hadley returned to the coffeepot, just keeping himself busy, Shady guessed, focusing on more practical matters as he brought it back to the table along with the mugs. He poured into each, but it was an action so half-hearted, so defeated, that Shady's heart ached further.

He sat too, took a sip from his mug and cleared his throat. "The police don't think she just disappeared but that she ran away. I don't know if you know this, but after visiting Batemans, the place she was last seen, she did something unusual and crossed the street. I say it's unusual because school is on the same side as Joe's store, a bit further down the road, and then you turn right. There's simply no need to cross the street. He also said she seemed to recognize someone, had lifted her hand as if waving. That's the sum of it, but…as baffling as it is, as bewildering, it gives us hope, doesn't it, darling? Maybe…maybe she *was* meeting someone and wasn't snatched. Who, though, we have no idea. The police have taken her computer and are also trying to track her cell, so far with no luck. I can't believe she'd just run away, though. We gave her everything, loved her, but maybe, just maybe, it's better than the alternative."

Despite the desperate optimism of his words, Mrs. Hadley started crying again, not the shuddering, howling tears of earlier but more silent, defeated too.

"Remember Alisa?" she said.

Josie glanced at Shady before replying. "Alisa Jones?"

Mrs. Hadley nodded. "Never found."

"That was a long time ago," Mr. Hadley pointed out. "Twenty years."

"Never. Found," his wife repeated, not just looking at him but glaring, her teeth bared. "Do you understand that? A pretty girl like her. Innocent. Out there still. On her own. After all these years. How?" Again, she shook her head, wildly, her husband reaching out a second time, having to swallow his own tears, to calm her when his nerves must be just as shot. "People don't just disappear," she continued to insist. "They don't."

As husband and wife at last clung to each other, Shady once more caught Josie's gaze, noticed how stricken she looked. It was now or never. She had to do this. Josie understood that, gave an almost imperceptible nod of her head.

Shady stood up, the sound of the chair scraping against linoleum catching both of the Hadleys' attention, surprise halting tears.

"Sorry," she said. "I…need to use the bathroom."

"The bathroom?" Mrs. Hadley repeated somewhat incredulously.

"I wouldn't ask, but…"

"Of course." It was Mr. Hadley, almost grateful for the interruption, Shady could tell. "The bathroom's upstairs, just beside…Brandi's bedroom."

"Thank you," she said, "and…sorry. I really am. I won't be long."

As she rushed from the room, found the stairs and headed up them, she felt bad. Not only for lying to the Hadleys but for leaving Josie alone to cope with them. But Josie *would* have to cope, keep them occupied for as long as she could, give Shady the time she needed to get inside Brandi's bedroom and touch.

The door to her room was ajar, something both hopeful and tragic in that, Shady thought, the Hadleys clinging on any way they could. Quickly she pushed it open and slipped inside. First thing she noticed was that Brandi's was indeed the room where the drapes were open, daylight streaming in. The second thing was the absence of the computer on a desk in the corner. The absence of many things, Shady imagined, notebooks, etc., that the police were trawling through, doing their best. Just as she must do.

Who were you meeting, Brandi? What secrets did you keep?

She had minutes, if that. Reaching out, she touched the bedframe and the bedside table next to it, the books that sat on top—*It Ends with Us* by Colleen Hoover, showing what…idealism? A tendency to romanticize things? Brandi had loved the book. Shady could see in her mind's eye how she'd devoured each and every page, not as sullen anymore but coming to life, the power of words stirring her. *Just* these words?

She moved over to the desk, pulled out the chair and sat down, placed her hands where the keyboard should be and, looking up as if the computer were still there, moved her fingers, tap, tap, tapping. *What were you planning?*

Because she *had* planned something; Shady could tell that much. This was where she'd sat and where she'd…dreamed. Those dreams idealized, as Shady had thought earlier, but not so sweet now, not so…normal, for a teenage girl, at any rate. Shady was detecting a darker tone to them, an…excitement…a thrill. That thrill…shared. Definitely shared. Did the police know this already? Perhaps messages had been exchanged via the computer or something? Or were they cleverer than that? Kids knew about computers these days, how to work their way around them, avoid detection. *What were you up to?* A flash of something else entered Shady's mind. An image. That of the Grand Willmott. Shady was startled by it, confused further. But also buoyed. How everything she'd found out so far—felt unease about—was connected, she didn't know, but this was further evidence it was.

Alisa stayed at the Grand Willmott. You knew that, didn't you? Were perfectly aware. You thought about her. Often. Why? And someone else, someone I can't quite get the name of. More male in energy. Missy's brother, Robert? Could it be? She sighed. *What is this darkness you've become tangled up in?* A kid, that's all she was, and therefore unwittingly entangled? A good kid, as Serena Hadley had stressed, so one that had been…groomed, as so many kids were nowadays. This interest…there were deeper layers to it. Spiritual layers. Something to do with myth and legend, with folklore. *Skin walkers?* The first time Shady had met her, she had, after all, shown an interest in that topic.

"We'll be on our way now, but thank you for seeing us. Thank you so much."

Josie's voice, much louder than normal, clawed Shady from her reverie. Downstairs, the three had clearly left the kitchen and were in the hallway.

Shady shot to her feet and hurried across the room, careful to leave the door exactly as she'd found it. She then entered the bathroom, flushed the toilet and left again.

"Sorry," she said as she descended the staircase, aware that their visit had consisted of apology after apology. "I was feeling a little faint. I don't know why, had to get my head together. I didn't mean to take so long."

Mrs. Hadley said nothing, didn't even glance her way, retreating back inside herself, but Mr. Hadley nodded, buying Shady's excuse, muttering that he hoped she felt better now, but his words were hollow, the visit from the two girls having exhausted them further.

They left the house, a ragged sigh escaping Josie when they were alone.

"Anything?" she said to Shady as they traipsed down the pathway.

"She may have been groomed," Shady said, "although who by, I don't know. But there's a connection with the Grand Willmott, with Alisa Jones." Shady had already informed Josie that Alisa and Brandi had gone missing on the same date. "Maybe even with Robert Davenport too, who also went missing on the twenty-fifth of April. There's something about that date. It has some kind of meaning. A dark meaning. That's the thing, Josie. I detected a fascination with something spiritual, and I don't mean the kind that enlightens you."

"Okay." Josie's frown deepened. "Do we go to the police with that?"

"Yeah, but can we do something else first?"

"What?"

"You have a library in Baker City, right?"

"Yep. Mom goes there all the time."

"Good, because that's our next port of call."

CHAPTER FOURTEEN

"If you'd like to follow me, I'll show you where we keep town records."

They'd arrived at Baker City Library and gone straight to reception, the desk occupied by a woman in her mid-fifties or thereabouts and diminutive, her red hair somewhat faded, her brow furrowed as she stamped a series of books piled high in front of her.

Lifting her head, she'd asked if she could help, Josie replying they wanted to do some research into Baker City's history.

As she led them through an area lined with bookshelves, desks interspersed throughout, some empty, some occupied, Shady was reminded of her own workplace. That was a long, narrow room too, although more light filtered in here than at the Mason Town Museum. The part where records were kept was right at the far end.

Ushering them into the annexed room, the woman—a name badge identifying her as Cassie Dupont—spoke again. "Anything in particular you're looking for?"

For reasons she couldn't quite fathom, Shady remained tight-lipped. What they were doing here was no one's business but their own. Josie, however, turned to face the librarian, her eyes only grazing Shady's—not enough time for Shady to signal a warning.

"We're researching people that have gone missing in this area, dating back twenty, maybe even thirty years. We also want to research the Grand Willmott and the kind of people who used to hold meetings there. We want to see if there's a connection, you see, with the teenager that's just gone missing. You know about her, I'm sure. Brandi Hadley?"

Cassie didn't answer right away; instead, the color seemed to drain from her face.

"Josie—" Shady began, but Cassie interrupted.

"A connection? In what possible way?"

"Because of the date," Josie blithely continued. "Alisa Jones went missing on the same date as Brandi, albeit twenty years before. And there's another, isn't there, Shady?" She might have asked her friend a question, but she didn't wait for an answer. "A Robert Davenport. He went missing thirty years earlier on that date in this area. I mean, it could be a coincidence, we accept that, but—" she shrugged "—then again, maybe not. And if not, then someone's responsible, someone…wild, who could still be alive."

"Wild?" Cassie swallowed hard. "Have you taken your concerns to the police?"

Shady at last interjected. "Not yet. Not until we have something more solid."

"I see." Cassie shifted her gaze from Josie to Shady. Time might have worn her, but Shady could see she'd been a very good-looking woman once, her features neat and even, her complexion clear and eyes unusual, almost amber. "Good luck," she continued, her expression now neutral, *carefully* neutral?

Finally, she left, Josie turning to Shady, a big smile on her face, still oblivious to any misgivings Shady might have had about her sharing their intent with Ms. Dupont, though even Shady had to wonder about those misgivings. Maybe she was getting paranoid, looking for fault with everyone, suspecting them. She had to narrow the net, not widen it.

The pair of them got to work.

"So, we're looking for people that have gone missing in this area on April twenty-fifth."

"Uh-huh," said Shady, following on-screen instructions and logging into the computer.

"Give or take a day?"

"Yeah. I suppose."

"And in the last thirty years right up to Brandi."

Shady nodded. "If you focus on that, I'm going to focus on the Grand Willmott. The types of events they organized, the meetings held there in the function rooms."

"You got this real thing about meetings, don't you?"

"It's got something to do with the bigger picture, I know it. Not just who Brandi was meeting, if in fact she was, but…secret meetings of other kinds."

"Not likely to be held in public rooms, then?" Josie challenged, logging in too.

"You wouldn't think so," Shady murmured. "Ordinarily."

Another hush descended, Shady grateful that they had the room to themselves and hoping it stayed that way. Most library records had been transferred to computer, including issues of the *Baker City Tribunal,* dating right back through the decades to the sixties at least, perfect for trying to get a feel for how the hotel had been used and by whom.

Yes, meetings had been held there and documented, town matters, it seemed, planning and expansion, votes being cast on how the town should evolve. Benign matters, she supposed, eminent townsfolk at the helm, whose names she scanned, slowly, slowly reading them, wondering if any would evoke a feeling in her—a suspicion. There'd been a series of mayors in the sixties, including Gordon Lyle, Leda Arzoni, David Hume and Lorrie Parker. She studied photographs of each, all classically posed and smiling, and reached out and touched the screen too but felt nothing. She moved on to mayors throughout the seventies. All had been popular, motivated to increase Baker City's fortunes, to create a sense of place for it in modern life. All were benign too, as far as she could tell. By the eighties, she was drowning in names and faces and minutes of meetings held, her brain stuffed full yet again.

She was about to turn to Josie, to mutter something like "needle in a haystack springs to mind," when details of another mayor, appointed in the early eighties, caught her attention. Jerry Hilt, who, with his wide stature, cowboy hat and bootlace necklace, looked like a Texan wannabe. But, oh, how Baker City had loved him! There was a profile written on him, listing his education, his achievements, his *hobbies*, one word in particular jumping out at Shady—*hunting*. Jerry Hilt was a man who loved to hunt the Oregon wilderness, the mountains and the wide-open plains that surrounded Baker City his playground. His photograph was as grainy as the one in the Grand Willmott, and when she touched it, she felt as chilled.

Josie clearly noticed. "You got something?"

"I think so. Maybe. This man…"

Josie slid over. "Jerry Hilt," she read. "Looks like a regular redneck."

"A hunter," Shady said.

"Yeah, I can imagine. Shady, what is it?"

134

"Something about hunting, about him. His eyes, look at them."

Josie did but then shook her head. "It's just a pair of eyes."

Eyes that reminded her of the masked men. Was he one of them? "What about you, you find anything?"

"Nope, would have said if I did."

"Shit," breathed Shady.

"Do we have to be so specific about the date?"

Shady thought for a moment. "You know what? I think we do."

"Your call, I guess," Josie replied, returning to face her own computer screen. "I'm not sure we should be happy or sad we can't find a pattern."

"A pattern?" Shady repeated before her voice rose in excitement. "Yes! A pattern! Of course! That's exactly what we're looking for. Everything has a pattern, *everything*, and Alisa, Robert, Brandi, that photograph in the Grand Willmott, the Grand Willmott itself, the mountains around here…goddamn it, this man Jerry Hilt is part of the pattern too."

Again, Josie was baffled. "Seriously? It all seems frigging random to me."

"Yeah, I know it does, but…Josie, the only thing I can do here is trust my instinct. It's served me well before."

"With Mandy and Gina's mirror?"

"Uh-huh. You know, none of that made sense when I was investigating it either until it made *blinding* sense. Sometimes it's like…a spider's web. Intricate. You get me?"

"Yeah, I suppose. There's only one trouble with that analogy, though."

"What?"

"You can get stuck in a web, Shady." She raised her hands and wriggled her fingers. "That big old spider can come out of hiding and eat you!" The girls laughed, but then Josie grew serious again. "You really think Jerry Hilt has something to do with it, a mayor?"

Shady turned back to the photograph of him, took in his smile too, found it to be…disingenuous. "I really do."

She searched his name, and more photographs featuring him came up, some attached to articles commending the good work he'd done for Baker City, picturing him at the opening of brand-new enterprises in and around the town and also with other eminent figures, the chief of police included, a man called Doug Saunders. One of these photos featured six men, though three more hovered in the background, eyeing the camera but unnamed.

Grabbing her cell, she took a photograph of the group; they were all big shots, farm owners, warehouse owners and the like. The three that weren't named, though, who were they? Two of them were tall and wiry, the third somewhat sturdier, something familiar about him that she couldn't quite place. She hadn't thought to count the people in the photograph at the Grand Willmott. Were there nine of them too or more? *These* people? Unmasked. She hadn't been able to find any details regarding masked events or festivals that the town had held over the decades; it didn't look like it was a thing here, something unique to Baker City. And yet, if it was some kind of secret event—a *ritual*—why was there a photograph on display at the hotel? An arrogance to it, the participants feeling that they were, what, above the law? Why? Because in these parts they *were* the law?

"Shady, Shady, hey, listen up, come here. I think I've

found something."

It took a couple of moments for Shady to register Josie's words. "What? Yeah, sure."

Closing the gap between them, she looked to where Josie was pointing at two words: *Mazuma Lake*. "It was around there that Alisa Jones went missing."

"That's right," Shady confirmed.

"Well, so did Robert Davenport. Did you know that? I mean, like, not just in the area but *precisely* there." She frowned, as if doing the math. "Within twenty miles of Alisa's camp."

"For real?"

"For real. There's an article here, not about him but Mazuma Lake. It mentions him, though. His disappearance. Just a couple of lines, but, hey, it's something."

"Another link," muttered Shady. "But there's no more reports of people going missing around April twenty-fifth in the last thirty years?"

"Nope, not on that date, in that area or otherwise."

"Okay, so what if we go back ten years *prior* to Davenport, to 1982."

Josie met Shady's gaze. "When Jerry Hilt was mayor?"

"Uh-huh."

Josie duly nodded. "Okay. Sure. Let's do it."

It didn't take long, maybe another twenty minutes or less, to unearth yet another nugget. Forty years ago on that date, in that area, around mighty Mazuma Lake, another person had indeed gone missing, no trace ever found. A man this time, in his fifties and another keen hunter, experienced like the others, who had somehow been lured from the camp he'd made, left everything behind, all means of survival. Had he stayed at the Grand Willmott before, like Alisa had?

Maybe even Davenport had stayed there too, Baker City's grandest hotel, its most historic, central to everything—*a gateway.*

They both stared wide-eyed at the information, at extracts in newspapers too, the *Baker City Tribunal* one of them, a big splash on the front page, a photograph not only of the man, Dud Hooper, but another of Jerry Hilt too, standing beside Doug Saunders, chief of police, as he read out a statement concerning Hooper, both their expressions so serious, so…concerned. Again disingenuous. It was Josie who broke the silence.

"I still don't get why we're doing this," she admitted. "These three went missing around Mazuma Lake. Brandi was last seen right here in Baker City, on Main Street."

"Meeting someone," Shady said, turning to her.

"Well…yeah. Maybe."

"What if they were heading there?"

CHAPTER FIFTEEN

It was early evening, Shady and Josie in Josie's room, as silent as they'd been in the library, each contemplating the events of the day so far.

Shady had written it all down, the people who had gone missing—they'd found no more prior to Dud Hooper—and the links, no matter how tenuous, to Brandi's disappearance. They'd then taken it all to the Baker City Police Department, explaining they might have information that could help with the teen's disappearance. They'd been seen quickly, told by the lieutenant and his supporting officer to take a seat in the interview room.

As if a gasket had blown, words had come pouring out of Shady as she'd told and shown them everything except the photograph of Jerry Hilt and the then chief of police. She'd held back that particular gem because in no way did she wish to imply the police were perhaps involved in this web that she was indeed creating, garnering disapproval before they'd even gotten going, maybe even risk getting sued for libel into the bargain.

The lieutenant, younger than Shady had expected, kind of good-looking with dark floppy hair and piercing eyes, had listened patiently while his officer took notes. Good, all good, it had been going well, then Shady noticed the officer had stopped writing and, like the lieutenant, was staring at her, a look of confusion marring his slightly more lived-in face.

"I know it doesn't seem to make sense," she began, but the lieutenant interrupted her.

"I appreciate what you've done. *We* do, the police. We never wish to discourage anyone sharing information with us that they think might prove useful. The most vital clue can be the most random, but this…I'm going to be honest with you. It's left-field."

"My friend's a psychic," Josie said, again blurting out information that Shady would rather have kept private. In fact, they'd agreed between themselves beforehand not to mention this particular fact to the police, not unless it was necessary. Clearly, Josie now thought it was *very* necessary, Shady wishing, though, she'd hung on a little longer, because there it was in the lieutenant's and his sidekick's eyes: disbelief, amusement even.

They were losing any credibility they might have had, and fast.

"This isn't just about insight," Shady said. "This is fact. That's four people who've gone missing from this area on that date, three of them never found. Cold cases."

"Decades apart," the lieutenant calmly pointed out.

"Yeah, sure, but—"

"You thinking it may be the work of a serial killer?"

"Well…yeah," Shady answered. "Or killer*s*."

"There's no profile."

"Excuse me?" said Josie.

"Serial killers usually have a type they go for—all women, for example, young men or older men. There's no type here."

"They were hunters," Shady stressed. "That's a type. Okay, not Brandi but the other three. All keen and experienced hunters who loved hunting in this area especially."

The lieutenant sat back in his chair, still calm, still collected. "You know how many people love to hunt in this part of the world? More than we can count. Plus, like you said, Brandi was no hunter, and neither were her parents. There's no relevance to her at all."

"But...the date."

"Is just a date, that's all."

"I know it's connected, that it has something to do with Brandi!"

"You know this because of your...psychic powers?"

Definite amusement in the lieutenant's eyes now—not unkind, though, Shady had to admit, although that realization did nothing to negate the sting of it. The man also didn't outright laugh her out of his office, no matter how much he might've wanted to. As tears formed in Shady's eyes from sheer frustration, he took pity on her instead.

"I understand how concerned you are for Brandi. We all are. We're throwing everything we have at the case, believe me. The Feds are involved too despite, at this stage, no foul play suspected. They monitor a whole range of missing persons cases, and I'll pass this information on to them. It may well be of interest. But regarding Brandi, there's no evidence whatsoever she was headed or was taken to the area around Mazuma Lake."

"So...you won't be checking it out?"

"We'll bear it in mind," he said, promising no more than that.

There had been no other option but to leave the police department and go home, Shady trying not to notice the sky above her, the darkness at the edges increasing.

Lulin had fed them dinner, despite neither of them being hungry, and then they'd gone to Josie's room to sit in silence, contemplating, contemplating, contemplating, the night falling in earnest now, the skies entirely black. Ray had texted, and Annie, both of them keen to keep up with any developments. She was about to reply, her fingers hovering over the keypad of her cell, when an idea formed. An urge that refused to abate.

She jumped up, startling Josie.

"Shady?"

"Do you know where Cassie lives?"

"Cassie? The lady from the library?"

"Yeah. Do you?"

Josie shook her head. "But Mom might."

"Can you ask her?"

"Really? She'll wonder why!"

"Think up an excuse. It doesn't matter what. We need to go there."

"To Cassie's house?"

"Yes," Shady replied. "She's connected to all this too."

* * *

Lulin Wong did indeed know where Cassie Dupont lived. Apparently, they would chat whenever Lulin visited the library, in hushed tones, of course. During one of these conversations, Cassie had mentioned she and her father, now deceased, had run a B and B on the edge of town, which had since closed. The Dupont B and B, "a home away from home," its address listed on the Net.

Having secured this information, Josie had then told her mother she and Shady were heading back into town for a drink. After strict warnings to be careful, the pair had left, Josie sitting in the passenger seat of Shady's Dodge, demanding to know why the heck they were doing this.

"She's connected," Shady reiterated, firing up the engine and pulling onto the road.

"Another one?"

She didn't blame Josie for being skeptical. She bet even Ray and Annie would be. Just before leaving, she'd replied at last to both of them, saying she was still on the case, trying to find a way through what seemed like such murky darkness. Ray had answered right away, repeating what he'd said before she'd left home to come here: *Say the word, Shady, and I'll be there.* He'd pressed home something else too. *Be careful, okay? Don't put yourself in unnecessary danger.*

Was this dangerous, what she was doing? Going to stake out Cassie Dupont's house. A woman in her mid-fifties. A librarian, for God's sake! What could possibly be dangerous about it? That feeling Shady had about her, that she was connected to the bigger picture, could be just that…a feeling. Totally unfounded. Yet when she'd locked eyes with Cassie, when Josie had blurted out what they were at the library for, she'd seen it, a *knowledge*. A secret held on to. And so, yes, Cassie Dupont was exactly that: connected. Somehow. One of the unnamed men in the photograph of nine also played on her mind and how she'd thought he'd looked familiar. If only the photograph had been in color and not black and white. If it had, she'd swear she'd see something else about him, amber eyes, perhaps…

"So, what's the plan?" Josie continued. "Do we knock on

the door, fabricate another excuse why we're here? Your turn this time. I did my share with the Hadleys."

"Maybe we don't knock on the door," Shady mused. "We don't announce our presence at all. All I'm aiming to do here is get the feels about her, and visiting her house, touching the walls, the sills, just being on her property, basically, might give me the insight I need." Josie was silent, causing Shady to add, "I know how crazy I must sound."

"Shady, you don't, but…I'm worried we're disappearing down a rabbit hole here. And, meanwhile, Brandi's missing. It's been forty-eight hours. Forty-eight *crucial* hours, and there's still no sign of her."

"Josie?"

"Yeah?"

"Do me a favor?"

"Sure. What?"

"Trust me, okay? You know I told you about Kanti?"

"Your grandmother?"

Shady nodded. "She guides me. And that's the impression I'm getting here, that I'm being guided."

"Okay." Josie's voice was solemn as she digested this, then she turned to Shady and smiled. "I guess it isn't just God who works in mysterious ways."

Shady smiled too. "Nope. Kanti does too. We won't be long at Cassie's house, I promise. I just want to see if there's any foundation to this feeling. Something a little more solid. If she has a porch, there might be a cushion on a chair I could borrow or a glass left out that she's drank from, something like that. I can take it, return to the car and just—"

"Tune in?"

"Exactly. Worth trying, huh?"

"When a kid's life is at stake, I guess anything is."

A little over ten minutes later and they arrived outside Cassie's. A double-fronted house in a green setting, it was slightly removed from other homes, surrounded by tall trees. Shady could imagine it as a B and B, a very pleasant place to stay, another base from which to explore the wilderness. It did indeed have a wraparound porch, with a table with a hurricane lamp on it and, yes—she could've punched the air when she saw it—a glass Cassie might have sipped from, enjoying a post-work beer or lemonade.

There were no lights on at the front of the house and no sign of a parked car, but that didn't mean Cassie wasn't home; lights could be on at the back of the property instead, where the car could be too. They'd still have to be careful.

Shady pointed at the porch. "That's where I'm heading. Can you keep a lookout?"

"Sure, but be quick. Nobody likes a snooper."

Shady agreed. "Needs must, huh?"

They both exited the car, Shady grateful for the night that aided them in their aim, the pair of them hunched and tiptoeing like cartoon cat burglars minus the loot bags. The glass was the only thing she wanted, that which Cassie had put to her lips. Maybe it had even lingered there while she'd been lost in thought, remembering two girls that had visited the library today, looking for missing people...

"Hurry," Josie whispered when they reached the foot of the porch.

"I promise I will. I'll grab the glass and then—"

"Jeez, I'm getting goose bumps already."

"We'll head home soon."

"We'll head to the bar!" Josie countered. "I need a shot of something to calm my nerves."

"There's nothing to worry about, but, yeah, I hear ya. Good idea."

"Okay, get going, then—go, go, go."

Still on tiptoe, still hunched, Shady climbed the stairs, six of them. The glass was in front of her; she had just a few more feet to go. Within easy reach. A heartbeat away…

"Shady?"

"Almost got it, Josie."

"No…Shady."

"And whaddya know, it's as fresh as I hoped it would be. I'll definitely be able to tell something from it. I can already, in fact, what she was thinking when she got home from work today. It was about us, Josie! Like I suspected. You and me were on her mind."

Excited, Shady spun around, holding the glass high for Josie to see.

What she saw instead took her breath away.

There was a woman behind Josie, a woman with red hair that had faded. Diminutive. Who held a secret and, right now, a rifle too.

Pointing right at the back of Josie's head.

CHAPTER SIXTEEN

"Ms. Dupont," Shady stuttered. "Really, I can explain. We...um...no, not we, *me*, just me, I was curious, about...about...I thought...um..."

If Shady was babbling, trying to explain their presence, Josie and the woman holding her hostage were mute, Josie through fear, Cassie clearly fuming.

This was no time for lies, she realized. This was crunch time. A rifle was at her friend's head, and who knew if the quiet librarian would do it, pull the trigger.

Shady came clean, telling her exactly why she was there, the people who had gone missing, a decade between them, and now—twenty years since the last one—Brandi.

"And despite the passage of time, there's a link between all of it, to the Grand Willmott too, to a photo that hangs in the hallway there of men wearing animal masks. To Jerry Hilt, mayor of Baker City in the early eighties, to Doug Saunders, who was the chief of police back then, and to other prominent figures—and to hunting. Hunting is definitely key in all this, up at Mazuma Lake. I'm not saying Brandi was heading there, but...there's a link. With you too. There are meetings. And there are secrets that have to come to light because a girl is missing, a kid, a teenager, and"—Shady recalled the strange skies of earlier—"time isn't on our side."

Her words might have come to an end, but her desperation was only increasing. What would Cassie do with this information? Train the rifle on her instead?

She didn't. She lowered the firearm, but only slightly.

"Upstairs," she barked at Josie, who, with an impressive swiftness, forced life into her limbs and obeyed, her eyes on Shady all the while, desperation in them too.

With all three on the porch, Cassie told Shady to open the front door and go inside.

Shady was also quick to obey, but not before giving Josie a quick glance, trying to reassure her. *It'll be okay.* This woman was a librarian and, before that, a B and B owner. An upstanding member of the community. She wouldn't just shoot the pair of them. *Please, God.*

Although the décor in the hallway was completely different from Missy Davenport's home—far plainer—the atmosphere reminded Shady of it, that same sadness permeating everything, an underlying anger too that was icy cold.

"Go into the living room," Cassie told them. "Go on, move!"

Still in the lead, Shady turned right, noting that on the left was a kitchen. Her hand held out slightly, she traced it along the wall, along the back of the sofa in the living room, and an armchair too, touching anything she could. *What is it with you, Cassie Dupont?*

Unmarried or divorced? She had no ring on her finger. The house did indeed have some masculine touches, but more historical than recent? There were several framed photographs in the room, Shady's gaze landing on the nearest one. It was of a young Cassie somewhere in her teens, as pretty as Shady had imagined her to be, an older man's arm around her shoulders, the pair of them grinning—father and daughter, it had to be, an easiness between them. Was he the man in the photograph she'd seen at the library? He was burly enough. She'd need to get closer to make sure, not an option at this stage.

"Sit down," Cassie said, the sound of her voice in such saturated silence making Josie jump and Shady flinch. As Josie took the single chair and Shady one end of the sofa, Cassie then lowered her rifle and headed to a sideboard, on top of which sat a crystal decanter three-quarters full with golden liquid, a set of shot glasses surrounding it.

After propping the rifle against the wall, Cassie upturned three glasses and filled them with hefty measures of the liquid—bourbon, Shady guessed.

She downed her glass in one, then took the other two over to the girls.

"Drink," she said, handing them over.

"Oh no, no," Josie protested. "Never touch the stuff."

"I said, drink!"

She did, knocking it back as fast as Cassie had, Shady joining in too, relishing the warmth it imparted and, if she wasn't mistaken, an ounce more courage too.

"We don't mean any harm," she repeated, wiping at the side of her mouth. "But I know you know what I'm talking about."

Cassie appraised her, those incredible eyes—like the eyes of a fox, or maybe even a wolf—narrowing to slits. "What did you mean back there on the porch, with my glass in your hand, that you could tell a lot from it, what I was thinking? Because, yes, it's true, I was thinking about your visit to the library earlier. But how could you possibly know that?"

Shady looked at Josie, saw her nod. *Tell her.* She would, she'd have to, and not be embarrassed this time but own her gift, be proud of it. Cassie was a proud woman; that much was obvious. To earn any chance of respect, Shady'd need to match her in that.

Shady gave her the same spiel she'd given Missy. "I can read objects. It's a gift, a psychic gift, if you like. The practice is called psychometry, and it's not all objects, just those where the emotions of those that have handled them is strong, the *energy*. And it's not all bad either. It can be a good experience that I detect, something…comforting."

"Comforting?" Cassie repeated.

"Sometimes."

"But not in my case. Whatever it is you sense about me is unsettling, isn't it?"

"You tell me," replied Shady, such boldness causing Josie to inhale.

There was a silence that dragged, Shady refusing to break it, not this time, and then Cassie laughed—a harsh, raw-edged sound. She returned to the sideboard and poured more bourbon, but just for herself this time. Was she seeking Dutch courage too? Shady wondered. She hoped so. She *prayed* so. If she couldn't make sense of this soon, fit the pieces together, she feared she never would. And what would that mean for Brandi? *Share the load. Unburden yourself. Please. You know how this all fits.*

At last, Cassie Dupont approached the seating area again, opting to sit at the opposite end of the sofa from Shady, her eyes on the empty grate in front of her as if there were flames leaping about in it, their flickering beauty mesmerizing.

"It was all such a long time ago," she said, her voice barely above a murmur. "Sometimes I forget it even happened. Life is so…different now." She raised her voice a little. "Other times, though, it haunts me, and I wonder at myself. How could I forget? How could I *possibly* forget? What happened and what I did about it, it defines me, and yet—" another bitter laugh "—no one knows anything about it but me. Until now."

Finally diverting her gaze, she glanced at Josie, then at Shady, the smile on her face indeed something haunted, cracking Shady's heart a little.

"You sure you're ready for this? Hearing how it's connected. Some of it, at least."

Shady nodded. Even Josie did, suddenly eager too.

"Okay, then. I'll do it. I'll tell you about Dan Turner."

CHAPTER SEVENTEEN

As Cassie shifted on the sofa, the air was electric. Her eyes were no longer fixed on the grate but on some invisible point in time way, way back.

"Mom died when I was a kid. Cancer, like a viper, struck hard and struck fast, took her out in the blink of an eye. At least that's what it seemed like to me, the ten-year-old Cassie. One minute she was there, and the next, she was…gone."

Cassie turned her head, such an abrupt gesture, and indicated another framed photograph on a cupboard toward the corner of the room. "That's her. It's one of those studio headshots everyone had back in the day. She's beautiful, isn't she?"

Shady and Josie both looked. The photograph in its gilt frame was far larger than the others in the room, black and white, and, yes, Cassie was right, her mother had been a beautiful woman, the smile on her face one of the softest Shady had ever seen.

Cassie cleared her throat, blinked a couple of times. "With Mom gone, it was just me and Dad when I was growing up, and Dad was a good man. We were close. He did his best by me, I want you to know that, to remember that. But…without Mom, he was lonely. He was a hunter, my dad, and so, for a while, was I."

As she said this, Shady inhaled, Cassie noticing, her eyes narrowing as they'd done before, but only briefly. She was in the moment now, truly captured, more words spilling from her.

"That's what we did, how we bonded. We'd go out together into the wild blue yonder, and we'd track and we'd hunt."

"Near Mazuma Lake?" Josie asked.

"Yes. Around Mazuma Lake."

"A sacred place," Shady said.

"It *all* is. It's supposed to be. A place to heal but also a place to die. Full of magic and full of terror. But back then, as a child, I could only see the magic. Me and Dad would head out there on the weekend or whenever we could, camping, stargazing, Dad telling me around the campfire about when he and Mom met, reliving the dream. We were careful, mind you. He took no chances. It was safety before adventure, always."

Having leaned back on the sofa, Cassie now sat forward, staring again at the grate, Shady wishing there were a fire made up, the chill in her bones increasing.

"You mentioned meetings," Cassie continued. "Well, a man came to town, not from Baker City, just beyond it, and meetings were held in the Grand Willmott, strictly men only. They were hunters, every one of 'em. Dad used to talk about the meetings. Heck, everyone who was anyone seemed to attend, but he didn't, not at first, not with a kid at home to look after. But, and here's the thing, as I got older, I lost the taste for hunting, revered life rather than wanting to bring it down. We had the business to tend to as well. This is a big old house, used to belong to my mother's parents. If we were to keep it, we had to make it work for us, so we turned it into a B and B, offering the best of the West, a real homey place to stay. As young as I was, that's what I became more preoccupied with. And Dad…well, Dad needed new playmates. I often torture myself about that, that I encouraged him to attend those meetings, to go hunting with the men of the town instead of me, to try to be someone too, more important when he was important enough already, in my eyes, at least. If I hadn't pushed him, things might have turned out very different."

Cassie rose, another abrupt gesture that again made both Shady and Josie flinch, Shady for her part wondering if she was heading for the rifle, done with talking, not wanting to venture any further down memory lane because it was simply too painful. She didn't, though; she went to another corner of the room, picked up another framed photograph—this one of a man, woman and child—and brought it back, showed it to them but didn't hand it over.

"This is us, the Dupont family, taken back when the world was a wonderful place to be. Look at Dad. Go on, look at him. He just wanted to belong, that's all. Wanted to find some meaning when meaning had been stripped from his life."

Shady reached out. "Can I take a closer look?"

Cassie refused. "This is precious," she said, seating herself back on the sofa and laying the portrait facedown on the cushion between them.

"So, Dad went to the meetings held every month, got a neighbor to sit with me when he did. He went hunting with them too, which also tended to be a monthly thing, all heading to the hills, no doubt whoop, whoop, whooping with excitement. He said I should come too, young as I was, that he'd fix it somehow so it was possible, that he'd told them all about me, had boasted what a good hunter his little girl was, as good as any man, a natural with a keen eye. An exception should be made, he said, for someone so talented."

"But you weren't interested?" Shady double-checked.

"No, I wasn't. Dad was the one who kept pushing this time, though, told me they'd allow it this once, that they were intrigued by me, this child who was nearly a woman, who'd suffered in life, lost her mom when she was just a kid, aged ten. The reason Dad pushed was because he was nostalgic, not wanting me to change. I knew that. I understood that. So I did it, I gave in, drove out with them to the mountains on one of their monthly meets. I was sixteen. And *that's* when I met Dan Turner."

* * *

Cassie was quiet for a while, Shady glancing at Josie, seeing a confusion that was surely mirrored in her own eyes but also a deepening curiosity. Just who was Dan Turner? The man she'd mentioned who was from out of town? What did he have to do with anything?

"Cassie," Shady prompted, growing more and more desperate to know, thinking of those black-tinged skies, of the clock ticking.

"I was sixteen, and he was…what…twenty? Something like that. Tall but skinny, dark hair kept short, clad in a jacket, jeans and boots, holding that rifle by his side like his life depended on it. A mountain man, like all the other men in the group, except for one thing."

"What?" breathed Josie.

"The look in his eye," Cassie answered. "Tall and skinny he might've been and, aside from me, the youngest there, but in among police commissioners, mayors and businessmen, he held himself well. He had this…way about him, you know? He was so self-assured."

"Charismatic," murmured Shady.

"Uh-huh."

"Do you know what he did for a living?"

"Nope, had no clue. All I know is that the other men, no matter what their rank, bowed to him. My dad—" Cassie grimaced, closed her eyes briefly "—was *obsessed* with him. The hunt got underway, and I don't know, that superior way of his, it riled me, along with something else in his eyes that I didn't like whenever he glanced my way. Fascination, maybe? Suppose you're thinking it's immodest of me to say it, but it was true. Although he never so much as said a word to me that day, for some reason I fascinated him.

"Like I said, I was sixteen, barely. Young, but I felt old too, had had to grow up a lot when Mom died. *I* was the woman of the house, cooking, cleaning and looking after Dad. That kind of thing takes its toll. But it makes something of you too. I was proud of myself, and Dad was right. I was a good hunter. Just a kid, but I'd show 'em anyways. And I did. It was me who brought down the first deer, quickly, effortlessly, almost…I'm gonna say it: *arrogantly*. Dan Turner appreciating that, *respecting* it.

"After that trip, time passed, so much of it. I never went hunting again, felt like I'd proved my point. I was done, truly. Tried to make a go of the B and B, but with the Grand Willmott in town, that wasn't proving easy. Folks went there no matter how much we advertised, no matter how nice our accommodation was, offering home cooking too, the works. As if—" Cassie frowned and inclined her head "—they were *directed* there. That's what I always felt. When folks came to stay in Baker City, it was the Grand Willmott or bust. And for no reason that I could see. It was shabby at the time, in ill repair."

"Forty years ago," Shady said, trying to get the timeframe right in her mind.

"That's right, forty, thirty, twenty years ago. We just couldn't compete. Our income from the B and B was too meager to survive on, and Dad, who also worked in construction, was working there less and less because of some injuries he'd sustained on the job years before. I was nineteen when I started at the library to supplement our income, working part-time to begin with, still trying to make the B and B a success. We got by, though, Dad and me. We lived our lives, him still religiously attending those meetings, still talking about Dan, all the damned time talking about him. And then one day Dan came calling.

"I was nearing twenty-six by this time. Dad was off somewhere. I was at home, and a truck pulled up. I went outside to see who it was and didn't recognize him at first, the man I'd met when I was sixteen. Like I said, I'd heard so much about him over the years, but I used to drown Dad out, pretend I was listening when I wasn't. And now there he was, standing in front of me. The man himself. Still tall, yeah, but no longer skinny. He was…*powerfully* built. That's the only way I can think to describe it. Broad. Muscles bulging beneath the shirt he wore. I was scrutinizing him, and he scrutinized me right back."

"Was there…an attraction?" Shady asked, wincing that there might be, although not sure why. Cassie, though, quickly put her right.

"Let me tell you this, there was no goddamned attraction on my part, okay? I liked men, I had flings with men, but I'd been looking after my father since I was a kid, and, as I've already pointed out, that took its toll. No way in hell did I want another man to look after. Flings were—and still are—good enough for me."

Shady was immediately contrite. "Sorry."

Cassie wiped her hand across her brow. "But…he was interested in me. Like he'd been when I was sixteen. It was there in his eyes, the way they kept looking into mine, not roaming like you'd expect, just fixed right here"—she lifted her hand and pointed to her eyes—"like he was bewitched or something. He was dropping a package off for Dad, but he didn't want to just hand it over. He wanted to stay and talk. Asked me all about hunting and whether I was still interested. I told him no, I was too busy for that. He wouldn't buy it, though. Outright refused to. 'Come to the meetings,' he said. 'The *true* meetings. I remember what you were like at sixteen, that…skill, that…hunger. You're born for this.'

"I was frowning by this time. 'The meetings at the Grand Willmott?' I asked. He laughed and shook his head, told me no, other meetings held elsewhere. I wanted to know if my dad went to those too, although he'd mentioned nothing about it to me. Again, Turner shook his head. 'There are strict rules, only so many permitted, but I can make an exception, replace someone,' he said, nodding his head all the while. 'Yes, yes, I'll allow that, allow *you*.' Well, that got my sap rising for sure. Who did he think he was saying *he'd* allow *me*? 'Ask my dad instead,' I told him, holding out my hand for the package, which he at last handed over before turning and just…sauntering off.

"Later, I told Dad what had happened, asked him about those other meetings, and, like I suspected, he had no clue what I was talking about. There were the meetings at the Grand Willmott that everyone attended and the organized hunts, which everyone was also invited to. He said he'd ask Dan what he meant, that Dan was sure to tell him, and that was it, the last I heard of it." She leaned back into the sofa again, her head on the backrest. "More time passed. Another ten years."

"Really?" Josie asked, and Shady sat up straighter.

"All this seemed to happen in increments of ten," Cassie told her.

Shady couldn't resist asking. "You know about Alisa Jones, right? She went missing twenty years ago. Before that, *ten* years before that, on the same date, so did Robert Davenport. And then ten years earlier, Dud Hooper, also on that date, April twenty-fifth, all in the same area, around Mazuma Lake. Less than twenty miles between them."

For a moment, Cassie simply stared at her. "That figures."

Shady failed to keep the desperation out of her voice. "How does it figure?"

Cassie's gaze grew harder. "That's what I'm trying to tell you."

Shady apologized again. "Please. Go on."

"Life carried on, but then he came back to visit me, just me, not Dad, no pretense of handing over any package this time. All he wanted was to see me, and, by God, he'd changed again. He was even more...powerful. His energy was raw. Basic. Animallike." Cassie shivered, as did Shady, remembering those masked men.

"The secret meetings," she murmured. "This is all about

159

that, isn't it?"

Cassie bit at her lip, seemed to hesitate before carrying on. "He repeated his invitation to join the select few, told me he hadn't forgotten I'd turned him down or how as a child I'd felled the deer. He...coveted me, I'm telling you. Ten more years had passed. Twenty in total. He was a hunter, a *patient* hunter, and what do hunters love most?"

"The thrill of the chase." It was Josie who answered, her eyes practically on stalks.

"The thrill of the chase. Exactly that. He promised me stuff, knew the B and B was failing, that we were ready to give up on it, me now full-time at the library. Said he'd send business our way, as much as we could handle, that we'd be inundated. Dan Turner was not from Baker City. I told you he lived out of town. I also told you I had no idea what he did for a living, but certain types revered him, and by 'certain types' I mean those in charge. He expected obeyance, and he got it. He *fed* off obeyance. A patient man, as I've said, but a man who craved nonetheless. There was not just a meet but a hunt that night, and he wanted me in on it. Gave me his address, wrote it down on a piece of paper, closed my hand around it like it was something sacred too, and told me to come there early on to prepare, that the hunt would begin later, at midnight. Again, he said how special I was, gazing deep into my eyes, a gaze that was...reverent. He told me I was more like him than I knew. Wasn't it about time I admitted it? Gave in. Bullshit! All of it!"

"Cassie, if this is distressing you—" Shady began.

"Yes, it's distressing me! But you want to know why, don't you?"

Shady nodded. "Yes," she whispered.

"Because…because it might help."

"With Brandi, yes."

"I don't see how, but…if there's a chance."

"I think there is, Cassie. I honestly do."

Josie, meanwhile, had dared to leave her chair and gone over to the sideboard, where there was also a box of Kleenex, bringing it back and offering one to Cassie.

"What?" Cassie said, surprised at first by the gesture, and then she reached up and touched her own cheek, felt that it was wet. "Thank you," she said, taking it from her.

"I told him I wasn't gonna join any hunt, any meetings, any *select* few"—how scathing her voice was when she said that—"until my dad did. 'He's loyal,' I said. 'You know how loyal he is to you. Take him on first, and then I'll see.'

"And he agreed. Just like that. He smiled and said for me to tell Dad to meet them at his ranch, something about strict numbers again, that he could take the place of someone just for the night. 'Something special's going to happen,' he said. 'Something…sacred.' Something that, apparently, only happens once in a while, in a blue moon, that he *permits* to happen. And if my memory serves me right, it was late April, springtime, just as it had been when he'd first insisted. I was thirty-six by this time. Dan must have been around forty. Later, when Dad came home, when he found out he'd been invited at last, he was the most excited I'd ever seen him. He hugged me, *thanked* me." The tears were coming in earnest now, Cassie taking more Kleenex, wiping at her eyes and blowing her nose. "He went. Oh God, he went! And when he came back, he was a different man entirely."

CHAPTER EIGHTEEN

They needed another shot of bourbon, all of them, Shady getting up to fetch both the bottle and the shot glasses, bringing them back to a low table in front of the sofa.

While Josie poured, Shady asked if she could light the fire—they also needed warmth, now more than ever. Cassie agreed to both, necking the bourbon straight back as she'd done twice before, the girls doing the same, Shady feeling warmth in her belly as well as on her skin. How long it would last, though, she didn't know. The story wasn't over yet.

"Dad came home. I'm not sure what time," Cassie continued at last. "It was just after dawn, I think. I'd lain awake all night listening out for him, wondering how this special type of hunt was going, and then the porch door was opened and banged shut. Another door opened and closed too, the one to his office. I was relieved he was home, could finally sleep. When I woke, I padded down to his office, saw the door was shut still and that all was quiet within. I didn't think too much of it and got ready for work. We could always talk later. When I came home that evening, however, the door was still closed. Not just that, it was locked, when it had never been locked before. I called out for him, asked if he wanted some dinner. He shouted back, said he wasn't hungry. I shrugged, put his behavior down to tiredness. I went back again a couple of hours later, but he yelled at me this time from behind the door, said to stop bothering him. I tried to argue, but he wouldn't have it. 'You have to leave me be,' he kept saying. 'Cassie, you have to.' And may the Lord forgive me, but I did exactly that. I didn't press further, although my anger at Dan Turner was growing, imagining all kinds of things. What if my dad hadn't made the grade? He'd gone along to this nighttime hunt, this *sacred* event, and been humiliated. If so, what could I do about it? If Dad wouldn't speak to me, I'd go see Mr. High and Mighty instead, get him to explain."

"And did you?" asked Shady. "Go see him?"

"Oh, I did," Cassie told her, gritting her teeth and swallowing hard, "but not before something else happened, something…terrible."

"What?" said Josie, hugging herself as if still cold despite the fire.

"In bed that night, I was tossing and turning. Couldn't sleep again even though I was dog-tired, too weighed down with worry, I suppose. And then I heard it. A gunshot. From downstairs, Dad's office. I ran there, forced the door open but too late. He was dead."

Silence followed this revelation, the weight of it hanging in the air.

"Shit," breathed Shady at last.

"Why?" asked Josie, also wide-eyed.

"That's what I wanted to know," replied Cassie. "*Desperately* wanted to know. When he'd left the house prior to the hunt, he was happy, positive. When he came back, he couldn't even face me, couldn't say what had gone on."

"Unspeakable," whispered Shady.

"What's that?" Cassie asked.

"Some things are unspeakable," she said, raising her voice a little, remembering other wild things, hunters, the skin walkers, whom the Navajo wouldn't be drawn on.

"It was all a blur afterwards," Cassie continued, her eyes glistening, just staring ahead again. "I was in so much shock. I knew I needed answers, I just didn't know how to get them. And then he turned up, a couple days after Dad killed himself, Dan Turner, offering his condolences. There was no sorrow in his eyes, though, there was…amusement, I was sure of it, a whole heap of that damned arrogance. He was so sure Dad hadn't said a word to me about this secret meeting, this hunt, that he'd remained loyal to the end. And in that moment, I hated Dan because this was as much his fault as mine. Whatever had taken place that night, what he'd organized, was far from sacred. It was…horrific.

"I told him outright he was responsible for Dad's death. Demanded he explain to me what had gone on. And you know what he said?"

"What?" both Shady and Josie asked in unison.

"He said the cause was a worthy one, that my father clearly hadn't understood that, but I would. Also, that it was entirely my fault what had happened to my father. That I'd created the situation due to my stubborn streak."

"Bastard," exclaimed Josie. "No way that's true!"

Cassie didn't answer. Instead, she refilled her shot glass, the decanter drained now, but she clutched the glass rather than drank from it, swirling the liquid around and around, her wolverine eyes glittering dangerously. "He invited me, yet again, to a meeting, to be held at his house 'in honor of what has gone before.' The 'after-party,' he described it as. I told him to get the heck out of my house, that no way I'd be going anywhere near him and to never come visit me again. He did as I wanted, he left, but he was still smiling, still sauntering, because he knew, you see."

"Knew what?" Josie asked.

"That I *would* go. That the time had come."

Shady breathed deeply, realizing they were reaching the crux of the story.

"The meeting at his home was taking place that very night, while my father lay cold in the town's morgue. Dan lived around thirty miles out of town, down several old dirt roads, right off the beaten track, and the closer I got to his address, the slower I drove, finally abandoning the car and walking the last ten to fifteen minutes. The darkness out there is different to how it is in town. It's much thicker, but through it I could detect a glow from the rear side of the house that drew me closer. Another thing, it was so silent, like nothing really existed, the night not alive with creatures, as you might expect, but somehow deadened, as if they didn't dare to be there. It was a situation I'd ordinarily run from, not towards."

"You needed answers, though," Shady said.

Cassie agreed. "Just like you, I had to make sense of what was senseless. There was a variety of trucks and cars parked there, but none that I particularly recognized. Didn't mean there wouldn't be some familiar people inside that ranch house, though. I crept right up to the window and peered in, expecting to see police members, the owner of the Grand Willmott, maybe—heck, even the mayor himself—but what I saw stunned me. No matter what I'd imagined, it wasn't that. Not even close."

"What? Who was there?"

Cassie eyed Shady directly. "Animals, that's what. Or

rather men dressed as animals, in furs from head to toe, bodies and faces clad in skins. Nine of them, all crouched around a circle that had been chalked onto the floor, and in that circle were drawings of more animals, horned animals, animals of power, the kind that men dread."

"Or seek to emulate." If Cassie heard Shady, she gave no sign.

"And then a tenth man came into focus, also covered in skins aside from his hands, but I knew from his build who it was. Dan Turner joined the circle, at the head of it, and there was something in his hands, something that…dripped. The night was dark, remember, and the light from inside the room was low, mainly candlelight. I had to get closer to see, had to squint. What the heck was happening? Dan Turner crouched along with the others, holding whatever it was in his hands, cradling it carefully, reverentially, his fingers stained from it. And then he held it up like it was an offering to the gods or something. And the others, the nine, they started chanting, their voices rising, a crescendo, a *howling*, and there was such—" Cassie's mouth twisted "—*triumph* in it. Dan laid what was in his hands in the chalk circle, stood again and beat his chest, the others remaining low but beating their chests too. I was horrified. Mystified. Terrified. It looked like some kind of…"

"Ritual?" Shady said when Cassie faltered.

"Exactly that," replied Cassie. "Something profane. Whatever had been in his hands a sacrifice. Even now I can hardly bear to say that word, to think it, because, you see, I felt like I'd sacrificed something too. My father."

"I'm sorry," Josie murmured. "So sorry."

Cassie pushed on, Shady admiring her bravery. "I would have left then and gone back to my car, headed into town, straight to the police, except for one thing."

"You had no idea who to trust?" ventured Shady.

Cassie nodded. "Here was a man who liked to dominate, who sought control. So many people were in his sway, but who would he want enthralled by him most of all?"

"Those who held the most power," Shady answered.

"That's right, he wanted to be at the top of the food chain in every which way. And so I stayed, tried to absorb as much as I could, take it out of town if I had to. There had to be someone clean who'd listen to me. What was going on in that room was wrong, plain wrong, *lethal*. That was the word that kept going around and around in my head, seemed to burst from it. What they were doing was lethal. It had killed my dad, but who else?

"My eyes went from what he'd laid on the floor to something else, something at his side on a belt or something, two things hanging there, and it clicked further. Oh God, oh shit, I'm just an ordinary woman! Not someone who wants to see stuff like this."

"I know, I know," Shady tried to soothe, at the same time willing her to continue, still needing the jigsaw pieces to slot together. "What were those things you saw?"

Cassie lifted her head, her eyes not only wet with tears but full of weariness too.

"Trophies," she said. "Two older scalps that had become shriveled with time and one that was completely fresh. What had been dripping from the fresh one was blood."

CHAPTER NINETEEN

Shady and Josie were sitting in the Dodge outside Cassie's house, shaking.

"Scalps," Josie muttered. "Three. Two dried, one fresh. You know what this means?"

"I know what it *could* mean," Shady replied. Something that Cassie had agreed with.

"He was a narcissist," she'd said earlier, "a psychopath, who over time grew ever more powerful, a man obsessed with rituals. Him and those others—the inner circle, like…a sect or a cult or something—they'd been hunting for years, for *decades*, so of course they could be responsible for the murders of those missing people, Davenport, Hooper and Alisa Jones, disposing of their bodies afterwards, digging real deep out there in that wilderness so they'd never be found. Them and probably many more."

"Maybe," Shady had said. *Maybe not.* There was something about the restraint that Dan Turner had exhibited that nagged at her. The way he'd waited so patiently for the woman he'd coveted, the ten-year intervals in which he'd shown up, growing more powerful all the while. All so bizarre. And yet sense was indeed emerging.

Cassie had told them another thing they were still reeling from, each in their own way trying to process it.

"Once I realized they were scalps I was looking at, that these men truly were beasts, I couldn't help it, I screamed, I stumbled. The nine didn't seem to notice. They were still making such a racket, their eyes solely on Dan, worshipping the master. But Dan, he noticed all right. As if his hearing was supernatural, his head slowly, slowly, moved towards the window. I stumbled again, fell right on my ass, scrambled to my feet and then ran hell-for-leather, didn't look back to see if anyone was following. I scooted like I was damn near possessed too. I reached my car and somehow drove home, racing down those dusty old dirt tracks. Once home, I bolted the door. He was going to come for me, I knew it. Not that night, maybe, but soon enough—for him, anyway."

Oh, how angry Cassie had been. How scared too, shaking even as she'd relayed this part of the story. "He didn't, though. He remained as elusive as ever. Didn't see any sign of him until the funeral, where he had the nerve to show up. Him and so many prominent people, all of them paying their respects, or pretending to. I couldn't make a scene, not at Dad's funeral. I had to be cleverer than that, think carefully about what to do, plan ahead. I hated Dan Turner so much, and the evil vermin that had elevated him. Not in my eyes, though! I'd bring him down, destroy him, leave him lying in the ditch where he belonged."

"Cassie," Josie said. "What did you do?"

"I went back to the ranch. Not right away, oh no, not for a while, a few months maybe. That's how long it took me to summon up the courage, although part of me was playing him at his own game too, making him wait. Because he was expecting me, let me tell you that. We *had* to meet again. Once I made my mind up that that time had come, it was late summer, nearly autumn. I went back, walked right into his living room, and there he was, pouring whiskey, two glasses, *expecting* me.

"I went up to him, and I told him I'd seen him that night along with nine others, seen what had taken place, and you know what he did? He laughed! I wasn't laughing, though. I told him he'd not only murdered my father, or as good as, but I knew he'd murdered others too. The night hunts, I'd worked out what they were. Their prey was human, bonus points if the victim was an experienced hunter too, from what you've told me. It'd make the hunt all the more exciting. No guns allowed, though. We know that Alisa Jones left hers behind or was likely forced to. It was clearly all about going back to basics, relying on your wits."

"Did he deny it?" Shady could hardly breathe at the vision Cassie had created.

"No, of course not! He just shrugged, said it wasn't murder, it was an *appeasement*. Those were his words exactly. Said his behavior wasn't reckless either, or gratuitous, just the opposite. It was considered. He said he *despised* recklessness. It might be the way of others, but not him. He said that who he appeased—the Great Beast, he called it—wasn't reckless either, or greedy, that greed was for the mindless, the base, the *unevolved*. He admired me, he told me, and my bravery in coming to him at last, that he was in need of an equal, a mate, and had marked me from the first time he'd seen me, when I was sixteen and he was twenty. 'We're so alike,' he repeated, reaching out to try and touch my hair, although I took a step backwards. 'Worthy.' I didn't understand a goddamned word spilling from his mouth, and nor did I want to, but he kept on talking. Said it may have taken time, but I was now ready to 'ascend,' to dispense with the trivia of life and embrace something more meaningful. Together we'd preside over everything, hold dominion."

"Dominion?" Shady said, frowning. "Jeez, that's dramatic! What did you do?"

"Oh, I hadn't come empty-handed to his ranch. No way on God's green earth would I do that, not a second time. So, I'll tell you what I did. I took the gun from the inside pocket of my jacket, and I shot him. Put a bullet right through his heart."

Silence. Again. Shady noticed Josie's eyes flicker over toward the rifle, similar thoughts likely running through her mind. *Cassie's murdered before. She could murder a second time. Now that she's confessed.*

No psychic, perhaps, but Cassie wasn't stupid. Following this startling revelation came a burst of laughter. "I'm not going to kill you! Don't worry about that. But if you're sitting there, thinking of rushing off to the police, good luck with that. Want to know what else I discovered?"

"What?" Josie's voice was a squeak.

"That officially Dan Turner didn't exist."

Revelation after revelation, and now there was pure bafflement.

"What?" Shady said.

"Having carried out what I went there to do, I returned home and waited, expecting the police to come knocking at my door this time, probably break the damned thing down if they had to. But here's the thing—no one ever did. I ventured out, worked my job, kept my ear to the ground and waited some more. No one breathed a word about Dan Turner having shown up dead. Digging as deep as I could, it seemed his death was never reported or even registered.

More than that, I couldn't find any local birth records that fit his profile either. Of course, it's entirely possible Dan Turner is a bogus name and, if so, lucky me. He was…what do you call it? Below the radar. As mythical as the creature he was trying to be. I got bold and began asking around, prominent people, you know, the hunters, said something along the lines of 'You still hold those meetings in the Grand Willmott? Dan Turner still something else with a rifle?' People made excuses rather than answer or mumbled something unintelligible before turning away. With Dan Turner gone—clearly the driving force behind the whole outfit—it all just…fell apart."

"Are you sure you killed him?" Shady asked.

Cassie was indignant. "Yes! Of course. Why?"

"What did you do right after pulling the trigger?"

"Right after?" She hesitated only briefly before replying. "I turned, got out of there. Listen up, he was dead! I shot him fair and square. He wasn't superhuman, despite what he and everyone else might have thought, Dad included. No man could survive that."

"It's just, as you know, Brandi Hadley's gone missing too, right around that date."

"Headed for Mazuma Lake?"

"I don't know," Shady admitted, "but she's got to be somewhere. Look, I know this doesn't make sense, there are plenty of variables, it's twenty years later not ten, but—"

"You feel there's a connection."

"Yes. Could others in the sect be responsible? Members who are still alive?"

"Here's the thing. After Dan's death, over a period of a couple of years, there was a spate of deaths in Baker City, and all were people of note. There was a suicide, a car wreck, a shooting, and some died of natural causes too, of cancer and heart attacks."

"How many deaths?" Shady said, although she thought she knew the answer.

"Nine," Cassie confirmed. "I want to help with Brandi, but I don't see the connection."

"Is the ranch still there?" Josie wanted to know, Shady able to see where she was heading with this and hope flaring in her too, which Cassie poured water on.

"The ranch is gone," she informed them. "It took months for me to find that out, to make my way back there a third time and discover it razed to the ground. It was just rubble and ash. Nowadays, a highway cuts right through it, although it's a route I tend to avoid."

"And what of the Grand Willmott?" said Shady. "Who owned it then?"

"One of the people that died. Jason Elliot. He was in the car wreck."

Shady nodded. So that explained the framed photograph on the wall—an heirloom, as the new owner, Wanda McIntyre, somewhat innocently viewed it, something from its glory days. But they'd been dark days too, the meetings held there spawning a terrible offshoot.

When Shady had asked if Cassie knew about the photograph in the hotel, she had shaken her head. "That's the last place I ever want to set foot in."

Now in the car, Shady reached a conclusion. "I need that photograph. I need to go right into the Grand Willmott, remove it from the wall, get it back to your house and tune in properly."

Josie screwed up her nose. "Why? It should be burned, like Turner's ranch, destroyed."

"It should, I agree, but not before I find out if she really did kill him."

"And you think handling it will tell you that?"

"No harm in trying."

"Jeez! Shady, what are we gonna do with all this? Our local librarian's a murderer!"

An unrepentant murderer. Cassie had been clear on that.

"I have no regrets about what I did," she'd told them, "because...because I stopped something big in its tracks. Something *wild*. If you want to report me, if you think you can trust the establishment round here nowadays, go right ahead. I can't stop you. But understand, I have no regrets about killing Dan Turner. Those were scalps I saw, human scalps. The hair on the fresh one, where it wasn't stained with blood, was bright blond, just like Alisa's hair was, like they showed on the posters everywhere. Whoever it was, that poor, unfortunate Alisa Jones or someone else, they hunted her like an animal, unarmed. They brought her down and then took her to that ranch in the middle of nowhere and scalped her."

"Shady," Josie pressed, "what are we going to do, about Cassie, about Brandi too?"

Shady gunned the engine. "First things first," she replied, heading back toward town. "I need to find out if Cassie really did kill Dan Turner. Only then can we decide."

CHAPTER TWENTY

People worshipped a variety of gods. Dan Turner, for one—the Great Beast—hoping to become a god himself, it seemed, but more and more Shady put her faith in Kanti. *I have to get into the Willmott tonight, somehow, someway. Help me do that.*

As they cruised downtown, Josie started pointing.

"There are lights on in the hotel. Someone must be working late."

"Yes!" Shady hit the steering wheel with her fist. "Let's hope the side door's open too."

Glancing at her friend, Shady noticed she was biting her lip, something Josie only did when stressed. Quickly, she reached over and gave her arm a squeeze. "Hey, I'm sorry about all this, you know. What we've discovered. Like the lieutenant said, it's left-field."

"It's that all right," Josie agreed, trying to smile. "Small towns, huh? And the secrets they keep. What Cassie was saying, about the men dressed in furs, do you think…"

"What, that they were skin walkers?"

"Or trying to be."

Shady nodded. "Something like that. Feeding into the myth because that's all they've got, Josie, a myth. Skin walkers don't exist. Only in people's minds."

"Do demons exist?"

"*Demons?*"

"That Mandy doll…"

"Ah, okay, I see what you mean. Mandy is a conundrum. She's also what you call a conduit. There's good energy attached to her, and bad. Energies exist, I know that much. I've *experienced* that, and this is bad energy we've got here, historically and right now."

"You know what?"

"What?"

"You kind of evaded the answer there!"

Shady laughed. "*Humans* are demons, and justice has to be done for Dud Hooper, Robert Davenport, and Alisa Jones. Closure. Maybe Cassie will realize that too, trust this new generation of police, go tell them what she knows instead of leaving it to us."

"Hand herself in?"

"Exactly."

"*If* she killed him."

"That's right. If."

They parked up close to the hotel.

"Josie, stay in the car—"

"What? No way! Someone needs to watch your back!"

Shady smiled again. Josie, like Ray, was an incredible friend, never doubting her even though the path she'd put them on twisted and turned, no clear end in sight still.

Even so, Shady was adamant. "It's easier if there's only one of us. Less chance of being caught. Seriously, I'll only be a minute."

"If you're not…"

"I've got my cell. I'll text if I need you."

Only slightly pacified, Josie agreed, and Shady left the

car, the night air chilly, causing her to pull her jacket tighter. As she hurried to the hotel, she glanced up. No stars visible in the sky. *They're there all the same.* Was that her thought or Kanti's? She hoped it was the latter, that Kanti was near, guiding her still, even though she was out of sight too.

Reaching the side door, Shady made sure no one was in the immediate vicinity—the streets thankfully still eerily empty at night since news of Brandi had broken—and tried the door handle. She had to be quick; she *wanted* to be, the memory of when she'd last been in there, the laughter she'd heard, mocking her, still fresh in her mind. This place had spawned evil from the minute Dan Turner had walked into it, a corrupted man who had gone on to corrupt others and so effortlessly, it seemed. *Why'd you do what you did?* One part of her was intrigued to find out, the other part wishing it wasn't necessary.

It was dark inside, and quiet. Closing the door, she crept along the corridor to reception, feeling exposed when she reached it, longing for the shelter of a hallway again. Step by step, she ventured forward, hardly able to breathe. She'd been in this hotel at night before, felt the weight of its history, the shadowy presence of those that had stayed there, knew now that among those guests had been Alisa Jones and likely Dud Hooper and Robert Davenport, gearing up for that great outdoors adventure, enjoying a couple of beers in the bar, meetings taking place again, encounters with who, exactly? Those that were out scouting? Looking for victims? She could almost hear the snatches of conversations that had taken place: *Mazuma Lake's pretty nice this time of year. Is that where you're headed? Good hunting there, always.* A male voice insisting, a friendly man, trustworthy.

On approaching the other corridor, she stopped and

listened some more. There was a brief burst of chatter, but it was distant, a few workers still in the function room, adding some finishing touches, perhaps? No time to linger, to even think, just to get the photograph and go, face the morning armed with yet more information. About to make the last few paces, her cell began to vibrate.

"Shit!" she breathed. She'd put it on silent, but the vibration still seemed loud.

Who was it? Josie? It wasn't. Ray was calling. And then Ray was texting.

Shady, where are you? What's the latest? I'm getting seriously worried here. Something's kicking off. I'm not psychic, but I can feel when something's not right.

Oh, Ray! She hated to do it, but she shut the phone down, resolving to call him later to calm him. She should have checked in with both him and Annie this evening, but she'd headed off to the Dupont house instead, had heard all Cassie had to say…

"Shit!" she repeated. The voices from up ahead were closer now. She had to double back to reception, hide behind a column there. Two men, it sounded like.

"Hotel's coming along, huh?" said one.

"Yep," the other agreed. "It's looking good."

"Be glad to get home, though."

"Me too. Been a long day."

"Anything on the agenda tonight?"

"Watch the game on TV with a few beers."

"Sounds good."

"Oh shit, hang on. I think I left my charger back there. Go ahead, I'll catch you up."

"No, it's okay. I'll come with."

"Don't like to be alone here, huh?"

"You fucking kiddin' me?"

They laughed. "It's creepy. When it's just us, I mean. At night. Y'know?"

"Like someone's here, watching us?"

"Yeah…third man syndrome."

"Say what?"

"Google it."

"Okay, I will. You know, it really does feel like someone else is here, especially tonight. Not sure I'll be working too many more late nights from now on."

More laughter. "You and me both. Come on, let's grab your charger and scoot."

As they retraced their footsteps, Shady stepped out from behind the column, raced along the corridor that the workmen had so recently occupied, and grabbed the framed photograph off the wall, then raced back across reception and to the side door.

Third man syndrome. She'd have to look that up too, she thought, heading back to the car, grateful for the chill of the cold night air now, feeling edgy from her expedition, by the prize she'd claimed and the fact that in this instance there had indeed been a third person, not a ghost, not an echo, just her.

* * *

Skin walkers might be myth, but in the darkness of Josie's room—Josie downstairs with her parents watching TV, giving Shady the space and time she needed to focus—Shady hoped that the other Native belief, that a photograph captured your heart and soul, like the ones at the museum and in the office at The Lazy Stay Motel, was true for this one too, that it had somehow trapped Dan Turner, not just a fleeting memory but his very essence.

Josie had been upset about it even coming into the house.

"It won't taint us in any way, will it?"

Shady had assured her it wouldn't, but she felt bad about that because it wasn't strictly true; she *was* inviting the darkness in, but they had to do it if they wanted to find Brandi, the police having issued no breaking news so far.

Once she was done with it, though, she'd take it outside, burn the photograph and bury the frame. Wanda might notice it had gone missing, but she might not. Either way, she'd never suspect who'd taken it. Shady was in the clear regarding that, at least.

Okay, Dan Turner, hit me up.

Having released the photograph from its frame, she ran her finger over his masked face and stared deep into his eyes, opening her mind, waiting for images to invade.

After a few moments, it began.

Trauma. She could sense that. Whose? His? Dan Turner's? Carefully concealed.

But it's in there, isn't it? Deep down?

Shame. Did he feel shame because of the trauma? Anger? Sadness? Hatred?

Dan…who are you?

A kid when he'd experienced trauma. A child beaten, starved or just plain neglected. Growing up alone on the fringes of society, not belonging to the human race, the human race seemingly not caring about that either. *What happened to your parents?*

Ten. A number with some apparent meaning. Shady frowned. Something had happened when he was just ten. *Did you kill your parents?* She shook her head. No. That wasn't right. He was a scared little boy, innocent, and yet something *had* happened, perhaps *to* his parents, because he was alone from then on…and it had changed him.

Reborn.

She inhaled. That was a repeat of what she'd heard before at the hotel—*Those who seek to ascend. Whose destiny it is. To be reborn. Reborn. REBORN.*

A select few. Those who'd been chosen. Who were willing.

Shady hadn't known who those words, those thoughts, had belonged to, only that they were ingrained into the atmosphere, a part of the hotel's history. She knew now, though. They were his. Dan Turner's. Aged ten, had he thought he'd been reborn? Because his parents had died? Just as Cassie Dupont had lost her mother, aged ten. *We're the same.* It had been a trigger for him, along with her wolverine eyes, perhaps.

A patient man.

He'd been that, sure enough; even Cassie had said so. She'd said he'd despised recklessness. As a kid, he'd had no control whatsoever, living with crazy, selfish people, those who were supposed to love and take care of him but did the very opposite. It was becoming clear now. He'd *feared* recklessness, that it might somehow be inherent in him. And so, to Dan Turner, restraint had been everything. A serial murderer but one who controlled himself as well as others. To the power of ten.

What a complex man you are, Dan Turner. But why the skins? Why the animals?

In answer, Shady saw an image of a fox, one with pups. She was grooming them, taking care of them. Dan Turner as a boy had loved the fox, saw that in the wild a mother could be something else, something nurturing. And then the fox was what…destroyed? Yes, she could see blood and bones and fur, not destroyed by Dan, though, by another animal, and in turn that animal had been destroyed too by something even bigger, more fearsome. Within the young boy, anger rose yet again, overwhelmed him. But so too had something else: fascination.

Skin walkers.

Dan had known of them. Dan had admired them. A creature that could walk on two legs, with glowing red eyes, that no one would talk about. *A great beast that held dominion.*

Oh, Dan, Dan. You never forgot what you saw, did you? This fascination led to…obsession, led to…worship. Something running riot in him after all, his imagination filling a void.

Shady couldn't help but feel sympathy, for Dan the child rather than the adult he'd grown to be. If anything, the force of her own anger was directed toward two other ghosts, his parents, two shadowy figures she only just caught a glimpse of; no more substantial than wisps of smoke, they quickly evaporated, deleted from Dan's mind and therefore her own. Even so, they were every bit as guilty of the murders Dan and the members of his inner sanctum had committed, for their cruel actions had birthed it.

A loner as a child, perhaps, but as Dan had grown, when he'd realized the admiration that not just his hunting skills could elicit but his core beliefs too, he was never alone again. Not when it counted.

Were Alisa, Dud and Robert your victims?

The hunt. She could see flashes of it now yet, strangely, no enjoyment. Not on Dan's part, anyway. It was more grim

182

determination instead. *An offering.* Dan had truly believed he had become something other and had cast a spell too—over his companions, made them believe they would also ascend. *It is our destiny.* And, therefore, must be fulfilled.

They were your victims; I know they were.

And with that acknowledgement, she felt both increased horror and relief. Horror that it had happened at all, that humans had been hunted by creatures masquerading as skin walkers, those that believed themselves divine, but also relief because with it there might come some closure for living relatives. If she could get anyone to believe her, that was.

What about Brandi? How are you connected to her?

Twenty years ago, the group had brought down Alisa Jones. A few days after that, Cassie had shot Dan, sending his dark ambitions up in smoke. No one in that area had gone missing on that particular date since. Until now. Brandi could have gone, or been taken, to Mazuma Lake. There was so far no evidence she had, and in no way was she a hunter. And yet Shady could not—would not—relinquish the possibility of a connection. As Josie herself had found, it was impossible to think of Alisa without thinking of Brandi too, Alisa who'd been very much on Brandi's mind before her own disappearance.

Shady needed to fast-forward to a time *after* the photograph had been taken.

Did Cassie kill you? Are you alive or dead, Dan Turner? Answer me!

Just as Ray had pleaded with her earlier, now she was doing the same.

Kanti, give me the insight I need. Did Cassie kill him, or did he take Brandi? Befriend her, groom her, lead her into the wild? How is he linked to all this?

He wasn't. Not directly. Because she experienced it, an impact to the chest, one that sent her falling backward onto the bedroom floor, after which there was nothing. Before, though, a few seconds prior, there'd been a smile on his face. Such certainty. Such arrogance. Had he believed the bullet wouldn't penetrate, that it would just bounce off him?

Because it didn't. It ended there. Afterward, there was only darkness.

CHAPTER TWENTY-ONE

"But, Shady, if he's dead, then there's no need."

"I know. I know it looks that way. Just this one thing, and then…"

"Then what?"

"We'll have done everything we can. Josie, please."

It was asking a lot, Shady knew that. They were as certain as they could be that Dan Turner was dead, also that he and his inner circle of friends—the nine who had subsequently died, most of whom they had names for—were responsible for at least three people's deaths. This was all further information that could be taken to the police, but, as Shady acknowledged when discussing this latest insight through the night with Josie, it didn't appear to have anything to do with why Brandi Hadley had gone missing. And because it didn't, the police wouldn't turn their attention to the area around Mazuma Lake. Shady would, though, and Josie too if she could persuade her, heading to the area where Alisa Jones, Davenport and Hooper were last seen.

"What's our aim, though? Just to get a feel for the place? What good will that do?"

Shady shrugged. "Truth? I won't know until I'm there."

"Will we be putting ourselves in danger?"

"I don't know that either. I don't think so. I just don't

want to leave any stone unturned, not now that we've come this far, found out this much."

Josie remained unconvinced. "With Brandi, it feels like we're clutching at straws here."

"Hazard of the job," Shady said, "but…I have to trust myself." *Trust Kanti.* Because it was her leading the way, she was sure of it, from beyond the stars, wanting resolution too.

The girls agreed to grab whatever sleep they could, then make a firm decision in the cold light of day. With Josie slumbering, Shady quickly dashed off texts to Ray and Annie, both along similar lines: *I'm ok. Some interesting things have happened. Gna try one more angle, after that will leave it to police to find her. I believe they're doing everything they can.* It was true, they were, apart from searching in the right place; she remained convinced of it.

Reading the texts back before sending, she raised an eyebrow at her use of the word *interesting.* What they'd unearthed here, courtesy of Cassie, was far more than that; it was *outstanding* and in the worst possible way.

The new day dawned, the third day of Brandi Hadley having gone missing. Both girls now awake, Josie was still reticent about striking out for Mazuma Lake.

"What will we tell Mom?" she whispered in the early morning light. "She's paranoid about my whereabouts right now."

"We tell her…we're heading out of town for a couple of days, going to stay with another friend of mine that lives close by, a few towns along."

Josie's jaw almost hit the floor. "We're going for a couple of days? Why?"

"You know that campground we stayed at?"

Josie nodded.

"That's near enough to Mazuma Lake. We'll head there this morning, make that our base, strike out from there and hope that that weather phenomenon, or whatever the hell Teddy called it, doesn't happen again. We'll come home the day after."

"Shit, Shady! I'm really not sure Mom's gonna buy this."

"Will she be awake now?"

Josie glanced at the clock on her bedside table. "Her alarm will go off soon."

"Okay, well, let's get packing meanwhile, be ready to leave as quickly as we can."

Lulin Wong didn't like the fact they were skipping town, but she bought it, telling the girls to be careful, to head straight to where they were going, not stop off anywhere. When she and Huan left for work, Josie got the family's camping gear out of the garage, confident they wouldn't notice its absence, hiding any obvious gaps with boxes. No need for the full works anyway, just the basic stuff. As they left the house, Shady tried not to look at the black that now edged more of the sky or acknowledge the increasing hopelessness that leaked from the Hadley house. She simply put her foot down and drove all the way back to Smoke Ridge, where they paid for their campsite before heading back out on the road. They'd put up their tent later, when they got back from the lake.

"No sign of weird fog so far," Josie said as they traveled onward.

She was right; they had that on their side, at least.

"Josie, I'm sorry," Shady replied, sighing as she rounded a curve in the road.

"Why?"

"I know how upset you are about Brandi. I came here to

support you, to be with you, and yet here I am dragging you into something I know you're uncomfortable with, making you lie to your parents too."

Josie shifted in her seat to face Shady. "You know what? I'm gonna say it. You have a gift, a gift that seems to have become something else entirely since our teenage years, which is awesome, it really is, I mean it. But I won't pretend I understand it. And, actually, I'm not sure I want to either. But you're my friend, my very best friend, and if this is what you want to do because you think you have to, because you believe it to be right, then I'm with you all the way."

"Thank you," Shady murmured, glancing at her and smiling.

"You act with good intentions because you want to help her, Brandi, and that's all I really need to know. And, Shady?"

"Uh-huh?"

"I've actually got a revelation of my own."

Again, Shady glanced at her. "Oh?"

"I've brought something with me other than camping gear."

"Yeah, what's that?"

"A gun."

Shady almost braked to a halt. "A gun? *What the fuck?*"

Josie reached into the backpack she had at her feet.

"Josie! What are you doing?"

"Showing you."

"It's in your backpack?"

"Well…yeah."

"No, no, keep it there! I don't want to see it, okay? What are you doing bringing a firearm along? Whose is it?"

"Dad's," Josie replied. "Look, we don't know what we're

up against here. We've discovered hunters, murderers and fricking nutjobs wanting to be something other than human. Skin walkers, for Christ's sake. *We need a gun!* First rule of thumb: you should not go into the wilderness without proper protection."

"Shit, Josie, but…yeah, I suppose. We're not gonna use that thing, though, okay? There'll be no need. We're just going to get—"

"A feel for the place. I know."

There was silence, more strained now, although she had to admit, if only silently, she saw the logic in Josie's decision. Out here they were indeed at the mercy of the elements, of wolves and bears and coyotes and cougars. It *was* a rule of thumb you go sufficiently equipped, but a gun… If her mom got wind of this, her dad too, she'd be in deep shit.

"Do you know how to use it? Ever fired a gun?"

Josie didn't reply but just gave Shady a nervous sideways look.

That was a no, then.

A sign by the side of road showed they weren't far from Mazuma Lake. They needed to make a right turn off the main highway and then continue a few miles down a logging road that led close to it and the mountains, dark, smoky monoliths in the distance becoming more substantial the closer they got.

"It's so quiet out here," Josie murmured.

It was. The world bereft of everything but nature—the *hugeness* of nature, Shady reminded herself. Breathtaking but treacherous too. She understood, though, why people were drawn here—you could clear your head, feel a part of something much bigger, like your troubles didn't count for much against all this, the whole of creation. Dud Hooper,

Robert Davenport and Alisa Jones had all loved the great outdoors; heck, Shady loved it! All those times spent in the Idaho outback with her dad, mostly, sometimes her mom joining them when she could abandon work or household chores, were memories she cherished. They were special. Just as Cassie being out here with her dad had been special too, giving back some meaning to life. But so quickly something so special had turned sour, for the Duponts, at least. Dan Turner was a hunter and, in search of other hunters, had turned them into prey instead, into sacrifices. The terror each victim must have felt sparked something in Shady, a terror of her own. She had to work hard to control what bloomed in her chest before it took hold, made her swing the car back around toward civilization.

The lake came into view—big and beautiful and sacred, it was all that and more. Glittering beneath the sun's rays, causing both girls to catch their breath.

Although remaining defiantly rugged, it was a known beauty spot, a place where people came to swim in summer, to soak up nature at her best, but which, for now, was almost deserted, just a few cars parked along the track, their inhabitants nowhere to be seen.

Shady parked too and stood with Josie looking at the vehicles, four in total: a Westfalia like Dorothea but in better condition, two Kias and a Ford truck.

"I wonder who they belong to," Shady murmured.

"Hikers," suggested Josie.

Shady went over to the vehicles.

"What are you doing?" Josie asked.

"Just looking in them, just…checking." She also reached out, drawn to the truck in particular, the back of it covered in a tarp. *Who do you belong to?*

Grabbing the door handle on the driver's side, she detected a masculine energy. A man who was...eager. For what? Hiking? Hunting? Likely, if he was out here. Really, *really* eager. Couldn't-wait-to-get-going eager. A little overkill, but could he be blamed for that? He probably lived for this.

"Shady, come on."

Josie was also keen to get going. And she was right, they should, because those blue skies up above were fading, and not just because of the blackened edges that only Shady could see—more clouds were coming in, a slight breeze picking up too.

"Okay, on it," Shady said, leaving the truck and heading back to her.

"Which way?"

Shady held out her cell, using the compass app. "We go just north of Mazuma Lake. That's where Alisa made camp, about four or five miles away."

"Four or five miles?" Josie repeated. "Jeez, Shady, you'll make a hiker out of me yet."

CHAPTER TWENTY-TWO

The terrain toughened far quicker than Shady had expected, becoming much wilder than it was around the lake's shoreline. Trees, bushes and scrub dominated, the blue of the water behind them only now visible if you turned and peered through the trees, the clarity of it still something jewellike. It was a landscape that only the experienced should attempt, heading toward the base of the mountain. That other family that Josie had mentioned, who'd been found elsewhere in the Oregon wilderness, their bodies savaged—was it truly a bear that had torn them apart or Dan Turner? She shook her head. Here was his preferred hunting ground, a place deemed fit for purpose. Also, he never left his victims to be found. Regarding this family, some other monster was responsible.

Not monsters, Shady, just people! She told herself this as she walked beside Josie, the pair of them searching, for what? What did they truly expect to find?

The truck in the parking lot came to mind, and the keenness of its driver. Why it should stick in her mind, she didn't know. Suddenly, though, she wished she'd handled the passenger side of the Ford, had tuned in there too—did he have a companion just as keen? *Rabid.* That word confused her further. She had to focus.

The Native Americans were trackers—she knew something about their techniques, had read up on them since discovering her ancestry, wanting to know more. They kept themselves alert to anything out of place. Nature was chaos, everything seemed to grow at random, but it was *organized* chaos. There was actually harmony to it, a rhythm, a pattern, a design. And so, if anything was wrong—damaged branches where there shouldn't be damaged branches, scattered twigs where there shouldn't be scattered twigs, a thread of cloth that had snagged on a branch, a deep impression in the ground from something heavier than wildlife—it should be detectible. There was another way to track, though, for a sensitive like Shady: by tuning in, by touching.

She dropped to her knees.

"What are you doing?" Josie inquired again, her frown deep. She was nervous out here. Shady was too, grateful now for the gun in her friend's backpack. Conversely, hoping it would stay there, never needing to see the light of day.

Shady tried to explain exactly what she was doing, trying to sense those who'd trodden these paths before—if the man from the truck had come this way, and his companion.

"You got something?" Josie asked. "Seriously?"

"I...don't know," she confessed, sighing. "But this path seems like the *only* viable one in this direction on the map."

Shady straightened up, continuing to scan every inch of the area, wanting to sniff the air too like an animal, although she refrained for fear of freaking Josie out further. Relying on instinct, though, and her Native American blood, especially out here, was everything. They continued onward, the distance and the route they were covering recorded with an app on their phones. People *had* trodden this ground recently; there were fresh prints, those of walking boots impacted against the earth but triggering nothing in Shady.

"Path's getting trickier," Josie commented a short while later. She was right. Although already an uphill path, it was getting steeper, Josie having to stop and catch her breath.

"Such a wild land," Shady breathed, a land too often seen from afar rather than close-up, a new respect, an awe growing in her because of it and for those that were determined to tackle this land, make it their own. They never could, though; it was untamable.

The sky had grayed entirely now, although the clouds remained thankfully intact. They continued to make tracks, two miles under their belt, another three to go—ordinarily an hour and a half's walk from here, but in this terrain, likely it would take longer to reach where Alisa had camped, closer to the river that cut through the land.

Determination spurred them on. Around half a mile from her camp, Shady dropped to the ground again, placed her palms on it and closed her eyes.

Josie waited, knowing not to interrupt, to just wait and see what Shady could detect.

"Footsteps," Shady said. "Two sets."

"No tread marks, though," Josie pointed out.

"I know, but even so…there's a pounding of feet. It's like…I can hear a rhythm of some sort, distant, but it's there, someone running and…someone following."

"Human or animal?"

"That's the even stranger thing."

"What is?"

"It feels like a mix of both."

Shady looked up, caught Josie's gaze, saw the confusion in her eyes…and the fear.

She stood. "Josie, you know that truck I was looking into back at the lake? I think…I think I need to go back there when this is done and try the passenger door handle too. The last sighting of Brandi, we know she crossed the road outside Batemans, seemed to walk towards something, her hand raised like…in recognition?"

"Uh-huh," said Josie, her confusion only increasing.

"Well…what if it was that truck?"

"Really?"

"It's just something to check, that's all. The driver was super excited about something. Maybe even…*weirdly* excited."

Josie's eyes widened. "Excited about something bad?"

"Maybe."

"And he's out here with us?"

"The point is, Brandi could be too."

Josie looked as if she were about to hurl. "Thank fuck we have the gun!" She swallowed hard. "Shady, are you sure about this? I mean—"

"You know I am, as sure as I can be, anyway. I think she met someone and came to Lake Mazuma willingly. It's a renowned scenic area, so why not? As good a place as any for a romantic date. But once here, something went wrong, really wrong. They took a walk, following the track we're on. Maybe, just maybe, they wanted to see Alisa's camp too because we know Brandi had a fixation with her. Maybe the camp is some kind of ghoulish attraction. Like, you know, the last known whereabouts of the poster girl." Another thought occurred. "It's like a shrine to some people. A place of…worship."

"Shit. This is so fucked up!"

"I could be right, though, huh? I could be onto

something here?"

Josie shrugged. "People *are* ghoulish. Plenty of 'em. But if it played out like you say, this was three days ago, so what's he doing? Returning to the scene of the crime?"

Shady nodded. "Look, if I'm right, if it's him and he's out here too, we'd better play it safe and not hang around. We go back to the lake, I get what I can from the truck, then we go to the police and try to persuade them again to come here, to comb this area. Josie—"

When Shady abruptly stopped talking, Josie frowned. "What is it? What's up?"

"Hang on. Wait," Shady replied, craning her neck forward.

"Why? Come on, don't do this, don't keep me guessing. Tell me what's going on."

"I thought I saw something. Just beyond you in the bushes. Wait. Just wait here."

"Shady, no!"

"I'm not going far. I'm just checking, that's all."

She crept forward. What she'd caught in amongst the trees and bracken was a glimpse of something. Something…tall. Like a human was tall. That walked on two legs. And yet…there was something different about it too. It appeared to be covered in fur. Was it something keeping track of them? Spying on them from the cover of the forest?

Skin walkers aren't real. Skin walkers are not real!

That was the mantra in her head as she continued onward. They weren't, but other stuff was real enough if her theory was right, like the man who'd brought Brandi here, who'd *kept* her here. Why, though? For what purpose? And what if he was wearing skins? Like Dan Turner had? A

196

worshipper in more ways than one?

Her skin tingled as she entered the trees, as she heard Josie telling her to turn back and then, admitting defeat, to remember that they had a gun with them.

A snap of branches. Something *was* close by. She could feel eyes upon her, searing her. Eyes that were red instead of white? Something not human after all but demonic.

Skin walkers aren't real...

There! Farther up ahead, just out of reach, something had stopped, turned and was now glaring back at her. For a split second only. A fraction of a moment. And it could be her imagination embellishing an already terrifying situation, but its eyes were indeed red.

Shit! Maybe...maybe...

It was as though her limbs took on a life of their own. Despite the danger, her legs darted forward, and her hands stretched outward to clear low-hanging branches from her path. Whatever was out there—man or beast—she had to get a closer look. Had to know. *There are some things not spoken about, too taboo, the skin walkers being one of them.* She knew that, had read words to that effect, but whatever it was, it was running from her, not attacking; there was comfort in that, at least. It didn't *want* to be caught.

"Shady!"

The sound of Josie's voice reached her but from far away. Too distant to heed the warning in it.

"Shady, please come back!"

Just a little closer, just a better look, that's all she wanted. If she had something more solid to take to the police, they'd take her more seriously. And a guy who'd been stalking them, dressed in skins, was definitely that.

"What the—"

She was falling suddenly, and hard, the ground rising up to meet her, shock reverberating as her body smashed against an unforgiving earth, a stone by her head that she'd missed, or had she? The world around her rocked; her eyesight blurred. It took a few seconds, but eventually she sat up, heard something too, a cry—not herself this time, so whose was it? She lifted a hand to her head, tried to focus, to gather her thoughts, but they became even more jumbled. *Three days. Ten. Twenty years. Thirty. Forty.* Figures that hurtled through her mind, each riding a wave of nausea.

Shady turned quickly to the side, her stomach heaving violently, vomit bursting from her mouth. When she was finished, she raised a hand and touched her head more exploratively this time. Pain immediately bit back, and on her fingertips was blood. She further studied the stone she'd fallen against. There was blood on it too.

Josie. She had to get back to her. That cry she'd heard, what if it was her? Something had followed them. That was it! Stalked them. *Third man syndrome.* Where had she heard that? She'd Googled it, hadn't she? Something about a presence, felt not seen, appearing during traumatic situations—a guardian angel, some people suggested, while others feared it was the opposite. Either way, it was something outside of normal...unnatural. Just what kind of danger were they in here? And what kind of danger was Brandi in too?

Brandi...

As Shady stood, her legs feeling as if they were made of cotton wool, she blinked rapidly as she looked around her. Brandi was why they were here. To save her. Three days missing—that was the significance of that number, at least. Darkened skies blackening around the edges, an indicator time was running out.

Where are you, Brandi?

It was as though she were looking at the world through layers and layers of gauze. "Brandi? Josie?" Two girls she had to find, and no sign of either. "Brandi?"

She hobbled forward, hoping she would reach the clearing where Josie was supposed to wait for her, but no way of telling. Not in this haze. She rubbed at her eyes as she continued walking. Why wasn't her vision clearing?

Panting.

Someone was panting close to her.

A harsh, ragged sound that filled her ears.

She spun on her heels, the action making her feel nauseous again, her stomach lurching, but she clamped her lips tight in a defiant gesture. She had to *see*. She realized that now. Out here, in a world removed from the one she knew, from civilization and all that anchored it, something was replaying, an echo in time.

Reaching a tree, she backed up to it, needing some support in case her legs did indeed crumple beneath her. Her hands holding on to the sides of the trunk, she craned her neck forward and opened her eyes wider. *What happened here? What took place?*

Brandi. The panting belonged to her.

She had happened here.

CHAPTER TWENTY-THREE

As well as panting, there was a crunch and a rustling—someone moving through the terrain, a wisp, a ghost, an insight into a moment in time that Shady cleaved to.

A person running—Brandi, it had to be, her breath harsh, labored, because…because someone was in pursuit of her, that was why. She was trying to reach safety.

Shady looked around. Was there any safety to be had out here? Any hiding place?

Brandi! Brandi!

Shady's own breath caught in her throat.

Someone was calling out for the girl—not a beast, something born of imagination like a dragon, a skin walker or some other creature. It was a man's voice, and demanding.

Brandi, however, refused to slow down.

There she was! Shady caught sight of her. A wisp, yes, but Shady recognized her dark hair, not hanging limp past her shoulders anymore but flying all around her.

"Brandi!" Shady called this time, but of course there was no response. Brandi carried on running, stopping only briefly to look around her, to assess her situation, her head turning from side to side, naked desperation in her eyes. Which way should she go? She couldn't turn back, burst out of a landscape that had so quickly become dense forest, for then she would risk running into his arms—the arms of a murderer? Is that what he intended? To kill her, a girl who was still only a child, sixteen?

Shady's hands clenched tight. The man in pursuit—who was hunting her—was he the man from the truck? That same sense of exhilaration was in the air, that...*keenness*. He'd come here to hunt, just as others had years before, their quarry something other than local wildlife, the humanness of his victim honing a razor-sharp edge.

Hunting. She found she loathed the concept. Saw it not as man's right but an abomination. Had to come to terms too with the fact that she was no innocent regarding it, remembering all the times she'd hunted with her dad in the Idaho wilderness, for fish, mainly, but sometimes small animals too. It was wrong, all of it, when done for pleasure rather than necessity. The true way was to live and let live. To respect. And yet there was no respect here, only the need for supremacy. That's what Brandi's pursuer sought, just as Dan Turner had. An irrepressible urge to dominate.

Brandi had started running again, coming closer to Shady but without seeing her, her gaze trained straight ahead, dirty tear tracks marring otherwise smooth cheeks.

She was heading north, higher up the base of the mountain, continuing to bat branches out of her way, crying out when one flew back at her and marred her cheek further.

Tears still poured from her eyes. She was panicked, that emotion giving her the power of flight, but for how long? She could quickly tire when the adrenaline ran out.

"Brandi!" Shady couldn't resist yelling again. "I'm here.

We've come looking for you. Brandi, you're not alone. Keep going. We'll find you."

She'd expected no response, for how can a shadow, an echo, respond? But the girl slowed as if she *had* heard, turning her head toward the spot where Shady stood.

"Brandi?" This time Shady lowered her voice. "Can you hear me?"

At first, the girl looked through her, but then slowly, slowly, she focused.

"Shit!" Shady breathed, unsure what was happening, the already surreal becoming something even stranger. How was any of this possible? Rather than give in to confusion or hesitate, Shady had to act. The girl, somehow, was reaching out to her. Not from mere feet away but across the great divide. Drawing on instinct, Shady held out a hand.

To her amazement, the girl's hand lifted in response.

Oh, her eyes! No child should have to endure such terror or such bewilderment. It caused her own to become teary. Such a moment. Such a connection. But what was it that Shady was really doing here, reaching for the dead?

"Are you alive?" she whispered.

Their hands didn't meet—still too much distance between them, Shady unable to close the gap, her feet, like the tree she held on to, seemingly having taken root.

"Tell me you're still alive," she said instead. "That you're more…substantial than this."

Suspended in time, the pair of them held fast. But it couldn't last. Already, the girl's hand was lowering, her head turning.

Shady grew as desperate as the girl. "Tell me you're alive! Please!"

Before Brandi could turn fully, Shady darted forward at

last, part of her knowing that if she tried to grab the girl, she'd clutch at nothing but thin air. "Brandi!"

Another moment, again all too brief. One word left the girl's mouth before she continued onward, so weak that Shady barely caught it, could even have imagined it.

"Help."

CHAPTER TWENTY-FOUR

"Help! Help! Shady, where'd you go? I need help!"

"Josie? Shit, I'm coming. Hang on. Hang on. I'm almost there."

Shady's head hurt like hell, the place where she had hit it throbbing.

Had she imagined all she'd seen, Brandi also asking for help? She couldn't think, only respond, this time to Josie, her voice all too real.

Shady broke into a run, still feeling nauseous but doing her utmost to ignore both it and the terror that was mounting. Had Josie been hurt as well?

She burst out of the dense foliage and into the clearing where Josie had waited for her, not as far back as she'd left her but closer to the forest edge.

Immediately Shady dropped to her knees, tending to her.

"What happened?" she asked.

"I…oh, it sounds so stupid. I just got spooked, that's all, standing here alone. Jesus, Shady, how do people do it, camp out here? No way I'd embrace this whole wild-living thing. It's just…too harsh, too hostile. I…I thought I heard something behind me, just like you thought you saw something, as if…as if whatever it was had circled around and was spying on me, getting ready to pounce. I ran, I tripped. Got my foot snagged on a root. I've twisted my ankle and, man, it hurts."

Shady looked to where Josie was clutching her leg. "Is it swelling?"

"Maybe. Should I take off my boot—"

"No! Don't do that. You'll never get it on again. Can you stand? If you can, lean on me, see if you can walk. If not, we'll have to call for help."

"Shady, I've already checked. The signal's crap. It keeps dipping. Right now, I don't even have one bar." As Shady's face fell, Josie reassured her. "I'm sure I can walk, well…hobble. If we take it slowly, I'll be fine. It's not as if it's broken or anything."

"You don't know that," Shady replied, still agitating.

"It's just twisted, honestly. You know what, I'll crawl if I have to! This place…sacred, my ass."

"Okay, come on, let's get you up. Put as little weight as possible on the injured foot."

Josie did as she was told, yelping but otherwise stoic, leaning heavily on Shady, and Shady bore her weight happily if it ensured her safety.

It was slow going, the pair having to stop regularly to rest and catch their breath. Shady worried for Josie, at how screwed up with pain her face was, her complexion waxy. It was midafternoon, and the clouds were still looming, turning grayer and grayer. *Blacker.* Shady's heart plummeted to see it. Eventually, though, the lake came into sight, a shining beacon in the distance, and Shady hoped they'd encounter some people too, *normal* people, hikers, but the place looked even more deserted, likely because the weather was turning.

"Damn!" she said, causing Josie to glance at her.

"What?"

"I just wish I'd checked the other door of that truck before. What if it's gone now?"

"Hopefully not, but even if so, it could have nothing—"

"No, it does. Josie, something happened back there in the forest. I fell too, hit my head."

"Shit, Shady! You didn't say."

"No, I know. I...we have to focus on you, not me, but...I'm sure what I saw was real." *What I heard.* "Josie, I saw Brandi—"

"*What?*"

"Not the real her, a...shadow, like...looking at the past, seeing what had happened. She was running from someone. She was scared."

"And only now you're telling me this?"

"Because...because, shit, I'm really aware of how crazy I sound. I've told you, this thing I have, it's hard for even me to understand. I'm normal, I really am. Just like everyone else, I'm trying to find my way through life, and yet...this path I'm on, there are times when it baffles me and when...when I wonder."

The two girls had stopped and were looking at each other.

"Wonder what?" Josie asked gently.

"How much further down it I should go. And just what else I'll discover on the way. Josie, the world and the people in it...it's all so dark sometimes. So bleak."

Josie's expression was grave. "This...vision, can we call it that?"

"It's as good a word as any."

"You think it could be real?"

"Uh-huh."

"And you saw Brandi?"

"Yeah, and she was just so incredibly frightened. It was just a vision, but for a moment it was like something more. Our eyes met, and she said something."

"Help?" Josie guessed.

"Exactly that."

"And the truck, you think she was brought out here in it?"

"I think so. I keep telling you, the eagerness I sensed was on the manic side, out of the ordinary. That's hitting home more and more."

"Did you note the license plate?"

Shady screwed her eyes tight with frustration. "Shit, no. Did you?"

"No. But if it's not there when we get back, we can describe it well enough. It was an Oregon plate, I know that much, still a lead, something to tell the police. So that's what we do. We go and see the lieutenant again, today, this evening, whatever, or if I can't make it, you go. Tell them about the truck and insist they check out this area. Shady?" Josie said when Shady didn't answer but kept looking at the ground instead. "You have to make them believe you!"

"Do you, though? Believe everything I'm saying?"

Josie didn't falter, not even for a second. "I've never known my best friend Shady Groves to tell a lie in all the years I've known her."

The two girls hugged, a fierce hug that drew yet more tears from Shady. A short while later, they reached the Dodge, now the only vehicle parked along the road.

"Where the hell did the truck go?" Josie muttered as

Shady helped her into the car.

"I wish I knew."

"If the driver was the one stalking us, then he did what I thought and circled back."

Shady shrugged, remembering the glimpse she'd caught, the strangeness of it. "Come on, let's get you home. That's what's important right now."

"Okay. Get me home, and then head to the police station. Right?"

Settled in the car now too, Shady fired the engine.

"Shady, *right*? You go to the police station, get them to step in, to intervene. I can't come back out here, not immediately, my ankle...I'm sure it isn't broken, but even so, I can't come back again. I don't want to. This whole area of land feels...ruined. And there's no way you can come back either. Shady, listen to me, will you? We've done all we can." She swallowed, then sighed a little. "I guess from now on, what will be, will be."

* * *

Josie was right. Her ankle wasn't broken, but the sprain was bad, and the pharmacist they'd just caught before closing hours on their drive back had insisted she put no weight on it for at least a week, give the tissues surrounding the bone time to heal.

That was the good news. The *only* good news.

As Shady had promised Josie, she'd also gone to the police station, relieved that the lieutenant she'd spoken to before was still there. He saw her right away, ushering her into the same room with the same sidekick in tow. She didn't mention Cassie Dupont and Dan Turner. Not yet.

She was still hoping Cassie would step up at some point, believe in the truth of her own words, that she'd been right to do what she'd done—stopping the possibility of more murders, *hideous* murders, scalpings. And never mind that they were ten years apart; a murder was a murder, period. But raising all that…Shady couldn't. She'd have to then explain why she'd been snooping around Cassie's house, and that would sound even crazier to the lieutenant's ears. She focused only on Brandi, blurting out instead all that had happened when she'd gone to Mazuma Lake, the truck that she thought was involved, describing it and cursing herself again for not having taken a photo of the license plate. Such a simple thing to do, such a big mistake to make.

The lieutenant sat there, as he'd done before, right across the desk from her, and listened, nodding in all the right places. Finally, Shady had come to a halt, spent.

"Well?" was the only thing left to utter.

"Well," the lieutenant repeated. "It's…interesting."

Reasserting herself, she leaned forward. "But do you also think it's possible?"

"That Brandi and this mystery guy—if it is a guy, this guy who may or may not have a pickup truck—went to Mazuma Lake?"

Shady nodded fervently. "He either forced her or, once there, turned on her. We know she was going to meet someone."

The lieutenant shook his head. "We *think* she was. There's no hard-and-fast on that."

"Sir, are you going to scour the area around Mazuma Lake or not?"

He also leaned closer. "We will open it up as a line of inquiry, Miss Groves. But it is just one avenue. There are many others to explore and only so many…" Here his voice petered out, igniting more frustration in Shady.

"Resources? Is that what you were going to say? There's only so many resources available, even for a missing kid? She's out there, sir, and I think…I think she's still alive. If you want to find Brandi Hadley before it's too late, then head to Mazuma Lake."

By the time Shady left the police station, another day was nearly done, causing yet more frustration to build up in her chest, becoming something of a physical pain.

She had no choice but to go straight back to Josie's, Lulin and Josie still up, and Lulin proceeding to fuss over them both now, believing the lie they'd delivered about how the accident had happened. Josie had tripped over a paving stone, plain hadn't seen it, taken a tumble and hurt her ankle. A stupid accident but one that could happen to anyone. As for the lump on her own head, Shady was only glad her hair disguised it.

Just before heading to bed, she managed to slip outside again to call a frantic Ray and an anxious Annie, who'd both insisted they wanted to talk no matter how late the hour was, Shady opting to FaceTime the pair of them in the confines of her car.

She wondered whether she should withhold some of what she'd learned just as she'd done with the lieutenant because… *It's so surreal!* In the end, though, she revealed all, watched as their eyes grew wider and their jaws dropped open.

"Their disappearances, this whole hunting thing, this wild ritual," she continued, "it's linked to Brandi somehow. She had a fascination with Alisa Jones and may even have known that Robert Davenport went missing in that same area ten years earlier."

Ray was the first to reply, his warning similar to Josie's. "You've done what you can. Leave it to the police now." When there was a heartbeat of silence, he pressed further. "You're coming home soon, right?" Another quiet moment and then, "You're not thinking about returning to Mazuma Lake? On your own?"

"Ray—"

"No! You can't do it. Just leave it now. It is most definitely a police matter."

Annie nodding in agreement prompted a passionate outburst from Shady. "She's still missing, guys! If she's alive, it's just barely. If the police don't act right now…"

"Doesn't mean you have to," Ray countered. "There's a ton of danger out there, not just whoever this guy is that you think has Brandi, but other stuff too, dangers that, to put it simply, you're not equipped for. Don't go back there alone. I mean it!"

"Ray's right," Annie interjected at last. "I understand your empathy. I've said it before that part of the greatness of your talent is how much you identify, but you mustn't go back to Mazuma Lake. I don't share your gift, not to your extent, but I also have a feeling."

"And?" Shady held her breath, half wanting to hear the answer, half not.

"It will indeed be a dangerous thing to do. You've been there, you've searched, you hurt yourself, as did Josie. Please, Shady, stay away."

"Promise us," Ray urged.

"Okay, okay, fine. Like you say, it's a police matter."

Annie smiled, trying to ease the tension. "Okay. So, what are your plans now?"

"Just going back inside. Grabbing some sleep."

"And tomorrow?" Ray wanted to know.

"I don't know. I'll come home, I suppose."

"Good, good," Annie said. "Museum's busy, isn't it, Ray? Plus, we've had a rather interesting object donated to us."

"Oh?" Shady replied, intrigue rising despite herself.

"A chair, of all things. Eighteenth or nineteenth century, possibly. Like a…a…"

"Relic from a castle," Ray said when she faltered.

Annie nodded. "It could be English or French, or American if a repro. It has all sorts of strange carvings on it. I mean…really, it's exquisite to look at. Solid oak—dark, though—a hard seat, no padding on it but regal, throne-like."

"Why was it donated to us?"

"The person who hauled it in here, a young man in his early thirties, I'd say, all he said was he thought it belonged here in a weird museum like ours—his description, not mine. I asked him to elaborate, but he didn't want to, started scratching furiously at his hands and arms instead. From what I could see, the skin looked very sore there, as if he has eczema or psoriasis or something similar. Before I could quiz him further, he made to go, said if we didn't want it, to burn it, that it wasn't his problem anymore, it *couldn't* be."

"Where is it in the museum?"

"Right at the back, under some sheeting. It's too awkward to take down a winding staircase to the basement, although Ray rather heroically tried."

Ray blushed, which Shady couldn't help but smile at. She missed these guys, found suddenly she couldn't wait to see them. "Have you taken turns sitting on it?"

"Uh-huh," Ray declared. "Seems fine to me."

"Annie?" Shady checked.

"I've taken a turn too."

"And?"

"I'm not sure. There's a frisson of something."

"More darkness," Shady murmured.

"What's that, dear?" inquired Annie.

"Oh, nothing. Nothing."

"Well, anyway, we need you back as soon as possible to see what you make of it. Wonderful if we can negate the energy attached. It'd make a lovely exhibit."

A yawn escaped Shady, for which she immediately apologized.

"No need, dear," Annie insisted. "It's been a long, long day, especially for you. You must be terribly exhausted. Did you get the pharmacist to check you out too? A bump to the head can have serious consequences, delayed concussion being one of them."

"It was just a little bump," Shady lied.

"Well…if you're sure. We're looking forward to seeing you soon."

"Maybe even tomorrow," Ray said a little more eagerly. "Everyone's going for a drink at The Golden Crown in the evening. If you set off early enough, you could join us."

"After six hours driving, Ray? I'll be good for nothing."

"Even so," he insisted. "You are leaving tomorrow? For sure?"

"Yeah, yeah."

"Okay, all right, then."

"Look, Ray, Annie, I need to see how Josie is…"

"Sure, see you soon, Shady," replied Ray.

"See you soon," Annie also said, a smile—or could it be

a frown?—on her face.

Shady ended the call, then sat for a while in the car, getting ready to face Josie, who would continue to do the same as her colleagues and insist she either stick close by her side the next day or leave town entirely and return to the sanctity of Idaho Falls.

Shady's shoulders slumped as she leaned back against her seat.

Josie, Ray and Annie were her special people.

How she hated lying to them.

CHAPTER TWENTY-FIVE

Dawn hadn't even broken when Shady stirred. Josie was asleep beside her, her back to her and breathing gently.

Despite a sense of urgency that felt like it was suffocating her, Shady quietly and carefully inched out of bed. As she did, she glanced over at the window, a phrase coming to mind, one which took on special significance: *The darkest hour is just before the dawn.* Not just a saying but a notion. Out there, with a new day about to begin, there was terror and there was loneliness, a young girl reaching out, trying to connect, to let someone know she was still here, still alive, and for someone to come and help her.

As Shady gathered her things, a backpack that she'd surreptitiously stuffed with essentials when Josie had first fallen asleep, she also noticed the framed photograph of the masked men close to her car keys on the desk. Josie had hidden it beneath notebooks and her iPad, but still a corner peeked out. When all this was done, they would indeed dispose of it, the frame and the glass buried deep within the earth, somewhere on the road back to Idaho Falls, perhaps, far from Baker City. The photograph itself she'd set fire to, watch as flames reduced it to ashes, which she'd then crush to powder and scatter to the four winds. The memory of Dan Turner and his legacy, extinguished forever.

Pulling on her jeans and a hoodie, again with exaggerated care, Shady picked up her backpack and crept out of the bedroom. She made her way down the stairs, grabbed her boots from a shoe rack by the door and her jacket from the back of a chair in the kitchen, and let herself out of the Wongs' house, only then pulling on her boots.

It was as cold as she had expected. Swinging her backpack over her shoulder, she hurried down the pathway to the Dodge, her arms wrapped around herself for extra warmth. At her car, she stopped and gazed over at the Hadley house. Today was the beginning of the fourth day that Brandi had gone missing, and every second was precious.

Stay alive, she breathed.

About to turn, Shady instead stared harder at Brandi's bedroom window.

Was that a shadow there? Someone staring back at her? Mrs. Hadley? Brandi's dad?

No, she didn't think so. It was too wispy for that.

Brandi, then? The essence of her?

She was nowhere, and yet she was everywhere too, it seemed. Her presence infusing the atmosphere, a bona fide member of a small-town community, which she needed to return to. And the good people of that community—for there were many, people like the Wongs who only wanted a simple, peaceful life—were ready to band together to try to heal her of whatever ordeal she had suffered. They'd be vigilant for a long time to come, not wanting another poster girl. One had been one too many.

Climbing into the car, she pulled the door shut as quietly as she could.

By the time she reached Mazuma Lake, the sun would be on the rise. She'd park and not just retrace her footsteps this time but go farther to the foot of the mountains, to where there would be hiding places, trying to second-guess the route Brandi had taken. If Annie and Ray knew what she was doing, there'd be hell to pay. But they *would* know, soon enough, in a few hours, in fact, because when Josie woke and found her gone, she'd tell everyone, Annie and Ray, her parents, the cops; the whole lid would come off. Shady imagined the scene as she continued driving, the concern and panic that would follow, and felt sorry for causing it.

How much longer, though, would it take for Josie to discover something else missing besides Shady? Because when she did, that's when the real panic would set in. The gun.

* * *

So still. A smokiness hovering just a few inches above the lake that lent it a true sense of otherworldliness. Little wonder those who had known this ground long before the white man had arrived considered it sacred. Staring at the lake, enchanted, Shady then lifted her eyes to look over at the mountains beyond it, tendrils of cloud drifting all around them, and deemed it *all* sacred, every inch. Yes, the land was something to be wary of, but it was also what gave meaning to life, an excitement, the thought of waking each morning to find you were still a part of something, such beauty.

The track around the lake was empty, which she was thankful for. As she left the car, her breath created another cloud of mist before her, the sun not yet warming the air on the shoreline. She wouldn't blame the others for being angry with her when they guessed her destination. She understood. This was madness. *Utter* madness. Reckless behavior that Dan Turner himself would despise and which she was supposed to avoid. What had Annie said to her once? *Recklessness is not an option, not for you.*

If saving a life depended on it, however, she was willing to face the consequences.

If the truck had belonged to the perpetrator, if the perpetrator had returned to the scene of the crime for whatever reason, he was gone now. Just a few hours was all she needed here to try to connect again.

Brandi, I'm coming for you.

With stubborn determination she turned away from the lake, already mourning the loss of its beauty, and headed toward the path she had taken the day before, this time alone. She'd go carefully, guard against falling again and making herself even more vulnerable than she already was. Her only security was the gun, and that only as a threat tactic. Unlike Josie, she might have fired a gun before—her mom had sent her for a few lessons when she was in her teens, and her dad had taught her how to handle a rifle when they were out together on their expeditions—but she'd never aimed at anything living, with lethal intent or otherwise, and she certainly didn't want to have to do that now, out here alone. If any small animals had been brought down on father-daughter hunts, it was Bill who'd done it.

The sun continued to rise in the sky, but the day refused to grow any brighter.

As Shady trekked along the path leading upward, she fought mounting anxiety. Would it be a dull day? Worse than that, a misty one? The smokiness that she had seen hanging over the lake and the mountains looked to be thickening rather than dispersing, expanding breadthways too, reminding her of the weather phenomenon they'd encountered en route to the lake in Dorothea. A fog that had suddenly grown more intense.

It wasn't like that here, not yet, at any rate. But what if it did come in? Such a strange fog, like nothing she'd ever encountered before. There was no real reason to think it would happen again and so soon after the last time. When the sun grew stronger, it would be able to penetrate, burn through what was there now and disperse it.

But if not?

If not, she'd be in trouble. *Big* trouble.

She was half tempted to turn back, listen to the advice she'd received: *Leave this to the police. You've done all you can.* She did indeed turn, cowardly relief flooding her bones, but then she stopped. Brandi was trying to reach out, and she'd done it, succeeded, connected with Shady and begged her. *Help!* Such desperation behind it. Because she was here, somewhere. She'd been hunted, and the hunter had returned, come back for her. And he wasn't going to give up. Not until he found her. *Gained dominion.*

For that was his goal. Just as it had been Dan Turner's goal.

"Fuck it," she murmured through gritted teeth as she pressed on.

Now Brandi had two people on her tail, tracking her, both with very different intentions. Shady only hoped she had the advantage. If her psychic talent gave her an edge, then she'd be more grateful for it than ever. She had to be brave, open her mind to possibilities and be hopeful that the closer she got to Brandi, the girl would be able to sense her and connect again. A far-fetched theory, perhaps, but it was the only one she had. The mist, though, as she climbed higher wasn't dispersing as fast as she'd hoped. It appeared to drastically reduce the world around her; no longer was it vast and unconquerable but more intimate than that. Shady picked up a hefty stick and marked the route in any way she could: scoring deep marks in the ground, just simple crosses, snapping branches on trees, picking up stones too and placing them in small piles at intervals, the equivalent of a Hansel and Gretel breadcrumb trail. It would hopefully lead her back to safety, maybe even with Brandi in tow. No way she could risk becoming disoriented. She had to stick to the path even if it became one of her own making.

Alisa Jones's camp, she was nearing it; it was off to the right, more toward the river. She felt the pull of it but also knew Brandi wasn't there, that she'd gone higher toward the foot of the mountains in search of shelter.

She pushed on farther, then, starting to call out Brandi's name after half an hour or so. Upon reaching the foothills of the mountains, she glanced behind her at mist that had become a fog and black at the edges, she noticed, double- and triple-checking to make sure it was true and not just imagination, her nerves getting the better of her. Fear, even.

"What the hell?"

It *was* blacker at the edges, no doubt about it. Part of the phenomenon Teddy had talked about or, again, something unique to her?

Turn back, Shady! Go home!

The voice in her head was screaming at her, but another quickly replaced it.

She's hurt. That's why she can't make it back down to Mazuma Lake. He hurt her.

Not just words infiltrating her mind, Shady could see how it had played out. Brandi had been hurt but somehow got away. And, as a wounded animal would do, she'd crawled into a tight space to lie low, drifting in and out of consciousness.

As before with Josie, Shady dropped to the ground and placed her palms on the dirt and gravel. The atmosphere was so quiet, whatever wildlife there was lying low too. She was glad of it, for what she sought this time was the beating heart of the land.

Closing her eyes, she tuned in. As before, a faint noise made itself known, not the rhythm of pounding feet this time, masking everything; instead, it was…soothing. Despite her fear and her misgivings about her own actions, she couldn't help but marvel. The hum was incredible. Full of magic. *Natural* magic. The earth not bent to the will of men but existing despite them, that would also outlast them, in the end regarding them as nothing but a passing nuisance. It was the beating heart of nature she was listening to, something majestic. Another heartbeat, though, she needed to hear that. A sound that overlaid it, hopefully with just as much rhythm. *Are you still breathing, Brandi, or is all this in vain?*

She listened and listened to the steady drum of the earth, the tribal quality of it. But gradually, and only after exercising a patience she didn't feel, that right now went against the grain but would make Dan Turner proud, she heard it—a second heartbeat, causing a yelp of joy, a triumph that rose, that peaked and then just as quickly ebbed. A heartbeat that was indeed faltering, nothing strong about it at all, nothing as enduring.

A third sound. A snap of twigs.

Shady's eyes flew open.

It was so quiet out here…*deathly* quiet.

She'd thought herself alone this time, but she wasn't.

She scrambled to her feet. Where'd the noise come from? Behind her? To the side? In front? She couldn't tell, and the silence fell back into place. What she felt, though, was this: there *was* someone close. Just as she was tracking, something was tracking her.

CHAPTER TWENTY-SIX

The sound of panting. Not like before, belonging to something ethereal, a ghost or a wisp, a mere hope of something. It was much closer to home than that—Shady's own panting, her breath wrenched from her throat as she ran farther up the rugged path, cursing how steep it was becoming and the denseness of the fog.

Panic was only going to make matters worse out here. She needed to keep a level head, imagining not something monstrous behind her but a foe as human and therefore every bit as fallible as she was. Hard, though, given what she'd seen only yesterday. A beast, a creature that walked on two legs, that covered itself from head to toe in skins.

Dan Turner?

Could it be? Returned somehow to haunt these grounds, his land, his domain.

She was being chased by a ghost?

Ludicrous. Too far-fetched, even for her. But this world she'd found herself in was nothing like the world she knew, packed with bars, restaurants, shops, and people, huge amounts of them just...getting by, existing. A world with dangers too, but dangers she understood. Out here, despite her blood and any Native DNA she possessed, she was a fish out of water. No Dud Hooper, Robert Davenport or Alisa

Jones—she didn't *seek* to tame the wilderness or immerse herself in it. She enjoyed the beauty of it, but then she was content to leave it behind and return to a more concrete jungle. No chance of that, though, not right now. She was convinced that whatever was stalking her was also *herding* her, farther up the mountain, the path becoming less and less defined, not as well used, most day-trippers having decided they'd come far enough and turning back. Only the hardened would continue to plow their way through. To go where? To do what?

Like Brandi, she had to find a hiding place, grab her cell, the gun, and wait for whatever was tailing her to lose her scent.

Toying with her.

That was the impression she had. The hunter was enjoying this; she could almost feel the glee emanating in waves toward her.

She could stop briefly, get the gun out now and wave it around, screaming threats. "Leave me alone. If not, I'll use it. I will. Just…back off."

Her mouth dried at the thought. She was no hunter, she was no tracker, and she was no murderer. Would she use it if she had to? She didn't know. Couldn't answer that question despite being so frightened.

As she continued to run, tears blurred her vision, which she angrily wiped at. This was no time to succumb to despair. She wasn't the only one out here who was trapped; Brandi was, a kid. She had to hold it together, push that little bit harder. For her sake.

Her progress wasn't as fast as she would have liked, exhaustion setting in. It was daytime, still only morning, and yet, because of the fog, time had lost all meaning. The something that kept track of her was still at her heels. She could hear the snapping of twigs as it ran, keeping effortless pace. It could easily launch itself at her, bring her down, but where was the fun in that? It was the chase that turned hunters on, the fear they could inflict, feeling themselves grow in stature because of it, become more powerful.

The path was gone. Vanished. Before her lay only a tangled mess of scrub and stones. As she slowed—had no choice to, this was ground that had to be carefully negotiated—she turned and looked over her shoulder, strained to see something, anything, but the fog was no ally of hers. Or was it? Was it concealing her just as much as the tracker? Once again, there was a temptation to shout out, to tell whoever it was to leave her alone, to quit this juvenile game, that she'd had enough. But if the fog was indeed hiding her, no way she wanted to give away her whereabouts. She needed to exercise stealth, just as the tracker would, try to outwit it, find a hiding place and think clearly about what to do. The higher she climbed, the more likely her phone's signal strength would improve, surely? Then she could call the police, get them out here at last.

The police… Josie would have woken by now, would be well aware she'd gone, put two and two together, know where she was headed. What if—and the thought brought with it almost giddy relief—she'd already called the police? Saving Shady the trouble.

"Yes! Yes!" Shady muttered as she scrambled onward.

Josie would do that, definitely. Help would come. They'd find her. Maybe Brandi too. All she had to was find a hiding place and wait this out, her gun poised.

There was something up ahead that the fog only grudgingly revealed. Something dark, cavernous even, the maw of a beast, this time cast in stone and yawning widely.

A cave! Perhaps one that hid Brandi too. How her heart clung to reason, to hope.

Not running anymore but crouching on all fours like an animal, she headed toward the cave. Being low down like this might conceal her more. She realized that in the cave she might be effectively trapping herself if her stalker should spot it too and enter, that there'd be no chance of getting a phone signal either. But, again, what choice was there? Options were running out, and fast. At least in the cave with her back to a wall, she wouldn't feel vulnerable on all sides. If there was someone after her, it would approach from the front. And she'd have her gun trained on it.

A plan. Something to cling to. More reasoning, more hope.

She continued to scramble, like a snake now, practically slithering. The cave closer still.

When she reached it, a sob burst from her, refusing to be contained anymore. It was as though she'd been handed a gift, a chance of survival.

Not daring to look back, she straightened up and entered it.

Dark, dank and wet. A sound that resounded but gentle, the drip, drip, dripping of water from the roof of the cave, perhaps. The cave wasn't huge, although it had seemed that way from afar. Deep, she guessed, though impossible to see by how much.

She needed her cell, could use the flashlight on it. Shunting off the backpack, her hands traveled to the gun first in one of the side pockets, felt the reassuring steeliness of it. Right now, though, a light was more essential. She couldn't take another step without it.

While retrieving her cell, she listened out for other sounds—footsteps, primarily, the tracker entering the cave too. Aside from the constant drip and her breathing, there was silence.

As she replaced the backpack, she switched on the cell's flashlight, trying to calm her heaving chest and breathe more slowly.

"Brandi," she whispered as she took a tentative step forward. "Are you here?"

The flashlight was not effective enough. It barely cut through the darkness. Each step she took was therefore measured, making sure the ground was indeed level and firm before chancing another. Suddenly, inexplicably, a memory returned, a happy one so at odds with her current situation but which refused to fade.

She'd ventured into caves before, beachside caves, on vacation with her mom and dad when she was young, just a kid herself, ten, eleven, something like that. They'd been on the West Coast, down California way, and Shady as a child hadn't wanted to enter the caves; she'd found them creepy, preferred to stay outside in the sunshine instead, building sandcastles and splashing in the blue of the ocean. Her dad had persuaded her, though, lured her in there with the promise of finding treasure, her mom playing along, and so inside the cave they had crept, one of several that lined that shore, the buzz and echoing chatter of fellow beach dwellers all too soon fading.

"See, it's not so scary, is it?" her mom had said, but the young Shady remained mute, her eyes growing wider, straining to see, daylight encroaching but only so far.

"Just a little further," her dad had said. "A few more steps. We gotta find the treasure!"

If there was treasure, Shady reasoned, this might be worth it, imagining the glitter of golden coins in a wooden chest, as she'd seen in countless illustrated children's books. They'd be rich, heading for Disneyland after this, her young mind calculating the possibility of moving into Sleeping Beauty's castle thanks to such riches.

A few more steps, that was all, just as the grown-up Shady was urging herself to take a few more steps in real time, deeper and deeper into the cave.

It hadn't been so bad after all. Her dad had used a small flashlight on his keychain, and, as she'd looked around, she could see how the cave walls, slick with moisture, glistened, sparkled even, like treasure themselves.

Then, as now, the ground beneath her feet was slippery. Both times she'd had to tread carefully, fearing falling, being stranded there.

As a child, she'd started giggling, excitement replacing fear.

"Does anyone else know there's treasure here?" she'd asked.

"They do," her dad answered, "but no one comes here anyway."

"Why?"

"Because no one truly believes it, that's why."

How indignant the young Shady had been. "Why don't they believe?"

"I don't know. People can be…cynical," her dad said.

"Suspicious," her mom added. "They think magic doesn't exist."

"But it does!" Shady insisted. "The world is *so* magical!"

Her mom laughed again. "That's it. That's right. Never let go of the magic, Shady, because it's here, all around us.

It's everywhere. Now, where could the treasure be—"

A scream. Her mom. From laughing and chatting, she was suddenly yelling, lifting her hands and flapping at the air.

"What is it? What's wrong?" her dad shouted, rushing to aid her.

"Mom?" In contrast, Shady's voice was but a pale whisper.

"Something flew at me! Something…black! It's in my hair! Get it off me! Get it off!"

Both her parents were flapping now, her mom completely frenzied, and then she had run—not farther into the cave but out of it, her dad initially in pursuit, leaving Shady alone and staring after them, listening as more screams pierced the air.

Screaming…

Her dad had suddenly remembered he'd left Shady there, returned and grabbed her.

Screaming…

It had been bloodcurdling.

Screaming…

When before there had been laughter, there'd been magic and belief.

There's treasure in here. Something precious…

The very reason both Shadys had entered both caves.

Not just screaming…a roar. No longer a memory but playing out in real time. That bounced off those slick cave walls and hurled itself back at her.

Not Brandi. Not even human. Full of horror and something else—a dark promise.

As she'd been in the cave when her mother had fled—it had been a bat that had flown at her, become entangled in her hair—Shady was frozen.

Something was with her, even deeper in the cave than she was, just ahead. Something that, like before, allowed only a glimpse of itself. Shady stared, powerless to do anything but stand there and hold her breath as slowly, almost leisurely, whatever it was turned its head toward the light, Shady knowing what she'd see: eyes that glowed red.

This creature was responsible for the roar, for what else could it have been? A creature that had seen her once before, weeks ago, that had locked eyes with her and marked her, that had sensed her again when she'd been here the previous day and also today. Not behind her at all, it had somehow skirted around her, there to wait in the shadows.

An animal but with human trickeries, human thinking, that was opening its mouth, no doubt to reveal the sharpest of canines and to emit another roar that would burst her ears this time, galvanizing itself to spring forward and land upon her and pin her to the ground, where she'd be defenseless, at its mercy.

She had to move, force life back into her limbs.

The cell dropping from her hand to no doubt smash against the ground, the only thing she clung to now was her backpack as she fled, remembering what was in it, although there was no time to retrieve it, not yet. She ran in the darkness toward the only source of light—the entrance—a pinprick that grew bigger, pulling her toward it, though she expected at any moment to be dragged backward instead. When she reached the mouth of the cave, she saw the fog still hovering, as thick as before. A blessing and a curse.

With no path to guide her and her vision hindered, she had to once again rely solely on instinct, heading downward and into the trees toward more shelter where she could rest, retrieve the gun and save herself.

A crazy idea, coming out here. How she cursed herself for it! For trying to play the hero.

And now she'd pay for it. What if this thing knew every inch of ground, every tree, every low bough, every bit of scrub? She, a city girl in contrast, had too little knowledge of what lay beyond man-made structures. This was a hunting ground, for both humans and those devoid of humanity. The best place imaginable and the worst.

A skin walker, that's what was in pursuit of her. A human dressed as a walker? Or the real thing? Her heart raced even faster than her feet. It couldn't be real. *They're just a myth!* And so, if human, a bullet would stop it in its tracks.

She had to catch her breath, get the gun out.

Darting behind a tree, she shrugged the backpack off once again. It dropped to the ground, but she quickly retrieved it. Her hands then flew to the side pocket where she'd stashed the gun, shaking so badly it took way too long to unzip it.

Come on! Come on! Please, Kanti, help me! Don't leave me out here alone!

Those glowing red eyes that she had indeed seen, were they contact lenses, maybe? The aim to *really* act the part, to terrify people further. Is this what Brandi had encountered? Someone eager to play a little dress-up, who enjoyed the most ferocious of games? And if so, was Shady deluded in thinking the girl was still alive? Misreading all the signs that suggested she was. That beating heart of hers growing fainter still, giving up.

She mustn't give up, though, Shady, but dig deep, find what bravery still existed.

Fingers finally closing around the gun, a moment of

triumph was all too fleeting.

She heard what was now a familiar sound. The crunch of leaves and snapping twigs as something approached her. Something bold that had grown tired of playing and now meant business. Something that the fog still concealed but not for long. Soon it would give way as her pursuer drew within inches of her, a demon in animal's clothing.

Her back pressed against the tree trunk, barely registering the sharp ridges of it, she sought only to keep her ears and her eyes focused, lifting her hand again, pointing the gun, the other hand coming over to try to steady the aim.

Fingers on the trigger, they began to squeeze, Shady plumbing the depths of other memories now, all the lessons at the gun range her mom had made her take. Not that she personally owned a gun, but her family did, kept for use in an emergency.

This was an emergency and then some. A legitimate reason to squeeze the trigger further, to deliver a shot, not to the heart but lower down if she could, to the leg, to slow the wannabe walker down, then get out of there, bring back the police if they weren't already on their way, swarms of them to arrest him and track Brandi, end this horror once and for all. Seek justice too for the ones subjected to similar terror years and years before. This had been a game played out through the decades. If it was not Dan Turner, then how this stalker knew about such a game, she didn't know. That was yet to be discovered. As Cassie had intimated, if there was a sect, it had ended with Dan's death.

"Shit! Shit! Shit!"

Like a theatre curtain, the fog was indeed parting, revealing the star of the show, the sum of every horror character combined.

You got this, Shady! You can do this! You have to.

A bubble of something erupted in her, a roar of her own, a war cry.

She screamed, and so did the figure in front of her. Louder than her, more horrified. Able to—miraculously—stop her from firing off a bullet. Just.

"Shady! What the fuck do you think you're doing?"

CHAPTER TWENTY-SEVEN

"Ray? Ray! Oh my God, Ray! Is it you? Are you real?"

Having cast the gun aside, Shady threw herself at the man in front of her, half expecting him to be as much an apparition as Brandi, nothing but thin air.

He was solid enough, his arms coming out to wrap themselves around her, hugging every bit as fiercely as she was hugging him.

"Thank God you're all right!" he murmured. "The gun, though. What are you doing with a gun? Who were you trying to shoot?"

Although she wanted nothing more than to stay within the circle of his arms, she forced herself to take a step back, to look around, her eyes scanning the immediate area. Her tracker, he couldn't have just disappeared, could he?

"There's someone out there—" she began.

"There are plenty of people out there, Shady. Everywhere."

"Huh? What? I don't think you're listening."

"Shady." Ray clutched at her arms, forced her to focus on just him and what he was saying. "The police are here, me, Brett, Teddy, Sam, Annie, all of us."

Unable to process this, not immediately, Shady shook her head. "Listen to me! There's a…there's a…shit! I don't know what to call it. Something that's as tall as you are, wearing skins and tracking me. It has been…like…ever since I came out here, today, yesterday, and also before that, when we were at the campground all together. It has these eyes, Ray, glowing red eyes, and it's always on my tail, and…and—" she had to swallow hard, take a deep breath "—I think it's got something to do with Brandi's disappearance too. She came out here with someone, someone in a truck. Whether it's them that's following me or whether this fucker is someone or something else entirely, I just don't know. I'm so confused, can't think straight, but one thing I'm sure of is this: it's evil."

Ray looked shocked, completely bewildered, trying to take it all in, the explanation falling so rapidly from Shady's lips, garbled even to her own ears.

"Ray," she tried again, "we're in serious danger here. We have to keep moving. How is it that the others are here? I don't mean the police. I figured Josie would call them when she found I was gone—banked on it, in a way—to get them out here at last, the help that was needed to find Brandi. Shit, Ray, how come you're even here?"

"Because I didn't believe you, that's why," he said. "Last night on the call, when both me and Annie said you shouldn't come back here, especially alone, and you shook your head and said you wouldn't, I didn't believe you, not for a second. And neither did Annie."

"And so, what? You recruited Brett and the gang? Why?"

"Mom's away. I couldn't borrow her car, and Annie's car is in the body shop, having work done, so…we had to recruit Brett, who was as worried about you as we were. He told Teddy and Sam you might be in trouble, and there was no stopping them either. We drove through the night. And guess what? Dorothea came through for us. She was great, no problem at all, got us down in one shot, going full speed too. Not so much as a wheeze from her."

Once again, tears formed in Shady's eyes. "Good old Dorothea," she said. "And you and Annie and Brett and…thank you for coming after me! I was so scared."

"No need to be, not anymore. But you're right, we need to get going, find everyone. Some of the police are down at the lake, a whole team of 'em, along with Annie and Sam. Teddy and Brett went with other police who are headed upward to where Josie said you'd gone yesterday, where Alisa Jones's camp was apparently found."

"A local gruesome attraction."

"Uh-huh, it seems to be."

"Did you veer off or something? Why are you alone?"

Ray swallowed too, then shrugged. "Well…I didn't mean to. I kept noticing things, though, stones on the ground and crosses, like a trail. Was that you?"

"Yeah! Yeah, it was. Taking a tip from Hansel and Gretel."

He smiled. "Fuck, that's clever! I began following them, only took a few steps away from the others, but then…when I looked over my shoulder, I couldn't see anyone. I was alone." He gestured all around him. "This fog again, it's screwing things up, can't work out where you are or where you've come from. It's just so easy to get lost in it."

She didn't need telling. "Which way is back? Do you know?"

He thumbed behind him. "This way, I think. We're not

too far off the track. Hopefully, pretty soon we'll find your stones again, then as long as we stick together, we'll be fine."

"Great, come on, let's go."

With her hand in his, they hurried on, the pair of them now silent, each trying to focus on their footing. Shady was also straining to hear, not just for sounds of leaves crunching and twigs snapping but for voices, of those trying to find her and, of course, Brandi. All was quiet for now, but that could change and hopefully for good reasons. If whatever was tracking her also heard voices, became aware there were other people on the mountain—an army of them—it might just quit and leave them alone. They'd escape this now, just when Shady had begun to believe there was no escape, that she was doomed.

They hadn't gotten far when she remembered something.

"Ray, the gun! I have to go back for it."

Ray, still concentrating, only half turned. "What? No way. Leave it."

"It's not mine. It belongs to Josie's family."

"So? It doesn't matter. All that matters is we reach the others."

She wriggled her hand out of his. It really wasn't that far back; she could quickly run and get it. Another reason for wanting it was that she could hear no sound from the others, the fog absorbing voices, maybe, swallowing them up, but what if it wasn't? What if they'd drifted farther away, and what if the tracker hadn't retreated but was still close?

"Ray, it's best we have it. Safer."

She turned and left him, retraced her footsteps—just a minute or two, that's all it'd take.

"Shady!" she could hear Ray call, but she didn't respond,

too intent on retrieving the weapon. He'd come out here, they all had, her friends, and put themselves in peril too, and no doubt about it, the danger in the Oregon wilderness was the kind that could snuff you out in a heartbeat. It was insidious. Calculated. Waiting to strike. Perennial.

And once lost, they might never find you. More graves here than could ever be counted.

The more she thought about it, the more she realized they needed the gun, just till they could reach the others and find the police, who'd also be armed.

"Won't be long, Ray," she called back. "Almost there—"

It happened so quickly, her brain couldn't comprehend. One minute she was running, the next it felt like she was flying, her feet barely touching the ground. Was she flying? And why was she unable to scream? To even make a noise? Every attempt muffled.

Christ!

Not a myth, not a monster, it was a man who had grabbed her, one arm around her waist, the other against her mouth, a man who…stank. Even though his arm also covered her nose, she could detect a terrible stench, one so base, so raw that she wondered at it until she also realized something else—she wasn't feeling skin against skin. It was fur, *newly hacked fur,* another sacrifice. They hadn't lost the tracker after all.

Initial shock wearing off, she kicked, arched her body, the arm that wasn't trapped by her side flailing too. It was no use. Just a man, but he was strong, dragging her farther into the fog, away from Ray, her only haven, to where? The cave? Was that indeed his lair? And had she been right in suspecting Brandi was also there, deep in its tunnels?

How far back did the cave extend, how many chambers did it have, how many avenues? Would the police be able to find and search it? And if they did, would it be too late? Ray had already said the fog was hampering their investigations here. If the day waned and the fog still persisted, what would they do? Call off the search? At least overnight or they'd risk putting more lives in danger. *Too late…* It definitely would be, for Brandi, at least. She had to continue fighting, but exhaustion was draining her.

Help me! Someone. Anyone. Help me! Please!

Shady was falling backward and without warning, again struggling to reason why. There was a yelp, not from her; it was too guttural, too…male. It was from the man who had hold of her, as surprised as she was, perhaps, by the fact they were falling. With all her writhing and bucking, had she somehow managed to land a blow?

The man hit the ground, another gasp escaping him, Shady's own landing beside him much softer. The impact caused him to release his grip on her, and immediately she drew in big lungfuls of air, gulping it down, desperate to reenergize herself. At the same time, she rolled away from him and tried to stand, hoping that he had hurt himself in the fall just as she had the previous day, his head hitting not a stone but a ragged-edged boulder.

She didn't stop to check.

Forcing herself onto her feet, she sprinted from him, her mouth opening to yell out Ray's name—he had to be nearby—cursing when the only sound emitted was tantamount to a squeak. She simply could not gather enough strength to produce anything more. No matter. She'd continue to run, put as much distance between herself and her attacker as possible. Ray had said this place was crawling alive. She'd find someone soon enough.

As hope once more sprang eternal, something else sprang too, right onto her back, bringing her back down onto the stony ground.

She was flipped over as if she were no more than a rag doll. She closed her eyes, almost too afraid to open them, to look into his, but she knew she had to. When she did, she almost laughed. The creature above her…it was…ludicrous. No other way to describe it. Animal skins covering his own, and a mask that had slipped, it seemed, hiding those strange eyes, but otherwise just like the mask Dan Turner had used in the photograph at the Grand Willmott. Only the edge of his mouth and chin, covered in stubble, was visible. Impossible otherwise to tell who he was or even his age.

Could it be…? Was it possible…?

"Dan?" she croaked. "Is it you?"

Could a man in his sixties be this strong? Like a wild bull.

"Cassie didn't kill you, then?"

There was a moment of surprise, this time on her assailant's part, a brief second of hesitation when she'd uttered Dan's name, Shady again taking advantage of it, kicking, punching, managing to slide out from under him and regain some ground. Once more, there was only brief reprieve, and then he was on her, a snarling, drooling beast of a man, his hands closing around her throat.

"You're not going anywhere." His voice was little more than a rasp. "The Great Beast demands a sacrifice. An appeasement. And it looks like you're it."

She was insane for coming here. And he was too. Deluded.

If only she could cry out, reason with him, reach up and rip that stupid mask from his face. Who was he? Where was everyone? He was spouting nonsense but such *determined* nonsense. He'd kill her if someone didn't help her, if she couldn't help herself.

Again, the world such as it was, this alien, mist-enshrouded universe that she had found herself in, was blackening at the edges. Is that what it had meant all along? The sign she'd thought might herald Brandi's demise was actually foretelling her own? If so, she'd gotten something right, at least, the connections that had seemed so weak, so…bizarre turning out not to be so crazy, but what a price she'd pay for it.

This wasn't worth dying for.

She loved her life, wanted it to continue.

But if she had to die, then she'd go with the knowledge of who her murderer was.

Her hands, from trying to loosen his grip, moved upward, the blackness continuing to increase, reducing her vision to a pinpoint just as the fog had reduced her world.

Fear, shock, disbelief and grief all subsided too, made way for anger that was white hot. *Just who the fuck do you think you are?*

If it was Dan Turner, alive and truly feral, more insane than ever, Cassie's bullet having indeed bounced off him, then the only thing she took comfort in was that the net was closing all around him. Maybe today his long and repugnant reign would end. *Let it end!*

The rage was burning.

You coward! Wearing a mask! Pretending to be something you're not. Hurting people. Murdering them. Not a part of the natural order but an insult to it.

As her hands grappled with the mask that was already lopsided, she pushed upward, thrilled when it yielded just a fraction. Buoyed by success, she reached with one hand to yank it off completely.

Is it you, Dan Turner?

Not an old man. Far from it. He was young despite the grizzled beard, younger even than she was, nineteen or twenty? Those eyes—blue not red, contact lenses discarded, perhaps?—were nonetheless dead, indicating something very wrong if even the thrill of the kill wasn't enough to enliven them. *Lost.* Not her, but him. Shady tuned in. *Looking for something. For meaning.* All this could be told from his eyes, that message not hidden but something graphic as his grip tightened. *You want to believe.* But believe in what? That he was a species apart, superior, that he could…ascend? Her frantic heart beat faster. That was exactly his aim, as Dan Turner's had been. Not the stuff of myth and legend but the danger lying in the fact they believed themselves to be.

A young man with blood on his hands. Whose blood?

The darkness might be increasing, blotting out her vision now, but in her mind's eye she could still see. It was *her* blood. Shady Groves. She was to be his first victim, not Brandi. Relief and, again, a sense of the ironic about that, that she'd worried about Brandi all this time, not herself. Never imagining what else she could see. More blood and more death. *He needs meaning!* And he believed this would give it to him, eventually, the senseless slaughter of others, innocent people he'd hunt down and destroy. All in the name of ascension. A horrific destiny, her death giving him the taste for it. *Was Brandi's supposed to?* Maybe, but she'd gotten away, was hiding somewhere. *You're a young man,* she wanted to say. *Don't give in to the darkness!* But he'd choked the words from her.

If only she could speak! If only she could fight harder!

He would prey on countless victims, far more than Dan Turner would have planned for. She could see them, for now just shadowy, anonymous figures, female, male and all ages. But, as time went on, they'd take shape, become real people with real lives, the loss of them mourned forever. Indiscriminate, just as Dan Turner had been, but unlike him, he'd show no restraint, no patience, no long-drawn-out, cunning pursuit. Unbound by anniversaries or rituals, he would strike whenever an opportunity arose, bringing instant gratification. That was his goal, an ambition to achieve, one that would slowly, by increments, inject life back into his eyes, the life that had been taken from others.

He has to be stopped!

But he wouldn't be. He'd dispose of her body out here in this foreign landscape, hidden by a traitorous fog that seemed the stuff of witchcraft, as if he did indeed have the magical powers he craved and could conjure it from nothing. This was the future she was looking at, helplessly and in despair. The last thing to see before her own end—not the sweet smiling faces of her parents, of Josie, Ray and Annie, those who were closest to her, just death at the hands of another psychopath, and yet more deaths to follow.

The visions were fading, the darkness almost complete.

She couldn't resist the cold caress of oblivion. She would close her eyes and lean back into it. There was no help coming and therefore no alternative. It was all too late.

What an incredible gift I have. Was this to be her last thought? *A beautiful, terrible gift.*

A roar. More terrible than the one she'd heard in the cave. And just when life was leaving her, it returned, was something that roared too.

Her eyes snapped open. More than that, *better than that*, she could breathe again, sucking at the air as if surfacing from a drowning.

What had happened? Had the police found her? Had Ray? Teddy or Brett?

Elation mixed with more confusion; she had to struggle to focus, to understand.

Who had torn this man, this creature, off her?

How terrible his cries were, the air exploding with them.

Shady rolled from her back onto her knees and crouched there, her palms flat against the cold, stony dirt. When she lifted her head, she saw what had gotten him. Something large and ferocious, its mouth at his throat as it shook him from side to side. He was the rag doll now, not her. What strength he possessed no match for it.

It was an animal…but unlike any she'd ever seen.

One that was tall, that could walk on two legs just like a human, fur *and* flesh covering its limbs and its face…oh, its face…it was horrifying. This creature had a long, thick snout, ears that were tall too, sharply pointed, and eyes that glowed red.

"Skin walker," Shady breathed. "You're a skin walker."

Something unspeakable.

The Great Beast.

The man in its clutches tried to reach out toward Shady, as if begging for help, a fountain of blood spraying from his mouth.

And she *wanted* to help, despite everything.

He might have murder in his veins, but she only had pity. If he should survive such an attack, there were other ways to deal with him, not this.

Still on all fours, she crawled forward.

As she did, the creature stopped its violent shaking of the man, although not for one second did it relinquish its grip. Those strange eyes—not feral but full of intelligence—continued to glare at Shady, boring deep into a heart grown cold with fear.

What are you? Who are you?

Not a man, but a man once?

Dan?

No, not him, but the creature he'd worshipped, that he'd tried to emulate, just as this man had too. Something…mysterious. Outside of nature, but still it existed, it had its place, in folklore and in reality. And this was it. The wilderness. The deepest pockets of it. Drawn out of hiding, *attracted* by the noise, the commotion. *The violence.*

Would it slaughter this young man and then come for her, tear her apart too?

The victim in its mighty jaw was gurgling on blood still, slight murmurings leaving his lips, but his hands were now limp by his side. With a gasp of horror, Shady realized that whatever shred of life he was clinging to was quickly deserting him. Also that there was nothing she could do about it. This creature would not suffer such an abomination to live.

As it was staring at her, she stared back, amazed that her curiosity was overriding fear.

Ancient. A hybrid. Responsible for other deaths too, no doubt about it, but nothing like as many as man himself, the most dangerous, most destructive beast of all. If it could see into her heart, she could see into its, a heart that was…lonely. It shied from attention, kept itself to itself and *showed restraint.* Just like Dan Turner. If not, these hills and mountains would run red; they'd be littered with bodies.

An animal that was also human. Other than bloodlust in its eyes, there was pain, torture and...sadness. A deep well of sadness. Whatever its history and if there were others like it, the reason for their transformation she would never know, never come this close again.

Something she tried to communicate.

I will never seek you out. I will never...tell.

Because if she did, people would swarm this territory. They would hunt it to extinction.

The man was no longer murmuring. He had fallen mercifully silent. Taken his last ragged breath as the pact was made.

The skin walker lingered but only for a second or two more, then it turned, taking the man with it, and disappeared as swiftly as it had appeared. The fog closing around it was an ally after all. Whoever the man was—and likely she'd find out soon—he'd be classified as missing because whatever the walker did next with him, there'd be no trace left.

On her feet now, Shady could only continue to stare, horrified but also awed.

In myth there was truth.

Ray. She had to find him, already developing a story in her head about the man who'd attacked her but whom she'd escaped. God, there'd be such a temptation to tell at least Ray and Annie what had truly transpired, but a promise was a promise, even if unspoken, and if she didn't keep it, who knew what might happen. She'd been marked. That's what she'd thought the first time she'd ever set eyes on the walker and several times since. Maybe it was true.

"Ray." The sound she emitted was pitiful still, barely a

croak, one hand going to her throat, which burned from the attack. "Ray," she tried again. "Ray. Ray. Ray."

No use, he'd never hear her. The adrenaline that had fueled her before was wearing off, more shock, more confusion setting in.

Would she ever find Ray, Annie, anyone?

Where have you all gone?

Tears blurred her vision, made it harder to see. Angrily, she tried to blink them away, weary now to the bone, tempted to collapse where she was. Sink down upon the ground, curl up in a ball as tight as could be and just lie there, become smaller still. A resting place whose beauty was stained with such intrigue, desire and death.

Her steps were faltering, her legs caving. She'd faced death but then been saved. She'd *condoned* death, but for the greater good. Something she suspected she would have to remind herself of over and over, like Cassie Dupont must have to. One man had died, two men, but because of that, others—*innocent* others—would live.

No need for tears, but still they came because everyone had been innocent once.

Even Dan Turner.

Moments from collapsing, she caught a movement, if only slight, in the fog. There were sounds too, a low rumble but becoming clearer the harder she listened, the shouts of others calling to each other, calling for her.

Was that Ray's voice among them? Sam's? Even Annie's. "Shady! Shady! Shady!"

Her legs held, renewed strength sustaining her limbs, renewed hope too. The shape in the fog coming closer.

She picked up speed, desperate to close the gap between them. But then she stopped, yet again unable to believe her eyes.

"Brandi?"

CHAPTER TWENTY-EIGHT

Something wasn't right. Something was far from right.

When Brandi came limping out of the fog, her dark hair awry, her cheeks smudged with dirt and blood, and clothing torn, she'd clearly been wounded. Not just blood on her face, the side of her shirt was deeply stained too.

Shady had indeed run to her, caught her as the girl collapsed, fell with her to the ground, Shady's arms tight around her, refusing to let go, half fearful she'd disappear again.

And yet before that, Shady had caught it, a glimpse of something not just in her eyes but in her expression...something at odds with the girl's tortured appearance. There'd been...a hardness. A few words muttered too.

"He's dead, isn't he?"

No relief in them but triumph.

Before Shady could wonder at it, look further into Brandi's eyes, connect with her, the world around them was suddenly heaving with people. Out of the fog, they fired from all directions. Ray and Annie, her friends, and others in uniform, some of them carrying guns. Cries and whoops punctuated the air. Quickly, Shady was separated from Brandi, police at each of their sides, tending to them, assessing the damage, police radios spoken into, urgent requests for backup and medical care. At one point, Shady was convinced she was in a movie rather than real life. Some of it she couldn't remember at all, being removed from the mountainside or the transit to the hospital. Whether she'd actually lost consciousness, she didn't know, but she became aware again in the hospital, the lights above her blindingly white, making her think for a moment she was elsewhere, another dimension entirely. Her eyes adjusted, however, to find Ray and Annie by her side.

"What's happened?" she murmured. And then with more force, "Brandi?"

Annie soothed her, reaching out to pat her arm. "Brandi's going to be all right. *You're* going to be all right. Rest now, Shady. You've done your bit. You found her."

But Shady couldn't rest, something that Ray and Annie likely suspected.

"Go ahead, tell her," Ray said. "About Curt Landon."

"Curt who?" Shady said, leaning back against the pillows but not before she asked them to check in her jacket pocket, to give her Kanti's scrap of leather to hold, needing it now more than ever for the comfort it gave.

Annie glanced at Ray only briefly before gazing back at Shady. "Okay, all right," she conceded. After a brief silence, she began talking again. "I just want to assure you Brandi's injuries, although significant, are treatable. She's in surgery right now. But, before that, on the mountain, she would not stop talking. There'll be police statements taken, of course, from both of you, but while we were waiting for the medics, Ray and I hovered, if you like, managing to catch quite a bit of what was being said. Look," she said, sighing, "we can do this now or we can wait. You've been through a lot. You're exhausted."

"Please," Shady implored. "I need to know. Who is Curt Landon?"

Annie pushed her glasses higher up her nose. "Curt, it seems, is a bit of a wastrel."

"A what?" said Shady and Ray simultaneously.

"A ne'er-do-well. A rogue."

"Oh. Right," Shady said, remembering how lost he'd been. "Go on."

"He was from the east side of town, from what Ray and I have gathered since, this time courtesy of a rather talkative policewoman. He rarely attended school, and had rather a troubled home life. He just…drifted. He was older than Brandi, nineteen, apparently. Somehow the two of them had gotten to know each other. They would meet, and he became obsessed with her. That's how she put it. She liked him at first, but he began filling her mind with stuff. 'It was him,' she said. 'Everything. It was all his idea.'"

"What idea?"

"That I don't know," Annie confessed. "But whatever it was, she was very insistent, very…animated. He lured her into the wilderness in his truck. She went because, by now, she was scared of him, wanted to appease him but also to persuade him to leave her alone, but then…once out there, he attacked her. She ran, but he cornered her again and stabbed her. Luckily, the wound wasn't as serious as it could have been. She escaped a second time, though how, she has no idea, and found shelter deep within a hollow, by water, thankfully, and then was in and out of consciousness. For days she was simply too scared to move, because, as she said, there was something out there. She could hear it, searching."

"Him?" asked Shady. Or could it have been the walker?

"I'm presuming she thought it was him," replied Annie, oblivious to the other question on Shady's mind. "And then finally she heard it, a commotion, you and Landon fighting. Heard the voices of others too, calling out. Knew it was safe to move at last, that she *had* to or she'd die anyway. That's when she stumbled on you. Was it Landon who did this to you, Shady, who tried to…strangle you?"

Shady nodded. "It was a man, a young man around that age, so, yeah, I guess he fits the bill. He was…dressed in skins."

"Thank God you fought him off!"

Although it was painful to do so, Shady swallowed. "I did. Yeah. But if he'd pulled a knife on me too, I'd have had no chance."

"The police are hunting for him. Right now they're out there, scouring the mountain. The helicopters and the tracker dogs are out too in full force. Don't worry, he won't escape."

Worry? Oh, it wasn't that which concerned her. She knew he wouldn't escape, that he would never trouble anyone again. But Brandi…something wasn't adding up with her story, her insistence. *Her shifting of the blame.* Was that it?

"Did he…did Curt drive a Ford truck?"

"Uh-huh," Ray confirmed. "He did. It's been impounded."

"It wasn't at the lake."

"It was," Annie told her. "It was parked behind your car."

So, he'd come to the mountain soon after her and, once there, had followed her. A girl on a mission just as he'd been.

252

Both of them determined to complete it.

She sighed, long and low, causing Annie to start fussing. "That's it, that's all we know. The police will want to question you soon, as I've said. Your parents will also be arriving—" she checked her watch "—very soon. You really must rest and gather your strength. It's over, Shady. Brandi's been found, and you're on the mend. This really is a matter for the police now, not you, not us, just the police."

She was right; Shady knew it. *Landon* was a police matter. Dud Hooper, Robert Davenport and Alisa Jones too. And yet her hands were tied regarding all of it. Closing her eyes, she felt hopeless, still praying Cassie would do the right thing and that remnants of Landon would be found, even if it was months from now, so many needing closure.

Please, Cassie…don't leave this to me.

But one thing *was* in her hands. And it filled her with the utmost dread to face it. Brandi Hadley was not who Shady thought she was, what she'd assumed. An innocent. A victim. *A kid.*

She was so much more.

The look she'd seen in Brandi's eyes, the expression she'd caught before they'd both crashed to the ground, was imprinted in memory like a photograph, adding to others in the gallery, all those that had led her to this point, a hospital bed in Oregon.

Way much more.

And, once again, Shady was the only one who knew it.

CHAPTER TWENTY-NINE

"That's it, you're all set."

Josie looked around her. "I think you're right. That's my life, right there. All boxed up. Amazing, isn't it? How little we really own."

"Um…Josie, there's the biggest van I've ever seen parked outside your house, waiting to transport all your stuff back to Idaho!"

"Mom and Dad's stuff! You know what a hoarder Mom is! That's why I'm hitching a ride with you. Their car's also full to bursting!" She laughed as she threw her arms around Shady. "I'm coming home! Can you believe it? Back to Idaho Falls."

Shady was just as thrilled as Josie; the place hadn't been the same without her there, life hadn't. Then again, she mused, life *kept* changing, and who knew where it would take any of them next. Her own path was certainly a precarious one.

As they hugged, Shady mused about Cassie Dupont's life path too. She'd done it, gone to the police station in the heart of Baker City and confessed everything. Shady had only just arrived back home when she'd first heard that news via Josie.

So many emotions had surged through her, including a

whole heap of worry because Cassie Dupont was *not* a bad woman but someone who'd found herself in a bad situation. Consequently, she'd done what she'd had to, what she'd felt to be right, and it *was* right—Shady still didn't doubt that. Dan Turner was a murderer, a murderer who showed restraint, perhaps, but what if that had suddenly changed? Also, regarding other members of his sect, what if one of them had broken free of his control and gone rogue too? That family that had been slaughtered all those years ago, was it a bear responsible, a skin walker or one of them acting the part? She'd since Googled when it had happened, the '90s, so around the time the group was active. With this new information now in the hands of the police, perhaps their case would be reopened. Also, the cases of others who had mysteriously vanished in that part of Oregon during that era.

On the plus side, because of Dupont's actions, finally, *finally*, there'd be closure for Missy Davenport—painful closure, admittedly, but was anything worse than imagining what had happened to a loved one who'd gone missing? All the different scenarios that would play in your head, each one nothing less than torturous. As for surviving relatives of Dud Hooper and Alisa Jones, closure might bring them a little release too one day.

The girls had only just finished hugging when Shady heard Lulin's voice calling them from downstairs, an urgency in it.

"Girls? Girls! Come here. You're going to want to hear this."

A frown on Shady's face as well as Josie's—what was so important?—they hurried to where Lulin was waiting. She was clutching her cell to her chest, her cheeks pink with what could only be excitement. As they drew closer, she thrust it at Josie.

"I got a text," she said.

Josie's frown deepened. "Yeah? Who from?"

"Why, my friend Darlene, of course!"

Still Josie looked confused. "Darlene who?"

"Oh, honey, I've told you about Darlene! She's a cop, a local cop, often comes into the store for a chat. Oh, she's a sweetie. I think I'm going to miss her the most, but we'll keep in touch, come back this way and visit." Here she paused before adding, "Maybe."

Josie's face softened. "Mom, I'm sorry it didn't work out for us here."

"Me too," replied Lulin, "but I have friends I can't wait to see in Idaho Falls too, and the store premises we found, the rent was more reasonable than expected." She sighed. "We dreamed of small-town living, thought it'd be a whole lot safer, but what's gone on here, well…I'm looking forward to returning to Idaho Falls, that's all."

Josie nodded, as did Shady. What had gone on here for decades had tainted it, small towns proving themselves to be not quite as attractive as the veneer suggested, the anonymity of a bigger city perhaps offering more of a detachment from the real world. Who knew? But as Josie held up her mom's cell for them both to see and scrolled through the text so they could read it, one thing Shady was grateful for was that small-town people always knew each other's business.

Hey, hun, hot news! Cassie Dupont's been released, pending further investigation! No charges made against her, not yet, anyway. Officially, Dan Turner, whom she claims to have shot and killed doesn't exist. We can't find any record of him.

There're no witnesses either, just a claim from a kooky woman. She is a bit kooky, don't you think? Keeps herself to herself. I've always thought so, anyways. Whether she's for real or a fantasist, we'll never know, but I think I might swerve the library, buy my books from now on.

Again, Shady experienced both relief and disappointment. Relief because Cassie Dupont didn't deserve to rot in jail for what she'd done, but what of the victims' families—they'd have no closure after all? Dan Turner might have existed below the radar, but he'd been real enough. He'd lived and breathed and walked this earth, a damaged child who'd grown into a dangerous adult. There had to be some evidence he existed. Somewhere.

No way she wanted Cassie Dupont imprisoned—and if there was no body, no official record of existence, only evidence *linked* to Dan, she could still escape being charged—but Brandi Hadley knew something. Brandi Hadley had *found* something, perhaps the only evidence still in existence, because that photograph of a masked Dan Turner and his dubious gang was gone, Josie having taken a lighter to it.

"Well…" Lulin said, clearly waiting for a response.

"Shady?" Josie said, glancing at her.

"I…um…look, do you mind? I actually have to go somewhere."

"Oh?" Lulin was the one confused now. "Where?"

"Yeah, where?" echoed Josie. "Do you want me to come with?"

Shady shook her head. "No, you're okay. I'm only going close by. I won't be long."

"Close by?" Josie asked.

"Uh-huh," was Shady's response. "*Very* close."

* * *

"Shady! Hello. How lovely to see you!"

As the woman who had led the police to Brandi, Shady was Mr. and Mrs. Hadley's hero, and, this time, they had no hesitation inviting her in. How different it was inside the house compared to what she'd seen before. Where there was darkness there was now light, and plenty of it. As for Mrs. Hadley, no longer pale and ravaged, she was bright-eyed and plump cheeked, her hair as perfectly coiffured as the first time Shady had seen her.

"To what do we owe this pleasure?" Mr. Hadley asked, equally as bright-eyed.

"I was…wondering, how is Brandi?"

"Oh," Mrs. Hadley said, her smile slipping but only slightly, "she's okay. She's in her room. Tired. Exhausted, in fact. As you can imagine. She'll take a while to recover."

Weeks had passed since she'd been found, and while physical trauma might heal, mental trauma took a lot longer to come to terms with. For a normal person, that was.

"Could I…would it be okay for me to go and see her?" Shady asked. "Just for a short while. I promise I won't tire her out further."

"See her?" At first Mrs. Hadley seemed surprised Shady should ask, reluctant even, but then she quickly changed her mind. "Yes! That would be a great idea. Maybe…maybe seeing you, her *savior*—" here she laughed, a somewhat nervous sound "—might help! She's frightened, you see, about Landon. Whether he'll come back for her."

"Lightning rarely strikes twice," Shady said. "Perhaps I can assure her of that. Landon's probably a long, long way from here now." *In hell*, thought Shady, *rotting*.

"Lightning rarely strikes twice," Mrs. Hadley repeated, slowly, thoughtfully. "I like that saying. I like it a lot. You know what? Go right on up. Her room's the one next to the bathroom, just to the left of it." Although Shady knew this perfectly well, she duly nodded. "It'll be a lovely surprise for her," Mrs. Hadley continued, beaming again.

Shady turned and climbed the stairs, certain she heard the click of a door when she was about halfway up. Brandi onto her, her appearance not a surprise at all.

At Brandi's door, Shady knocked lightly. When there was no reply, she let herself in.

Before, this room had been the only one with light in it, the last glimmer of hope, Shady had guessed, the darkness elsewhere indicating how much hope had been on the wane. Now it was quite the reverse—the drapes were closed only in here, a sign of her tortured mind, or was Brandi embracing the dark?

Having entered the room, Shady gently closed the door behind her.

"Brandi?"

The girl was sitting in a chair by the desk, the one that Shady had previously searched. She was silent, although she inclined her head in Shady's general direction.

"You okay?" Shady continued.

"Uh-huh." It was little more than a teenager's grunt, the kind Shady had been guilty of herself when younger.

"Okaaay." Shady moved farther into the room, toward the drapes. "Mind if I throw a little light on the situation?" she said, reaching up to yank them apart.

That got Brandi galvanized. Crying out for Shady to leave them, she jumped up from her chair, intending to do what? *Force* her to if necessary?

Shady swung back toward her, triumphant. This was what she wanted, not the apathy of before. For a moment, all they did was stare at each other, Shady searching Brandi's eyes and even in the gloom finding what she needed, that defiance, that…anger.

It burned in the girl; it fueled her.

Shady strode toward her, forced her back into the chair, then leaned over her.

"Where is it?" she asked.

So quickly Brandi's defiance faded as she nervously pushed black hair from her face. "Where is what?" she said, a slight tremor betraying her.

"You know about Dan Turner!"

Her dark eyes widened. "Dan Turner?"

"Yep, you heard me. You know about him. How? Where's the evidence?"

"I… What the fuck are you talking about?"

Shady straightened slightly. "Okay, we can do this the easy way, just you and me, or I call your parents in and tell them you know about him too."

There was a tremble of her bottom lip. "My parents?"

"Yep, your parents who think you're so saintly. They're going to be shocked to find out otherwise."

"You're crazy! I don't know what you're talking about! I've never heard of Dan Turner!"

"You have, because you found something. Something to do with him. And you became…obsessed. That's it." She was the fantasist, Shady realized, not Cassie Dupont, this girl right here, Brandi Hadley, aged just sixteen. "You're obsessed, and that obsession…it's dangerous." Reaching out, she took hold of the girl's arms, not a tight grip—she was careful to be gentle with her—but she had to know.

Brandi didn't fight. She froze, enabling Shady to do what she needed and tune in.

A kid. A crazy kid. Not a monster. Not yet. But it was there, the potential, equal if not surpassing Curt Landon's potential, Shady's blood curdling on realizing it.

"You went willingly with him to Mazuma Lake, didn't you? Up to the mountain?"

No reply, but the truth was obvious in her eyes.

"You went because it was the anniversary...April twenty-fifth, the day a sacrifice was needed if you were to ascend or transform or whatever it was you thought would happen."

Brandi was frightened. That was also obvious. *Amazed* that Shady knew this stuff. Too amazed, perhaps, to bother denying it.

"You were in this together. The two of you. A sect all of your very own. A sacrifice." Shady inhaled. "Were you going to do it? Really? Murder someone?"

Was that a flicker of something besides anger in the girl's eyes? Remorse? Shame?

"Brandi, tell me! Were you really intent on murdering someone? Scalping them? Because that's part of the ritual too, isn't it? It completes it."

"I...I..."

"You're a fantasist, Brandi. Christ, you're a kid! From a good home, with parents that love you. What do you have to be so angry about?"

Again, the girl couldn't answer, only continued spluttering.

"But Landon wasn't from a good home. God knows how you hooked up with him, but you did, the pair of you a lethal combination, two angry fantasists together. Playing dress-up. I wonder where you hid your furs, Brandi, and if they'll ever be found one day."

The girl swallowed, hard, as well she might.

"Both fantasists, but one more intent than the other. A sacrifice had to be made, and there was no one around, no lone hiker, none that fit the bill. But it had to be made. On that date. It's been clearly specified. Such a special date, sacred. To Dan Turner. To you. But especially Landon. Who bought into the whole sorry shebang, down to the last detail. So, he turned on you. Even though...even though you thought you were the one in control, the one who was steering everything. What a shock that must have been! You're crazy but not as crazy as Landon was right then, nowhere near as troubled, as desperate or lost. He was looking for meaning, and you gave him that, or rather Dan Turner did, the man you told him about. That's what sects and cults are all about, wanting to belong. You played with fire and almost got burned." Should she do this, go ahead and tell a lie? Why not? If it helped to drive this home. "You escaped, but so did he. He's out there, Brandi. Right now. Still determined. You know what I'd do if I were you?"

Brandi shook her head, tears freely rolling down her cheeks now.

"I'd persuade my parents to move, to get far, far away from here, into a city somewhere, away from the wild. Because Landon is out there, a wild thing too, subhuman, and he'll stay in the mountains, sure enough, but every so often, he'll come down, and I don't mean like Dan, every ten years. He'll come far more often than that, and he'll be looking for you. But not in the cities. Cities will grow more and more alien to him. You'll be safer there."

"You...really think he'll come for me?"

"Yes," replied Shady. "Him and others like

262

him…monsters, if you don't change your ways. If you mess anymore in things that are simply too big for you. If you don't find another outlet for your anger, a more positive channel. Brandi, listen up, and listen well. Change the path you're on, okay? Like calls to like. That's what happened with you and Landon, I guess, two lost souls who gravitated towards each other. Change your path and find *yourself*. Attract the right people, good people, who'll lift you and help you on your way. There's a great life waiting out there, one that you're lucky to still have. Live it."

It was almost imperceptible at first, the nod of her head, but as Shady's words sank in, it became more certain.

"Good," Shady said. "Now show me what you found."

Breaking the connection at last, Brandi turned to the desk, moved a few items, and there it was—a folder where it hadn't been when Shady or the police had searched the room.

Her shame more obvious, Brandi handed it over to Shady, who took it, albeit gingerly. Backing up, she sat on the corner of Brandi's bed and opened it. It contained photographs. All of men in masks. Ten of them. Easy to tell who Dan was, the kingpin, the pack leader; he was taller and broader than the rest, and, even in print, he burst with an arrogance disguised as charisma. There were photographs too of the room they would meet in, the circle on the floor, the strange and mythical beasts chalked within it that they wished themselves to be. Of Dan again at the head of the circle, raising his arms upward just as Cassie said he had, something blurred and stringy in his hands. She held the photograph closer, examined the man's waist and what hung there too, again blurred, but Cassie would be able to identify it sure enough.

The folder also contained a diary, that belonging to George T. Hadley, his name upon it in gold lettering that had faded with time.

Shady lifted her head. "Who was he?"

"My grandfather," Brandi confessed.

"*What* was he?"

"He worked at a factory around here."

"*Just* worked at it?"

Brandi's shoulders slumped. "He owned it."

"That's more like it." Her tone was sardonic.

She opened the diary but only briefly, knew all too well what was in it—the worship of Dan Turner but in words this time, the man George had seen as a god, whom he'd hoped would make him a god too.

"Are there names in here?" Shady asked, snapping the diary shut.

"Names?"

"You know whose names I mean. The men involved."

"Yes." Her voice had become something very small indeed.

"What about the victims?"

Brandi nodded.

"And your father, does he know about this, about the true nature of his own father?"

More tears and a desperate shake of the head. "Please don't tell him."

"So where did you find it?"

"In a box in the attic, right at the bottom. I was up there one day, looking for Christmas lights, and noticed boxes that were still sealed. George…my grandfather…I'd never met him. He'd died when Dad was young. A gunshot, accidental, we think."

Shady nodded. They'd all died after Dan, all nine of them by various methods, allegedly. But mostly suicide? Only two had made it obvious. They couldn't live without their god; it was as simple as that. Refused to.

"Why were the boxes in the attic sealed?"

"I don't know...because...his death hit Dad hard, maybe? I know his momma was never the same afterwards. According to Dad, she just...deteriorated, died two years later."

A woman who couldn't live without her god either.

"And so things got boxed up. Lots of things. When Dad met Mom and moved house, Dad kept those boxes but never looked into them, didn't want to disturb the past, I guess."

"I guess," Shady repeated. "You sure your dad didn't know about this?" Or maybe it was because he *did* that, unlike his daughter, he never delved further.

"I really don't think so," Brandi insisted.

"Only you. Because you went snooping."

Brandi swallowed. "Because I went snooping."

The diary and the photographs placed back in the folder, Shady stood and then, still clutching it, began making her way to the door.

Brandi leaped up again. "What are you doing? Where are you going with that?"

"I think you know where," Shady said, halting just before the door.

"The cops? No, you can't! Dad...it'll destroy him."

Once more, Shady rounded on her. "What about the people they destroyed? Dan, your grandfather and the rest of them? The lives they took for their own deluded purposes? Bodies that were never recovered, the bones of people probably beneath that highway that now runs through where Dan Turner's property used to be. They didn't just destroy their victims but all those who knew and loved them, committed them to a living hell. And when you went missing, hiding out from Landon, do you know how distraught your parents were? Can you appreciate that? If you'd remained missing, they would never have recovered. They'd have been destroyed too. Is that what you wanted for them?"

More tears flowed from Brandi's eyes, which pleased Shady; she wanted the grief of realization to rain down on her. Teenagers could be self-centered, but sometimes they needed to see the bigger picture, be made to.

"The relatives of their victims need closure, and I'm going to give it to them." Dan Turner existed, and he, along with nine others, were partners in crime. This proved it. This would blow the lid off it, maybe the entire town. And yet still Cassie might escape punishment. Shady hoped so. She also hoped Cassie would approve of what she was planning to do, because of all people, she knew what it was like to leave a wound festering.

"Dad'll kill me," the young girl moaned as Shady opened the bedroom door.

"He won't because you'll still be the victim in all this. I won't implicate you."

"Really?" Hope gave color to her cheeks, even in the gloom.

"The blame will lie squarely at Landon's feet." Landon, who'd remain missing. "Like I said, you need to move, get away from here. This will give you the motivation to do that."

"Th…thank you."

Shady's nod was imperceptible now. "Choose another path, okay?"

"I will," Brandi whispered. "I promise."

"And one more thing."

"What?"

"Open the goddamned drapes. Your time in the dark is done."

CHAPTER THIRTY

"So, this is the chair?"

"Uh-huh. You gonna sit in it?"

Shady looked at Ray, who'd asked her the question, then at Annie, who was standing by his side, all three of them not in the basement of the Mason Town Museum but toward the rear, near the staff room. As Annie had said, no way they could get this chair down the winding metal staircase into the depths of the building, where most new additions were stored until they could get a handle on them.

"Shady?" Annie interjected. "Don't feel that you have to, not right now. Do it in your own time, when you're ready. You must still be reeling from all that's happened recently."

She was. Having taken the folder to the police, the lid had indeed been blown off the whole Dan Turner affair, family members of those involved in the murders—upstanding members of the community who'd come from a long line of upstanding members, or so most of them had thought—likewise reeling from the shock waves that just kept reverberating. No one had known a damned thing about it. And if they had, no way they'd admit it. Cassie Dupont came forward again, insisting it was all true, giving more evidence, cooperating in any way she could. And still no charges had been levied against her. No body, no crime, not as far as the police were concerned.

Landon's body had also been found—not hidden forevermore in a dark gully or cave but right out in the open for anyone to stumble across, which they had, a young couple on their honeymoon, who'd wanted to embrace the wild and the free. What they hadn't bargained for was encountering a horribly mutilated corpse, identifiable only by DNA.

Shady felt sorry for the young couple, hoped it wouldn't leave them with a lifelong scar, but she was personally grateful that Landon's body had been found. Everyone deserved closure, even those who couldn't bring up a kid properly or give them the home they needed, who never helped steer them down the right path. That his body had been in such an open space she found curious. Had the walker done that deliberately, knowing the burden she would otherwise carry? Had it realized how hard that would be and empathized? Stupid to think so, it really was, and yet…

As for the Hadleys, they had left town, sold up and moved to Philadelphia, just about as far away as they could get, to start a new life there. It was Cassie who'd told Shady this, who had called and thanked her for her intervention, had said that regarding burdens, she'd carried Dan Turner long enough and was grateful he was no longer on her back.

In the end it all seemed to turn out well, with closure for just about everyone. Shady hadn't been back in touch with Missy Davenport, but she could imagine, even so, that the weight she carried had lifted a little too. If Shady should ever pass that way again, hitching a ride with Dorothea on another road trip with her friends, she half suspected the motel would be a whole lot busier. Missy would come out to greet them, and on her face would be a smile, genuine this time, her eyes a little brighter. Robert's grave at the family plot would lie empty still, unless they dug up that highway where Dan's ranch had once stood, but the mystery was solved, at least. The Lazy Stay Motel was where all this had begun with a photograph, such a strange and winding journey. And it had ended with photographs too. Those of the murderers, exposed at last, finally held to account.

"Shady?" It was Annie again. "You do look a bit peaky, you know."

Shady smiled. "Annie, I'm okay. Stop fretting. Although…I like that you fret."

The smile Annie returned was indulgent. "You know how responsible I feel—"

"Don't!" Shady said. "I'm nothing but thankful I met you, that I'm here. It's for a reason, Annie. A good reason. Lives have been saved. Not Landon, but I truly believe we got to Brandi in time. In a big city there's lots of opportunities, so she'll change, channel her energy." Shady rolled her eyes. "Rid herself of all that teenage angst. Live a good life. A harmless life. Not because of me but because of this gift, because of you and Ray helping me to understand it when…I don't know, there's so much we can't understand."

"'My own suspicion is that the universe is not only queerer than we suppose, but queerer than we *can* suppose.'"

Shady grimaced. "Say what, Ray?"

As Ray tended to do, he blushed. "You never heard that before? A biologist said it, Haldane, I think. Similar to Shakespeare, 'there are more things—"

"'In heaven and earth than are dreamt of in your philosophy.' Yeah, yeah, I know that one. In fact, I think about that one all the time. But Haldane, that's a new one for me."

"True, though, huh?" Ray said.

"God, yeah."

"Look," said Annie, "why don't we call it a day? It's not quite closing time, but I don't think there'll be any more visitors today. No harm in knocking off a little early."

"Knock off early," Ray repeated. "I love your little sayings, Annie."

"Glad I amuse you! Come on," she said, grabbing the white sheet that had previously covered the chair, intending to replace it, a barrier of sorts.

"Okay," Ray said, but Shady stayed where she was.

It *was* a beautiful chair, oak that had darkened with age and was carved with strange symbols, ones she didn't recognize, personal to someone, maybe—a take on the Hermetic alphabet, Annie had suggested. A throne. That's what it reminded Annie of, and Shady too. A stunning piece. Unique. Perhaps not quite as old as they'd thought, just made to look that way. It had been treasured once. *For all the wrong reasons.*

On a deep breath, Shady reached out, laid her hands on the chair's sturdy arms, then closed her eyes.

Only darkness at first, inky in texture, but slowly she began if not to see, to hear.

There was screaming.

A sense of suffering.

Of pain inflicted.

Pain that was limitless, that caused unleashed pleasure.

She screamed too as she snatched her hands back.

"Shady? What is it?"

Annie tossed the sheet aside as she hurried closer to

Shady, Ray at her heels.

Dan Turner had been a false god, but whoever had owned this—the *original* owner—had not been interested in anything godly and hadn't pretended to. Evil was his obsession. Pure evil. Two words so at odds with each other but nonetheless conjoined.

Annie had told her that the man who'd brought it in had kept scratching at his hands and arms, marking the skin there, leaving it red raw. Shady didn't blame him. She too felt like ripping the flesh from her palms, wherever her skin had touched it.

"No," she breathed. "Goddamn it, not again."

Ray's eyes brimmed with concern and wonder. "What did you sense?"

"Too much," Shady told him. "Just…way too much."

"Shady," Annie said, "what do you want to do? Do we try and understand—"

Shady shook her head. "We store it. I don't mean here at the museum but somewhere on its own until…until…I can deal with it."

"A self-storage unit or something?" Ray suggested.

Annie nodded. "That can be arranged. Easily."

"Good, good," Shady murmured. "And we bolt the doors on it. Seal it in."

"And then?" Annie asked.

"Then we thank our lucky stars."

Ray frowned. "Thank our lucky stars? Why?"

"That we three exist to stop evil in its tracks. Because you know what? This kind of energy…there is such a force behind it. And if it falls into the wrong hands, a person that's…lost, that's looking for something, it'll take hold, and so many will suffer as a result. Annie, Ray, it's *infused* with evil, created for that very purpose."

There was a terrible wonder in Annie's eyes, and a hesitation.

"Annie, I'm not sure we can *ever* understand it."

"And so we lock it away?"

"For now. We surround it with crystals, with salt, with whatever. We send love towards it, a tidal wave of positivity to break it down bit by bit."

Annie conceded. "It won't be the only object whose fate it is to be contained in such a way. There'll be others right across the globe, in all four corners."

Ray had taken a step back, perhaps involuntarily. "Guys, why don't we just burn it?"

"You know why," Shady replied. "Energy doesn't dissipate. It adds to the load, can tip the balance, even, and not in our favor. But it can be subdued, made harmless. Mostly."

"Mostly," he repeated as he shook his head. "The things we have to deal with, huh?"

As Shady nodded, she recalled the glare of red eyes and the way they'd stared into hers, her concern also regarding the path she was on and what lay further along it.

"The unspeakable," she murmured. And maybe something else too if she didn't falter, if she believed in the stars, in fate, in Kanti. Something that existed after all, that Kanti was proof of.

True ascension.

A NOTE FROM THE AUTHOR

As much as I love writing, building a relationship with readers is even more exciting! I occasionally send newsletters with details on new releases, special offers and other bits of news relating to the Psychic Surveys series as well as all my other books. If you'd like to subscribe, sign up here!

www.shanistruthers.com

Printed in Great Britain
by Amazon